ALL SAINTS?

Ellie Carter

Ellie Carter
(Lisa Goodridge)

instant
apostle

First published in Great Britain in 2020

Instant Apostle
The Barn
1 Watford House Lane
Watford
Herts
WD17 1BJ

British Library Cataloguing-in-Publication Data

A catalogue record for this book is available from the British Library.

This book and all other Instant Apostle books are available from Instant Apostle:

Website: www.instantapostle.com

Email: info@instantapostle.com

ISBN 978-1-912726-21-9

Printed in Great Britain.

Acknowledgements

I would like to thank the team at Instant Apostle for all their help. Particular thanks must go to Nicki Copeland, who took a risk in publishing an unknown author, and to Sheila Jacobs, for her wisdom and encouragement and for always being at the end of the phone. Special thanks go to my family for their amazing patience and support, especially my husband and my sister.

One

It was Christmas Eve afternoon, just one more sleep until Christmas. The weather was mild and the sky shone a clear pale blue over the Staffordshire village of Oxley. Sophie Ashton negotiated the potholes of the church drive, accompanied by Henry, aged two and a half, in his smart outfit, new shoes polished. Sophie was feeling remarkably relaxed. Presents were wrapped, seasonal thank-you gifts (a nice bottle of red) had been distributed to the 'official' church helpers, the vicarage was as clean and tidy as it was going to be, the larder was stocked and all was well… for the moment. Audrey, chief of the flower ladies and self-appointed chief of the church kitchen, was bearing down on her from behind.

'Hello, Sophie, dear. Are you all set?'

'Yes, I think so, thank you,' said Sophie, just as Henry pulled his hand from hers and began running towards the church doors. Sophie turned around just in time to see one of his new shoes disappear into one of the larger potholes and sink into a couple of inches of mud. 'Oh no! Henry! Stop.' But it was too late. Henry had tripped and was sprawling in a large muddy puddle. 'Well, I *was* all set,' said Sophie sadly, as she bent to pick up a wailing Henry. 'I wish we could get this drive fixed, to be honest. It's a bit of a hazard for everyone, especially the older members of the congregation.'

'Ah, well. This happens every year, you know. I think they're all used to it by now. Besides, it would be far too expensive to

7

fix.' With that, Audrey expertly circumnavigated the remaining potholes and disappeared quickly into the church, leaving Sophie to struggle with the muddy Henry. She carried him into the church porch and got to work on him with a packet of wet wipes.

Once inside the church, Sophie spotted Dominic, her husband and the vicar of All Saints, putting the finishing touches to his well-planned children's service. The older members of the congregation liked the more established midnight communion service, which was to take place later, but Dominic had wanted to have something for younger people on Christmas Eve. The service had been advertised at the village school and the local toddler group, but one could never be sure whether people would come or not.

Sophie walked towards Dominic, still holding Henry firmly by the hand. Audrey appeared from the church kitchen and overtook them in the centre aisle. 'Ah, Audrey,' said Dominic, 'I've made a backdrop for the stable scene at the front of church, but I need some drawing pins to secure it to the pinboard. I thought there were some in the vestry, but I can't seem to locate them. Any ideas? Otherwise I'll just pop home and get some.'

'No need to use drawing pins. I've got something better. I put the drawing pins away so no one would use them on the new board.'

'But it's a pinboard,' said Dominic, looking puzzled. 'It's meant to have drawing pins stuck into it.'

'Yes, but we don't want to damage it. It is new and it was quite expensive, you know.' Audrey disappeared into the vestry and reappeared with a small envelope. 'Now, put these pieces of sticky-backed Velcro onto the back of whatever it is you want to stick on the board,' she said, offering the envelope to Dominic, 'and they will stick to the soft side of the pinboard.'

'OK, are you sure they will stick?' asked Dominic, doubtfully, taking the small Velcro pieces out of the envelope.

'Yes, they'll be fine,' Audrey reassured him, and then took them back out of his hand. 'Now, to be more economical, we cut them into quarters. There we are.' She snipped them into small pieces with a large pair of scissors and handed them back. 'We must be frugal. It's the church's money, after all!' She whizzed past him back into the vestry with the scissors, leaving him with the tiny Velcro quarters in his hand.

Dominic, looking dubious, placed them in the corners of his painted stable scene and pressed it onto the newly acquired pinboard.

'How are you doing?' Sophie asked him.

'Not too bad, stable scene constructed, hope it stays in place. Manger full of straw, star attached to fishing rod, costumes ready for children. No actual children yet, but I'm sure they'll be along soon. The music group sound good. Hayley has been very organised.' He paused. 'I thought Hayley looked a bit down, though.'

'Oh,' said Sophie, turning to look for her friend. Hayley McDurney was sitting at the piano, deep in conversation with Mike, the guitarist. She had her back to Sophie, her long blonde hair cascading over her shoulders. Sophie remembered that Hayley had hinted about an important appointment with the doctor that week with Paul, her husband. Hayley, the secretary at the village primary school, was very good at publicising church events with families, and the headmistress was very friendly towards the church.

Sophie decided to speak to Hayley at the end of the service. 'What needs doing?' she asked Dominic.

'I think it's just a question of catching the parents of the children taking part in the nativity, getting them into costume and making sure they sit near the front,' said Dominic. 'Ah, here come the Hendersons.'

John and Belinda Henderson with their three boys, Noah, Jonah and Boaz, were a new family at church. They had lived in the village for some years, but had been travelling eight miles into Stafford every Sunday in order to attend one of the churches there. It was unfortunate for All Saints that many of the younger churchgoing families in the village chose to drive past the village church on a Sunday morning to go to one of the bigger churches in town. Most of them did it because they wanted to take their children to a church with plenty of young people. It was immensely frustrating, thought Sophie. If some of them would just join them, then others would find it much more inviting! With a few more families they could do so much more. Dominic often said that churches were like parties that people only wanted to come to after they had warmed up, but no one actually wanted to do the warming up.

When John and Belinda had walked through the door one Sunday morning, halfway through November, Sophie and Dominic had hardly been able to believe their good fortune. True, the Hendersons had said that they wanted to 'try the church out' for the moment, but six weeks later they were still coming. Three more children in the Sunday school doubled their numbers. This afternoon Noah, aged eight, was to be Joseph, Jonah, aged six, a wise man and Boaz, aged four, a shepherd. The rest of the parts were to be played by children and grandchildren of members of the congregation, and it was hoped that children from the village would come and join in with the singing. Dominic and Sophie had briefly toyed with the idea of including Henry in the nativity, but decided he was a bit too young and unpredictable. There would be other years.

Sophie walked back up the aisle, smiling. She felt a little in awe of Belinda Henderson – her children were so well behaved. Today, though, she was feeling more confident and excited about the service. She greeted the family and invited them to come to the front, showing them the costumes that had been laid across the pew.

Gradually more families began to arrive. The church had been beautifully decorated by members of the congregation. Holly and candles adorned the high windowsills that sat beneath the stained-glass windows, the wooden pew-ends had been hung with arrangements of red velvet roses, and a large pine tree in the corner sparkled with tinsel, coloured baubles and fairy lights. The under-pew heaters that had been installed a few years previously were keeping the ancient church warm and, that afternoon, it felt alive and full of excitement. All the children were given a musical instrument to 'play', and seasonal refreshments were being prepared in the kitchen for after the service by Audrey's team. Sophie went to sit near the back, her usual place of safety, with Henry, who liked to shout a lot during quiet parts of church services and normally needed to be removed quickly.

Dominic welcomed everyone and the service began. Sophie knew Dominic would lead everyone through the nativity well, and she was right. Dominic loved Christmas, despite the long hours and lack of sleep it entailed for a vicar. He guided the children expertly through the story of the Saviour's birth, while their delighted parents looked on. Each scene was interspersed with a carol, led by Hayley and Mike, and everyone joined in. There was so much noise and jollity that even Henry managed to stay engaged and Sophie didn't feel the need to rush him out to the back room. The only slight hitch was when Jonah Henderson, resplendent in his wise man outfit, came forward to say his line, 'We bring him gifts of gold, Frankenstein and myrrh.' There was a kind of strangled noise, as every adult in the church tried very hard not to laugh, while all the children remained oblivious. Unfortunately, or perhaps fortunately, at that moment the backdrop to the stable scene released itself from the pinboard, the tiny Velcro pieces able to hold on no longer, and floated gracefully down over the heads of Mary, Joseph and the baby Jesus. Dominic rushed to stick it back up, apologising profusely, and the congregation were able to laugh to release the tension.

At the end of the service there were mince pies for the adults, Christmas cookies for the children and copious amounts of orange squash. Sophie was encouraged to see some of the children from the toddler group, which met in the village hall. She managed to get Dominic to hold Henry at his station by the door, while she went to chat with some of the parents. She hoped there would be some among them who might feel encouraged to try church on a Sunday.

Dominic and Sophie's prayer for All Saints was that they would be able to bring more young people into the congregation. They knew that if they did not, there was a chance that the church would eventually die out and close altogether – their greatest fear. Then there would be no Christian presence in the village at all.

Half an hour later, church was emptying. Sophie checked Dominic was still managing Henry. They both seemed fine. Dominic was chatting with John Henderson and Henry seemed happy being held in his arms. She turned and walked back down the aisle to the front of church, where Hayley was sitting on the piano stool, looking downcast.

'Thanks, Hayley. You and Mike did a splendid job this afternoon.'

'Thank you,' said Hayley. 'Paul didn't come, though. He said he would, but he didn't.'

'Oh,' said Sophie. 'That's disappointing.'

'That's not the only thing,' Hayley went on. 'Our appointment with Dr Payne didn't go very well.'

'What did he say?'

'It's Paul.'

Sophie's felt a twinge of anxiety. 'What's the matter?'

'Dr Payne said…' Hayley took a deep breath. 'He said that it isn't impossible for us to have a baby naturally, but it's highly unlikely.'

'Oh, Hayley, I'm so sorry.'

'I know. We both feel really upset about it, but Paul has taken it very badly. He doesn't want anyone to know… well… I can tell you and Dominic, of course. He's taking it very personally, almost like a personal insult. We had a row before I came out, actually. It's as if he thinks it affects him more than it affects me, but it doesn't. I mean, I know it's not Paul's fault, but it's me that can't have a baby, not him. He needs to understand that.' Hayley had tears in her eyes.

Sophie knew how Hayley felt, having been in the same position herself. She gave Hayley a hug as she measured her words carefully. 'I'm so sorry you have to deal with this. I do know how hard it is, you know I do.' Hayley nodded. 'But I'm sure Paul will be struggling with this hugely. I know Dominic did. It wasn't just that we couldn't have a baby; obviously we were both really sad about that. But it was more than that for Dominic – it was as if it emasculated him somehow. Do you see what I mean?'

Before Hayley had a chance to answer, her mobile started buzzing on top of the piano. She picked it up and read a text message. 'Paul,' she said. 'I'd better go.'

'Let's meet up for coffee soon.'

'Yes,' said Hayley, gratefully. 'That would be nice. We can talk properly then. I'll see you in the morning, though. Paul said he would come in the morning.'

'OK,' replied Sophie, thinking she would believe it when she saw it.

Hayley and Paul lived in one of the flats in the newer part of the village. Paul's parents lived in Oxley and Hayley's parents lived in a neighbouring village, in a house they had shared with Hayley's grandparents since Hayley and her sister had moved out. Paul and Hayley had been married four years earlier at All Saints, by the previous vicar. Sophie had suspected for a while that they might have been trying for a baby, but she hadn't liked to assume. Then, six months ago, when Sophie and Dominic had adopted Henry, Hayley had mentioned that she and Paul had been hoping for a baby too. It seemed to Sophie that Paul loved Hayley very much, but he wasn't a Christian and Hayley seemed to be in constant battle with him over his church attendance.

Eventually the church emptied of all but Dominic, Sophie and Henry. 'Well done, darling,' said Sophie. 'You did well.'

'God's work,' said Dominic. 'I do feel quite tired, though.'

'Three more services and then you've done it.'

Dominic shut the heavy, wooden church door. Henry couldn't escape now, so it didn't matter if he ran around the church – after all, none of the older people was there to complain. As Dominic began to tidy the manger away, Sophie got to work on the biscuit crumbs with the vacuum cleaner. Twenty minutes later they were walking back to the vicarage for tea.

When tea was finished and the kitchen tidied, Henry bathed and put to bed, Sophie and Dominic sat down with a cup of tea. This was the difficult bit. Apart from arranging the presents under the tree and preparing the vegetables for the next day, there wasn't a lot to do and Dominic needed to stay awake in order to go back over to church at eleven o'clock, for midnight communion.

'It's awfully quiet,' remarked Dominic. 'Do you mind?'

'What? Oh, you mean do I mind that Mum and Dad have gone to my brother's for Christmas? No, they came to us last year and it's their first Christmas with the new baby.'

'It's our first Christmas with Henry too!'

'Well, maybe it's nice that it's just the three of us this year. We've waited a long time to do this. Anyway, when we go down on Friday we'll see everybody, won't we? Do you mind that your parents aren't here?'

'No, they always want to drive and, if the weather's bad, it's such a long way to travel from that part of France. I'd much rather see them in the spring or summer, when we can spend a bit more time with them. Nicholas will be home from university, so they're not alone.'

'You're right.'

'I had a good chat with John Henderson at the end of the service.' Dominic smiled slightly.

'Go on,' said Sophie, hopefully.

'They've decided that they want to join All Saints and support us in our work here. John said that they felt things were going well and they really wanted to be part of their local church.

Belinda has been chatting to mums in the school playground and she feels it would be so much easier to invite them here than to a church eight miles away. They like the way we're doing things here and they want to commit. He said whatever we decide to do, they will be behind us. How about that for a Christmas present?' He was grinning broadly now and Sophie had the impression he had been bursting to tell her this for some time but had been waiting for the right moment.

'I can't tell you how happy I am to hear that! That really is a wonderful Christmas present.' Her heart, already light from the afternoon service, soared. John and Belinda's presence would certainly help attract other young families. Maybe God was answering their prayers!

She took the empty cups out to the kitchen and returned with her arms full of presents. 'He's asleep,' she said. 'Let's put these under the tree and then I'll sort the veg out for tomorrow.' A few minutes later she sat down with a tray of vegetables and a peeler. 'I wanted to talk to you about Hayley. I know why she looked upset.'

'Don't tell me – Paul said he would come to church and then he didn't?'

'No… Actually, they went to see Dr Payne this week. It looks as if they have a similar problem to us. About having a baby… They probably can't.'

'Oh no, that's sad. Is it, you know… Do they know why?'

'Yes, same as us. We didn't have long to talk, so we said we'd catch up properly after Christmas. It might be good for you to talk to him when he's ready. I think it's all a bit new right now. They're probably still in shock.'

'Yes, of course,' said Dominic. 'Poor chap. Well, poor both of them.'

'A bit of me wonders if Henry might not be the only adopted child in our church in the future.'

'Let's not jump to conclusions. Adoption isn't the right thing for every couple who can't conceive naturally. You know that.'

'I do,' said Sophie. 'Let's just try to be there for them.'

Just before eleven o'clock Dominic got up to go back over to church. 'I hope it isn't raining.'

'I'll have a look.' Sophie pulled back the thick curtain that covered the front door and peered outside. There was very little street lighting in Oxley, but the moon was bright and she could make out the shape of the fourteenth-century church in the darkness. The church sat on one side of the village and was so close to the vicarage that it was almost impossible to tell where the front garden ended and the ancient graveyard began. 'No, not raining.'

'Good, it puts people off coming if it's raining.'

'You don't mind if I go to bed, do you?' asked Sophie.

'Of course not.'

'Thank you. I promise that you can put your feet up tomorrow lunchtime and not have to do another thing all day.'

'Then I definitely don't mind if you go to bed,' he said, opening the door and walking out into the darkness of the cold, crisp night. Sophie closed the front door and shivered. She picked up her tray of prepared vegetables and took it out to the kitchen.

The vicarage kitchen felt chilly. In keeping with the rest of the house, it was large and old, but had a rather solid feel about it. The house was brick-built and had five bedrooms, but seemed to have got stuck in a time warp around the 1960s. Sophie kept it clean and tidy, and they had decorated most of the rooms when they had moved in the previous January, before Henry came to live with them that summer. However, the old-fashioned kitchen with its painted wooden cabinets remained, along with the antiquated bathroom with the old enamel bath. There was even a small, damp cellar, accessed from a door in the kitchen. A previous vicar had kept paperwork down there, but it had been ruined by mould. Audrey had once suggested putting a table tennis table there: 'It might encourage young people to join the church, dear,' but Sophie and Dominic had kept the door firmly locked.

Sophie put the vegetables into the fridge, switched off the kitchen light and climbed the stairs. She was vaguely aware of Dominic crawling into bed at one o'clock.

'How did it go?' she mumbled.

'Fine, go back to sleep,' he whispered.

She did.

Two

The next morning Sophie woke to the sound of Henry shouting, 'Out, out, out.' She groaned and stretched and looked at the clock. Half past six; it could have been worse.

'Coming,' she called. Slowly she got out of bed and put her dressing gown on, then went to Henry's room, checking the doors and the safety gate at the top of the stairs on the way. Henry loved to slam doors. The vicarage doors had very high handles, well out of Henry's reach, so as long as they were shut, he couldn't slam. 'Happy Christmas, Henry,' she said, as she lifted him out of the cot.

'Happy Christmas, both of you,' came Dominic's slightly gravelly voice behind her.

'Happy Christmas, darling. I thought you were still asleep.'

'Too much adrenaline,' said Dominic, 'and I'm starting to lose my voice. I've been talking too much and I've still got two more services to go.'

Sophie decided talking should wait until lunchtime in order to save Dominic's voice for as long as possible, and busied herself changing Henry's nappy and dressing him. Dominic went out for the early morning communion service and Sophie went to have her shower, leaving Henry on the landing with all but his own bedroom door shut. He could come to no harm there.

By the time Dominic returned from the early service, Sophie and Henry were sitting at the kitchen table eating breakfast,

Henry in the highchair. A fresh cup of coffee had been poured for Dominic.

'How did it go?' asked Sophie, as he joined them. 'Just the usual two customers?'

'Just the one, actually,' Dominic replied. His voice seemed to have recovered a little. 'Only Will… Florence has gone to her daughter in Leicester for Christmas.'

'How about last night?'

'Last night… I thought it went well, but Geoffrey seemed disgruntled. He said that numbers were much lower than last year.'

'Did you tell him about yesterday afternoon? Audrey was there – I would have thought she'd have told him that it went well. I mean, they are married, you would think they talk to each other!'

'I did mention it, but he didn't seem interested.'

'Never mind, it's just Geoffrey being Geoffrey. He always seems disgruntled about something. I've forgotten his background. Wasn't he in the army before he retired?'

'Yes, I think he was quite high ranking. He retired early, though. Audrey told me once that retirement hadn't suited Geoffrey and he needed a new challenge. Audrey, apparently, came up with the idea that retirement might be a good time for them to join the church. They both joined the choir and then, twenty years ago, he became churchwarden because nobody else wanted the job. He's been running the show ever since!'

'Running the show?'

'Well, he certainly seems to think he's in charge!'

'I think Audrey could give him a run for his money.'

'What, as chief of the flower ladies?'

'She not just the flower chief, you want to try being in the church kitchen with her! Woe betide you if you put too much water in the kettle or a spoon goes missing.'

'Let's not be horrible about Audrey and Geoffrey. They do an awful lot for the church and we must remember that. Anyway, it's Christmas!'

Henry had finished his breakfast and was squirming in the highchair. After wiping him down, Sophie lifted him out. 'Shall we go over to church?' she said. She knew Henry was still too young to really know what was going on, but she had been looking forward to their first Christmas as a family for a long time. Her plan was that after church they would all go into the living room together to see whether Father Christmas had been. She needed to get Henry out of the house before he wandered in by himself.

'Let's go,' said Dominic.

The Christmas morning service was a very happy one. Dominic's voice held out and he gave a short message. Mrs Fowler-Watt, the organist, did a great job with the carols, the church was full and there was a buzz.

We have much to be thankful for, Sophie thought, as she looked around at the congregation. She spotted Robert and Catherine. Robert Watson was a retired vicar from a nearby village. He and his wife, Catherine, had moved to Oxley for their retirement and were very supportive towards Dominic and Sophie. They had offered to lead the services on the Sunday after Christmas, so Dominic and Sophie could have some time away to visit family. Then Sophie spotted Lucy Shackleton, a young physiotherapist who worked in Stafford. Lucy was sitting with her parents. She looked tired, but happy. However, Sophie couldn't help noticing that neither Paul nor Hayley had made it to church that morning and she made a mental note to message Hayley later.

Lucy caught Sophie in the church doorway, just as she was leaving. 'Can we have coffee together sometime soon?'

'Yes, of course.' Sophie thought of Hayley and instantly felt a prickle of alarm. Had something happened to Lucy too? 'Are you OK?' she asked.

'Yes, I'm fine,' Lucy smiled. 'I just wanted to see you.'

'Great,' said Sophie, relieved. 'We have some days away after Christmas, but let's get together when we get back.'

When Sophie and Dominic, each holding one of Henry's hands, walked back to the vicarage, they felt positive about the coming year, despite their worry for Hayley and Paul. A full church on Christmas Eve afternoon and on Christmas Day and a new family ready to join them. Dominic opened the vicarage door. 'Let's see if Father Christmas has been,' he said.

The rest of Christmas Day turned out to be everything that Sophie had hoped for. Henry had the attention of one of his parents all of the time and both of them most of the time. He didn't seem to want to play with any of his presents, but he showed great enthusiasm for ripping off the paper.

In the afternoon Sophie sent Hayley a message: 'Happy Christmas to you both. Missed you this morning, but hope to catch up soon. You are in our prayers.'

A little later Sophie's phone buzzed. She picked it up and looked at the message. 'Hayley,' she said. 'She says they were sorry they weren't there this morning and thanks for our prayers. Then she says that she won't be in church on Sunday, but Mike's happy to lead the music on the guitar and she's told Robert and Catherine.

'I know why she can't come to church on Sunday,' said Sophie, suddenly. 'Paul's work Christmas party is always on the Saturday after Christmas and they're staying in a hotel in town on Saturday night. She won't want to get up on Sunday morning and rush back to church.'

'That's a very odd day to have your work Christmas party!'

'I know, that's what I said. Apparently, years ago someone didn't manage to book a venue before Christmas, so they were offered the Saturday after Christmas at a cheaper rate. Everyone loved it because it wasn't part of the mad pre-Christmas rush, so they've done it like that ever since.'

The day after Boxing Day, Dominic, Sophie and Henry set off in the car to Eastbourne, to spend a few days with Sophie's parents. It took a while to pack the cases (Henry kept taking things out) and a bit longer to get everything into the car. They put Henry in his car seat first, to stop him escaping, and then piled the cases, travel cot, highchair and pushchair in around him. Gone were the days of a quick getaway.

Sophie felt excited. She hadn't seen her family for a couple of months. It was too far to go for a day trip. Their last visit was when her brother Steve's girlfriend, Jane, had given birth to Freya. That visit had been a little fraught. It was the first time they had taken Henry away overnight, and Sophie was very aware that seeing her brother's first baby was going to make her feel wistful about the baby she had so wished for herself. Seeing Freya and holding her in her arms had brought a lump to Sophie's throat, but she had been determined to contain her emotions, so as not to spoil the excitement for everyone else.

That visit was also the first time that Steve and Jane had seen Henry. They were, understandably, a little apprehensive. Adopted children often came from quite difficult backgrounds, and Henry was no exception. His behaviour could be a challenge, but Sophie and Dominic had managed to keep him well under control and the visit had gone reasonably smoothly. Steve and Jane, although not really engaging with Henry, had gradually learned to relax around him.

This time, Sophie didn't feel so emotional about seeing Freya. Henry was quiet in the back of the car, looking out of the window, and Sophie and Dominic chatted happily. Dominic mentioned that John Henderson wanted to discuss some ideas he had for church when they got back. It pleased Sophie to hear how encouraged Dominic sounded about this.

As it was a long journey, they stopped for lunch at a service station just outside Oxford.

'I ought to get some flowers for Mum before we go,' said Sophie. 'I just need to pop to the loo too.'

'You go to the ladies and I'll get the flowers with Henry, and meet you back at the car.'

However, when Sophie arrived back at the car, Dominic and Henry were nowhere to be seen. It was cold and she didn't have the car keys. She started to walk slowly back towards the service station entrance. Once inside she looked around but couldn't see them, so she walked to the car again. After a few more minutes of waiting, she spotted Dominic coming towards her, looking red in the face, Henry over one shoulder and a squashed-looking bunch of flowers in the other hand.

'All right?' she asked.

'Kind of,' Dominic replied. 'Let's get back into the car and I'll tell you.' Sophie took the flowers from him to allow him to strap Henry back into his car seat.

'Go on then,' Sophie prompted, as they drove away.

'He got away from me,' Dominic began, quietly. He clearly didn't want Henry to hear what he was saying. 'I was looking for a nice bunch of flowers, which wasn't easy because of the time of year, I suppose. He kept grabbing at everything in sight.'

'You know the golden rule,' Sophie reminded him in a hushed voice. 'Never let him get within an arm's reach of anything on the shelves. The best way is to have him secured at all times. Move him directly from seat to seat – car seat to shopping trolley, pushchair back to car seat, etc, etc. Always, always keep him contained. Anyway, carry on.'

'So, I picked him up and carried him to the checkout. But then I had to put him down to get my wallet out and he gave me the look. You know, the look?'

'Oh, I do know the look.'

'I asked him to stand still for a moment while I paid for the flowers, but he made a run for it. I had to chase him right out of the shop and through the service station. I left the flowers on the counter and had to go back for them. The lady obviously thought I had no control over my child… because I didn't. It was so embarrassing. I'm sure he would have run straight out into the car park if he could have got to the doors before I caught him.'

'He has no idea about safety. I'm a bit worried about how he's going to behave at Mum and Dad's. There are no safety gates around the stairs or kitchen. I did mention maybe bringing something with us, but they were very dismissive. Mum just said that she hadn't needed anything like that when we were little. We're just going to have to follow him everywhere. He burned his fingers on the oven door the other day, you know.'

'You didn't say.'

'Sorry, I meant to. I probably forgot because it wasn't too bad in the end. He managed to get his arm through the bars of the gate across the kitchen doorway, while I was taking a cake out of the oven. I told him not to touch, that it was very hot and would hurt him, but his desire to defy was too strong. He managed to touch the edge of the oven door. I held his fingers under the cold tap until he stopped crying and there was no visible damage. I shouldn't think he'll try that again, but I still wouldn't trust him not to try to touch the iron or run into the road.' Sophie turned round to look at Henry. 'He's asleep now.'

'Do you think there's something wrong with him?'

'I don't know. He doesn't behave like other children. Perhaps it's us. Is it me?'

'I'm sure it isn't us. No, you're great with him.' Dominic thought for a while. 'He just seems to look for naughty things to do. Like when people come to the house and we have to keep reminding them not to put things down because Henry will grab and throw anything he can.'

'Or when the postman comes and he wants to stuff the letters back out of the letterbox before we can get to them.'

'And in the bathroom, when he wants to turn all the taps on and keep flushing the toilet.'

'A lot of it is just toddler behaviour. It's just that Henry's kind of toddler plus, if you know what I mean,' said Sophie.

'I certainly do know what you mean.'

Eventually they arrived and parked on the drive of the semi-detached house in which Sophie had grown up. Glenda, Sophie's mother, had obviously heard the car and opened the front door before they had even got out. 'Hello, darling,' she said, embracing Sophie. 'How's my favourite grandson?'

'Your only grandson is just waking up,' said Sophie, 'so he's a bit grumpy.'

'Hello, Dominic, how was Christmas?'

'Fine, thanks, Glenda.' Henry was crying, with his head on Dominic's shoulder. Dominic was rubbing his back. 'Sorry, he doesn't like being woken up.'

'Patrick's in the kitchen. Steve and Jane are coming over for lunch tomorrow. I'm doing a Christmas dinner for all of us then, as we'll all be together. Oh, here comes Dad.'

'Happy Christmas, Sophie, darling. Bit late I know, but here you all are. Hello, Dominic, how was the journey?'

'Not too bad – five hours including a stop for lunch.'

They went into the living room and sat down. Moments later Patrick appeared with a tea tray. Henry stopped crying and sat on Dominic's knee, watching the adults chat for a moment. He looked around the room at the many ornaments and framed photographs on the shelves and tables. There were a few new ones: one of himself, one of Freya with Grandma and one of Freya with Grandad. Glenda and Patrick were, quite rightly, delighted with their new granddaughter. Sophie couldn't help noticing that with the arrival of the baby, her parents had clearly cast off their previous feelings of indignation about their son and his girlfriend living together unmarried.

Henry slipped off Dominic's knee and toddled across the room. He picked up a frame containing a photograph of Sophie in her wedding dress. Glenda jumped up from the sofa. 'No, Henry, give that to Grandma.' But Henry had seen her coming and, with a glint in his eye, he threw the photo on the floor. Glenda picked it up and replaced it, but Henry was going for a crystal swan on an occasional table in the corner, a grin on his face. Sophie and Dominic both jumped up. Sophie made a lunge for the swan and Dominic grabbed Henry and sat back down with him clamped securely on his lap.

'I'll just move a few of these,' said Sophie, swiftly clearing the shelves and tables and putting the delicate objects onto higher shelves out of Henry's reach.

'You could just tell him not to touch things,' said Glenda, reprovingly.

'Children do need discipline, you know,' added Patrick.

'Saying no doesn't work with Henry,' said Sophie. 'If you tell him not to do something, you've set him a challenge.'

Grandma and Grandad's house may not be so well adapted for Henry as the vicarage, but at least, Sophie thought, she would be sharing the burden with Dominic.

The rest of the afternoon and evening passed with Sophie and Dominic taking it in turns to follow Henry round the house, closing doors to avoid slamming and taking things out of his hands, while the other one chatted with Glenda and Patrick. Dominic emptied the car and took the luggage upstairs. Sophie and Dominic would be sleeping in Sophie's old room and Dominic put the travel cot together in Steve's childhood bedroom. He wouldn't be able to escape from that.

After tea, when Henry had been bathed and put to bed, the four adults sat down together.

'Jane and Steve will come over just before lunch tomorrow,' Glenda reminded them. 'Freya is just adorable at the moment. She's such a good baby. She's sleeping through the night already. I think she looks like Steve, but Dad thinks she looks like Jane. It will be lovely for you to see her again.'

'Yes, I'm looking forward to it,' said Sophie, truthfully.

Her mother thought for a moment, then said, 'Jane was quite worried, you know, when she became pregnant. She was frightened of telling you. I think she thought it might upset you, but I told her you would be fine. I told her that you had got over not having a baby and that you're quite happy the way you are now, with Henry.'

Sophie glanced at Dominic, feeling a mixture of surprise and hurt. She wondered whether her mother really thought she had got over her sadness or whether she had just been trying to make Jane feel better. She didn't say anything, but she wished her mother would sometimes ask her how she felt instead of telling her.

The following morning Henry woke up bright and early. The weather was cold but dry and, in order to avoid chasing Henry round the house all day, Sophie and Dominic put Henry in the pushchair after breakfast and took him for a walk, while Glenda and Patrick made preparations for dinner.

Steve, Jane and Freya arrived just in time for lunch. The table was beautifully set and the food cooked to perfection. During the meal Henry sat in the highchair between Dominic and Sophie. Eating wasn't one of Henry's challenges; it was something he thoroughly enjoyed. Sophie sometimes worried that he didn't seem to 'do full', but on this occasion it was very helpful that he sat and ate quietly and continuously. It allowed everyone else to linger over their meals and enjoy each other's company. Freya was passed between the adults, so everyone had the opportunity both to hold her and to eat.

After lunch Glenda ushered everyone into the living room to sit down, and said that she and Patrick would clear away.

Dominic took the first shift looking after Henry. Jane passed Sophie a bottle of milk, so she could feed Freya. After Freya had been winded, Jane picked her up and placed her in her crib and she drifted off to sleep. Steve picked up the paper and Jane sat back in her chair.

'How's it going with your new job?' Jane asked Sophie.

'New job?' asked Sophie, unsure whether she was referring to being Henry's mum or something else.

'Yes, I mean, I know the vicar's wife runs the WI and the Mothers' Union…'

Sophie was momentarily speechless. 'Which novel from the 1950s are you getting that information from?' she managed to say, after a pause.

'Oh, isn't that what you do? My mum said that that was what vicars' wives did.'

'Not really,' said Sophie. 'The WI isn't part of the church, although some of the ladies at church are members. We don't have a Mothers' Union in Oxley.'

'Oh,' said Jane, looking confused. 'Maybe Mum got it wrong, then.'

'Actually, a lot of people in my position have jobs outside the church. I chose not to have a paid job in order to work alongside Dominic, but since Henry arrived I've had to stop doing quite a lot at church. I used to lead some of the Bible studies at the women's group we have on Thursday mornings. There were some people I used to visit and study with one to one, because they found it easier that way, and others that I just used to visit. Now I spend most of my time looking after Henry. I still go to the Thursday morning group, but now I sit in the crèche. Henry can be a bit tricky sometimes; I'm not quite ready to leave him with someone else yet.'

'I love being a mum,' said Jane, curling her legs up underneath her. 'Are you enjoying it?'

Sophie thought about the many coping strategies that filled her days. 'Well, I'm doing it,' she said. 'If I'm honest, I find it quite a challenge, but I have come in straight at the terrible twos, I suppose.'

At that moment, Glenda came into the room with a tray full of cups of coffee. 'You see, Sophie,' she said, 'a little baby like Freya is very hard work.'

Sophie stood up. 'I'll just go and relieve Dominic,' she said, 'so he can come and drink his coffee.'

The next day was Sunday and their last day in Eastbourne before the journey back to Staffordshire that evening. Feeling somewhat guilty, Sophie decided not to go to church. In many ways it would have been nice to visit the church where, as a teenager, she had joined the youth club and discovered her faith. She knew there would be people there who remembered her from all those years ago. Maybe, she thought to herself ruefully, it would have been different if Henry had been... well... different. She realised that she simply couldn't face the Sunday routine of sitting down, waiting for Henry to scream. Then she wondered whether that was a problem for young families visiting All Saints, Oxley, and what they could do about it. Really, Henry saw church as another opportunity to be naughty. He had learned very early on that the quickest way to be taken out of the church service and into the back room was to start shouting as soon as the service started.

In the end, Sophie took Henry for another walk in the pushchair and Dominic went to church alone. Sophie knew that he really appreciated the opportunity to simply be part of a congregation sometimes, rather than always having to lead one. She wanted him to have that special time. She took Henry to the park and arranged to pass by the church on the way back, so they could walk back to the house together.

They opened the front door in time to hear a lot of shouting coming from the living room. Going in, they found Glenda and Patrick watching *Countdown* on the television, both holding pens and pads of paper. 'Is that on now?' asked Dominic, sounding surprised.

'No, no,' said Patrick, not looking up from the television. 'We recorded it.'

Sophie smiled to herself and made a mental note to speak to Dominic later about her parents' *Countdown* habit.

After lunch, Sophie suggested that they all go for a walk together. Dominic put Henry on reins for safety, hoping he would walk some of the way with them, while Sophie pushed the empty pushchair. They all wrapped up and took a walk towards the beach, enjoying the breeze and the salty air. After a few yards Henry laid himself down on the pavement and wouldn't get up, so he ended up back in the pushchair again.

'You're very lucky that Henry is such an easy child to look after,' said Glenda.

How could her mother be so lacking in observation? 'I do find him quite hard work, you know.'

'But he eats everything,' said Glenda, as if that settled the matter.

'He does eat everything,' agreed Sophie, 'but I find him hard in other ways. He seems to be looking for the next naughty thing to do all day long.'

'Oh, he's just a normal little boy, with lots of energy,' said Glenda.

'He just needs discipline, that's all,' Patrick added.

Perhaps he was just a normal little boy who needed discipline, thought Sophie. Perhaps she just wasn't very good at coping. Other mums seemed to manage a lot more easily.

After tea, they packed the car, put Henry into his pyjamas with his coat on top, secured him in his car seat and said their goodbyes.

'Thank you so much,' said Sophie. 'It's been lovely and you've looked after us so well. I hope we haven't exhausted you too much.'

'Thank you,' said Dominic. 'Do come and visit us when you can. You're always welcome.'

'I'll ring you tomorrow when we get back from Bridge Club,' said Glenda, 'to check how the journey went.'

They began the long journey home. Henry dropped off to sleep quickly, leaving them to talk.

'It was lovely and I love them very much,' said Sophie, 'but they can be a bit funny sometimes.'

'Seem pretty regular to me,' said Dominic. 'They like looking after their family, playing bridge and then rushing home to watch *Countdown*.'

'Ooh, that reminds me, I must tell you about *Countdown* later. No, what I mean is, my mother doesn't always use her eyes. Or, come to think of it, her ears. You weren't there, but she told me she thought a small baby was hard work. I don't doubt that Freya *can* be hard work, but we spent the whole time we were there taking it in turns to stop Henry demolishing the house. And then she told me what an easy child Henry was, because he eats everything.'

'Well,' said Dominic, thoughtfully, 'she thinks Henry is easy because, let's be honest, your mother's mission in life is to feed people. As for the other things she said, she's your mother and she loves you. She wants to think you're happy. Thinking that Henry is an easy child and that you don't mind about not being able to have a baby any more means that she can think you're happy and content with the way things have turned out. In her own funny way, she's trying to make it true by telling you it's true.'

'I suppose,' said Sophie. 'I suppose it's a bit like when I first took Henry to the toddler group. It was horrible, because Henry didn't want to play with any of the toys and kept trying to escape out of the door to make me chase him. All the other mothers kept looking at me, but pretending they weren't looking at me. Anyway, I said that we were adopting him and one lady said I was lucky, because I didn't have to go through pregnancy and labour. I wanted to scream at her, "No, I'm not, I'm not, I'm not lucky," but I couldn't because I'm the vicar's wife and I have to be nice to everyone.'

'No, you're a *Christian* and you have to be nice to everyone.'

'OK, fair point. But what I was trying to say was that the lady at the toddler group was trying to make not being able to have a baby into a good thing, to make me feel better. She wasn't saying it to be unkind.'

'Exactly. Lots of funny things people say are kindly meant. Anyway, tell me about *Countdown*.'

'Oh, it's only funny because they record it so they can cheat. They've always done it. They record it and play it back, so they can pause it and give themselves time to work out the answers. Then they compete with each other to see who can work it out first. That was what all the shouting was about.'

Three

Hayley and Paul were getting ready for Paul's work Christmas party. They were both feeling rather low after Christmas. They had spent Christmas Day with Paul's parents in the village, but they had had another row in the morning and ended up missing church and being late for lunch.

Hayley had felt irritated when Paul had woken up on Christmas morning looking miserable. He had wished her a happy Christmas in a sad voice. Why, she wondered, couldn't Paul see how much worse this was for her than for him? She felt he really ought to be showing sympathy towards her, pampering her, even. After all, she reasoned, women had babies, not men.

'Happy Christmas,' she replied. 'Shall we have a cup of tea?'

Paul's usual morning routine was to bring Hayley a cup of tea in bed.

'Mmm,' came the reply, but there was no movement.

'Church is at ten o'clock and we don't want to be late.' Still no movement. Annoyed, Hayley got up and made two cups of tea herself. When she returned to the bedroom Paul still hadn't moved. 'I've made you a cup of tea, so stop sulking and sit up.' She sat down at her dressing table and started pulling hairbrushes and make-up out of the drawers. She glanced at him in the mirror.

'I'm not sulking,' Paul replied, rolling on to his back and looking at her. 'I'm just sad.'

'I know, but… well, I'm sure you're not as sad as me and I'm not lying in bed being grumpy.'

Paul rolled back on to his side, away from her. He pulled the duvet over his head. 'I'm so sorry. Sorry I've made you so sad, sorry I can't give you a baby. My body doesn't work properly. I feel useless.'

'Well, that attitude's really not going to get us anywhere, is it? It's no good moping about; we've got to tackle it. Dr Payne said he would refer us to the fertility clinic at the hospital. They might be able to help us. Dr Payne said our chances are reduced, not impossible.' Hayley could feel her anger rising. What was Paul playing at? He should be trying to make *her* feel better. She shouldn't be having to chivvy him along.

'But we've been trying to have a baby for ages, Hayley. Two whole years. And now we know it's all my fault it hasn't happened. I feel terrible.'

'Will you stop trying to make this out to be about you? It's not about you; it's about us. It's more about me, really; *I'm* the one who might not be able to have a baby.' She banged the dressing table drawer shut. Clearly Paul didn't understand how she was feeling. 'Stop being so selfish!'

'I'm not being selfish. I'm just trying to make you understand how I feel.'

Hayley turned, infuriated. 'I do understand how you feel. How could you possibly think I don't? We might never have a baby and it's terrible. It's the worst thing that's ever happened to me.'

'And it's my fault.'

'It's not about whose fault it is. It's about what we're going to do about it.'

'Hayley, can't you see, it's not just about not having a baby? Yes, I'm really sad about that, but can't you understand how awful it feels as a man, to know that that part of your body, the part that makes you a man, doesn't do what it should do? I feel inferior… embarrassed… ashamed.'

'So that's what it is, is it? You're worried about what people think of you. Well, get a grip of yourself, we'll get Dr Payne to refer us to the fertility clinic and see what they can do about it.'

'Hayley, I'm not sure there's much they *can* do about it. When the problem is with the man, I'm not sure they can do anything at all. There isn't a magic pill to make them... stronger swimmers.'

'Well, I've been doing a bit of research. Apparently keeping everything cool down there is supposed to help. Perhaps you could sit in a cold bath for an hour each morning. Or you could just pop a couple of ice cubes into your pants.'

'Oh, that would look great when they melted, wouldn't it?!'

'Or are you scared of the fertility clinic doing something worse to you? You are, aren't you?'

'No, it's not that... not that anyone really wants to have their private parts prodded with a scalpel, but...'

'So that is what this is about – you're scared of having treatment. Paul, it's the least you can do to make this better for us, really. Otherwise... otherwise we'll just have to adopt.'

'I just don't know how I feel about adoption,' Paul said, sitting up. 'I don't want to end up being a long-term babysitter for someone who goes back to their "real" parents when they're eighteen.'

Hayley didn't argue. She didn't really know how she felt about adoption either. She just wanted Paul to understand how desperate she was to have a baby.

'Anyway, that's not what I mean. If there's anything they can do to help, I'll have it done. It's just... I don't think there is going to be anything. And I'm sorry I've let you down, that I'm a rubbish husband, that I can't do what a husband ought to be able to do. I'm sorry we can't have a baby.'

Hayley looked at the clock, 'We're not going to make it to church.'

'Sorry,' said Paul again. 'I'm sorry about the baby and I'm sorry about church.'

'We can't give up,' she said. 'I can't not have a baby. We'll get through this somehow.' She walked over to the bed and sat down, putting her hand in his.

'I know. I just woke up feeling so sad. Hayley, do you still love me?'

'Of course,' she said, finally looking at him. 'Of course I love you.'

By the time Paul returned to work on 27th December, they were both feeling subdued, but were no longer arguing. Hayley didn't have to return to work until school reopened after New Year, so she turned her attention to preparing for Paul's work party on Saturday night.

She had been feeling a little nervous about the impending party. Paul worked in the IT department of a large firm in town. She had visited his workplace on a couple of occasions and felt a little overwhelmed walking into the plush open-plan office with its big desks, swivel chairs and coffee machines. It was so light and airy, with its large windows and high ceilings. It seemed like another world compared to her cluttered desk in the poky office of the primary school, next to the crowded staffroom with the mismatched chairs. She had worried that the party would be full of immaculately turned-out career women and she didn't want to feel out of her depth.

Deciding to tackle the problem, Hayley had been shopping and spent more than she should have on a dress for the occasion. The dress had quite a low-cut neckline and she had bought an uplift bra to go underneath. Then, on the Saturday morning of the party, she booked a spray tan and arranged to have her hair put up into an elaborate style at the hairdressers. In the afternoon, her sister, Chloe, who lived in a neighbouring flat on the estate, arrived to help with make-up, bringing some costume jewellery and shoes for her to borrow.

'You look great,' said Chloe, reassuringly. 'Send me a message later and let me know how you're getting on.'

'I will, I promise. Thank you so much for your help,' said Hayley, as her sister left. She went back into the bedroom and looked at herself in the mirror with some satisfaction. She had achieved the effect she had wanted. A new feeling of confidence rose inside her. Maybe, just maybe, tonight would be the night she would conceive her baby. After all, Dr Payne had said unlikely, but not impossible, and it was definitely the right time of the month. There was always hope. She just had to get Paul out of his negative thought bog and in the mood.

Paul walked into the bedroom and stopped to gaze at his beautiful wife. 'You look lovely,' he said, 'although you are showing quite a lot of cleavage!'

'I thought you liked my boobs,' she said.

'I do. I just don't want everyone else to like them.'

'Oh, I'm sure no one else will be looking. I've packed the overnight case. Are you nearly ready to go?'

They got into the car and drove to the hotel in town. For Paul and Hayley it wasn't far away, but the firm had lavishly decided to pay for rooms for guests so that no one would have to drive home. Hayley felt quite excited as she walked through the hotel doors with Paul holding their little suitcase. It felt as if they were going on a mini holiday.

They checked in and took the case up to their room on the second floor, then went down in the lift to the function room, where the party was to be held. Looking at the seating plan, they found the table with their names. Employees from the IT department, together with their guests, had been allocated places on two tables near the bar.

Hayley and Paul crossed the dance floor. Most of the guests were already seated. Hayley was positioned between Paul and a sandy-haired man with a nice smile, who introduced himself as David Stubbs. It seemed that David had not brought a guest. Hayley quietly surveyed the people sitting around the table. She needn't have worried about sophisticated career girls. Apart from the rather attractive girl sitting on the other side of David, whom Hayley recognised from a visit to Paul's office, they appeared to be sitting with a group of IT geeks. One man, she noticed, was even wearing a diamond-patterned V-neck jumper under his dinner jacket. She picked up her phone to message her sister, but someone had stood up to call for quiet by tapping a spoon on the side of a glass, so she slipped her phone under her napkin.

'Ladies and gentlemen.' Mr Wainwright, a rather distinguished-looking man in his late fifties, known as the Big Boss to his employees, had stood up from his place at a long table on the other side of the room. 'Welcome to our wonderful Christmas celebration, a small thank you from the company for all your hard work this year. Food is about to be served and I have asked Rufus Parsons to say grace.'

A fair-haired young man further along the table stood up, beaming at them all. 'Good evening. For those of you who don't know me, I'm Rufus Parsons and I've recently been appointed as manager of IT,' he said, confidently. 'Let's give thanks for the food that has been prepared for us.' He bowed his head, and most of the people in the room followed suit, some a little awkwardly. 'Dear God, we thank You for this time to celebrate together and for the food that has been prepared for us. Amen.' There was a quiet mumble of Amens from the room. He lifted his head and beamed at them again. 'May I wish you all a very pleasant evening.' He sat down and began talking to the man seated next to him.

Paul leaned across Hayley to speak to David. 'New manager?'

'Nice of them to let us know.'

'He looks very young to be a manager. He's certainly very sure of himself.'

A team of waiters and waitresses arrived and began pouring wine into their glasses from the many bottles on each table. Then the meal arrived. It was a set menu.

'Oh no, not turkey again,' Hayley heard the pretty lady on David's left exclaim.

Hayley had eaten quite a lot of turkey recently too, but she was hungry and she didn't mind. Paul was talking to a work colleague on his right. She turned to talk to David.

'Did you have a nice Christmas?'

'Yes, thank you. I went to stay with some friends near Shrewsbury. We had a nice time. What about yourself?'

Hayley didn't feel inclined to talk to a stranger about the Christmas Day upset or their fertility problems. 'Lovely, thanks. We went to Paul's parents – they live close to us. We went to my family last year. We try to take it in turns.' She cast around for something else to say. 'Do you have family?' Possibly not the best choice of question, she thought, given the fact that he had just told her he had spent Christmas with friends.

'No, not any more. I was an only child and my dad didn't stick around for long after I was born. I can't really remember him. Mum died in October, so it's just me now.'

'I'm sorry to hear that,' said Hayley, inwardly reproaching herself for her gaffe. 'I haven't been in your position, but I imagine the first Christmas without a loved one must be very difficult.'

'We were very close,' David went on. 'She always suffered with her health – she had a weak heart. I went away to university when I was eighteen, but then I moved back in with Mum. She really needed me to look after her. In the end, I found I was worrying every time I left her, even to go to work. She did pass away peacefully, though. I found her sitting in her armchair when I came home from work one day. She looked as if she was sleeping.'

'I'm sorry you've had such a hard time. There can't be many young men who would move back in with their mum to be her carer.'

'No, maybe not, but she was very important to me.'

'And you work in the IT department?' Again, not the best question, given the table they were sitting at.

'Yes, I've been working in the IT department since I left university. It's an easy drive from where I live and it's a good company to work for. How about you? What do you do?'

'I'm a school secretary at the primary school in Oxley. Do you know Oxley?'

'Yes, I've heard of it. About ten miles away, isn't it?'

'Probably more like eight, I think.'

'And what do you like to do, when you're not being school secretary?'

'Actually, I enjoy music a lot, especially the piano and keyboard. I play at the church in Oxley, All Saints.'

'Oh, that's interesting,' said David, sounding as if it wasn't. 'Have you got children?'

'No,' said Hayley, looking away. 'Not yet, anyway.' She stuffed a piece of roast potato into her mouth to give herself time to think of another change of subject, but at that point David turned to talk to the pretty girl on his left. Hayley didn't mind – she had been polite and made small talk. She hadn't really come to make friends with Paul's work colleagues; she had come to enjoy time with Paul and try to raise his spirits. She needed him to be in a good mood for later.

Paul was drinking quite a lot, although he appeared to be handling it quite well. 'Don't drink too much, darling,' Hayley whispered. A bit tipsy would be OK; drunk wouldn't be.

'I'm fine,' said Paul. 'Nice turnkey, turkey, I mean. Are you having a nice time?'

'Yes, I just don't want you to drink too much.'

'Don't worry, it's fine, just fine. I haven't got to drink, I mean drive, until tomorrow.'

It wasn't going quite according to plan, Hayley thought. She poured Paul a large glass of water. 'Drink some water too.' Christmas pudding was being served. She hoped it might soak up some of the wine in Paul's stomach.

Out of the corner of her eye, Hayley became aware of someone approaching the table from across the dance floor. She looked up. It was Rufus Parsons. Paul may not be about to make the best of first impressions on his new boss. 'Here comes that new IT man,' she hissed out of the side of her mouth.

Paul turned and stood up. Rufus held out his hand. 'Rufus,' he said, enthusiastically. 'Pleased to meet you.' He was a tall, slender man with a young face, and glasses. His fair hair was curly and Hayley thought he looked a little bit like an overgrown schoolboy.

'Paul,' said Paul, shaking his hand, 'and this is my wife, Hayley.'

Hayley stood up and shook Rufus's hand too.

'Lovely to meet you both. I'm sorry we weren't introduced before. I'm afraid I only arrived yesterday.'

Paul looked a little lost for words. How much had he had to drink? Hayley decided to take over. 'You mean you only arrived in Stafford yesterday? Or only arrived at the company yesterday?'

'Both,' he said to Hayley's chest. Then, realising what he was doing, going slightly pink and looking up, he added, 'I think, technically, I started to work for the company yesterday, but I actually moved up from Surrey yesterday and didn't make it into the office. That will be next week.'

'Oh,' said Hayley. 'You must have a house full of boxes.'

'No actual house at the moment, I'm afraid. I'll start looking around for a house as soon as possible. It was a bit of a last-minute appointment. They're putting me up in the hotel for the next few weeks, so I have a *room* full of boxes.'

'What, here?' asked Hayley.

'Yes, quite handy, really. I didn't have far to come this evening! Lovely to meet you.' He smiled and then bounced along the table to chat to David.

Hayley and Paul sat down.

'He seems nice,' whispered Hayley.

'We'll see next week,' whispered Paul.

At the end of the meal, coffee was served and music began to play. Couples started moving towards the dance floor. Paul didn't look capable of dancing, so Hayley sat close to him and held his hand. She hoped the coffee might sober him up. She could hear David trying to chat up the pretty girl. She heard the words 'my mother'. After a while the girl extracted herself from him and scurried across the dance floor to chat to a friend. Hayley watched them. They started giggling and the friend turned to look across the room at David. Hayley glanced at David, hoping he hadn't noticed, but unfortunately he had. He had also noticed Hayley watching them and then looking at him. She felt embarrassed. She also felt angry with the silly women.

Rufus seemed to have finished his round of enthusiastic introductions and seemed to be looking for his next move. Hayley watched him check the whereabouts of the people who had been sitting at the IT department tables. Most couples were slow dancing. Paul, Hayley and David were the only ones left at the table. Decisively, he strode towards them.

Then, addressing Paul, he said, 'May I ask your lovely wife for this dance?'

Paul looked surprised. 'Sure.'

'Don't forget to drink your coffee before it gets cold, darling,' said Hayley, as she got up to join Rufus on the dance floor. But as she walked away, she was aware of Paul picking up not his coffee cup, but his wine glass. There was nothing she could do.

Rufus turned out to be quite a good dancer. He expertly guided Hayley around the dance floor and engaged her in easy small talk at the same time. She felt herself warming towards him. There was a question she wanted to ask him and she found that she wasn't afraid to do so, but how to start?

'It was nice of you to say grace before the meal,' she began. 'It's quite unusual for people to do that these days, at functions, I mean. I was glad you did, though.'

'Oh, I'm glad you were glad,' he smiled at her. 'I asked Mr Wainwright if he was going to do it. He looked quite surprised, but then he asked me to. He knows that sort of thing is important to me – it came up at my interview.'

This was going to be easier than she had anticipated. Hayley decided to wade straight in. 'So, are you a Christian?' There, she had said it. She wasn't usually so direct when asking people about their beliefs. It was normally something she would have skirted around for a while, but Rufus obviously wasn't backwards in coming forwards.

'Yes,' he said, looking pleased to be asked. 'Are you?'

'Yes, but I don't normally ask people that question when I've only just met them. Have you had any thoughts about churches in this area?'

'I expect I'll try a few of the ones in town before I decide where I fit in. Have you got any recommendations?'

'I go to All Saints in Oxley. That's the village where we live, about eight miles from here. I really like it. The vicar and his wife are quite young and they're trying to make the services more up to date, to attract more young people.' She added, 'I expect it would be too far for you, though.'

'Well, I don't know where I'm going to end up living yet. I'll keep it in mind, though. Thanks.'

The dance ended and Hayley wandered back towards the table. Paul wasn't there. She searched around for him and saw him leaning against the bar with a pint in his hand. He was talking to a couple of men she didn't know. She sat down at the table and hoped Paul would notice and come and join her. His coffee was still on the table, untouched.

Hayley noticed that David was still sipping from his wine glass. He didn't look as if he'd had quite as much to drink as Paul, but he did look morose.

'Are you OK?' she asked, feeling concerned.

'Oh, I'm fine, thanks,' he replied, looking across the dance floor. The girl he had failed to chat up was now dancing with Rufus.

Hayley had had a couple of glasses of wine herself and her conversation with Rufus had made her feel bold. If she could talk about her faith with her husband's new boss, she could talk to David about anything. 'Don't take any notice of that silly woman,' she said. 'You can do much better than her.'

David turned his gaze to Hayley. 'Really?' he said. 'What makes you say that?'

'I don't think she was very nice to you,' said Hayley, simply. 'She obviously thinks she's a cut above everyone else and she doesn't care about other people's feelings. You wouldn't treat anyone like that, would you?'

'No, I wouldn't,' said David fervently.

'Well, then, you can do better.' Hayley was getting into her stride now. 'You want to find someone nice, someone kind and caring. Those are the important qualities.' She tried to think about what Sophie might say on the subject. 'My friend Sophie, from church, would say that all people are equal in the eyes of God. Actually, I think it's the Bible that says that.'

'You really take the God stuff seriously, don't you? Where is it you go?'

'I do take it seriously,' said Hayley. 'And it's All Saints, in Oxley where we live.'

'Does Paul go too?' asked David, curiously.

'Do I go where?' asked Paul, sitting down beside Hayley.

'David was asking me about church.'

'Oh, no, not really. I go when Hayley drags me along,' said Paul. Then, turning to Hayley, he added, 'How was your dance with Mr Rufus?'

'Nice, actually,' Hayley replied. 'He's a good dancer. In fact, I think he's really quite charming.' Then she added, 'And he goes to church. He told me.'

'Really?' said Paul, looking incredulous. 'Hey, David, you know we were having the problem uploading that php file to the web server? It turns out Gary had changed the TCP-IP password on the client side.'

'You're kidding? What a moron. He should have told us.'

And that, thought Hayley, was the end of the conversation about church. She had no idea what Paul was talking about, but at least it seemed to have livened David up. Two plugs for church in one evening! Sophie would be impressed.

Paul and David kept up their work-related conversation for the rest of the evening, both still drinking. Hayley conceded that tonight was not going to be the night and amused herself by watching the dancers.

At midnight, the music stopped and the lights went on. 'Come on,' said Hayley, standing up, 'let's go upstairs.' Paul was red in the face and his eyes were bloodshot. He stood up and started walking unsteadily across the dance floor, towards the doorway to the entrance hall and the lifts. Hayley linked arms with him, for his sake rather than hers. They walked slowly into the entrance hall. Hayley's shoes were pinching and she was hoping that Paul wasn't going to be sick. They took the lift to the second floor. Paul got the key out of his pocket but didn't seem to be able to coordinate unlocking the door of their room.

Hayley took the key and unlocked the door. 'How much have you had this evening?'

'Maybe a bit too much. Sorry. Was just feeling fed up. Sorry. I love you. Sorry.' He lay down on the bed and shut his eyes.

Hayley kicked her shoes off. 'These shoes I borrowed from my sister are killing me,' she said. There was no response. She looked at Paul. He was unconscious on the bed, fully dressed. Her sister... she had been going to message her sister at the beginning of the evening. Where was her mobile? She looked in her bag, but it wasn't there. Then she remembered – she had put it under her napkin. It must still be on the table. Without putting her shoes back on, she picked up the key and left the room, returning to the function room on the ground floor.

David was still sitting at the table. She walked over and started looking under the napkins and general mess that had been left on the table. Ah, there it was. She picked up the phone. 'You OK? Aren't you going to bed?'

'I'm fine, thanks,' David replied, standing up. He looked a little wobbly, but nowhere near as bad as Paul. 'Thanks for, erm, thanks for being nice earlier.'

'Oh, that's OK,' said Hayley. 'It's what anyone would do.'

'No,' said David, 'it isn't what anyone would do. You're kind. You're a nice person.'

They walked out of the room together. Rufus was standing in the entrance hall. He pressed the button to call the lift. He looked at David, then at Hayley's feet.

'My shoes were hurting and I realised I'd left something on the table,' Hayley explained.

'I see,' said Rufus, as the lift doors opened and they all went in. 'Which floor?'

'Second please,' said Hayley.

'Same,' said David.

'Me too,' said Rufus, smiling. He pressed the button for the second floor, the doors closed and they all went up together.

Four

Dominic and Sophie had settled back into vicarage life after Christmas. Dominic had been unable to resist going back into the study when they had arrived home from Sophie's parents, despite the fact that he wasn't really due back to work for a few more days. It was always so much harder to switch off from church life when they were at home – one of the consequences of living and working in the same place.

Lucy was enjoying a few more days of freedom before going back to work at the physiotherapy clinic in Stafford town centre. She had worked right up until Christmas Day and taken some leave afterwards. On the morning of New Year's Eve, which was a Tuesday, Sophie was looking forward to Lucy visiting for coffee.

Henry had made an important step forwards after Christmas. He had learned the delights of paint. He had little interest in toys, apart from the large plastic ride-on variety. He enjoyed sitting on these and propelling himself around using his feet. Sophie and Dominic had realised this very quickly and planned accordingly. A plastic sit-on car had been put downstairs and another one upstairs, behind the safety gate. There were a couple in the garden. These seemed to keep Henry happy, apart from the time when he had wanted to ride the car up the stairs. The safety gate had been left closed and Sophie had done her best to explain why riding the car up the stairs wasn't a good idea, but a major tantrum had ensued.

Yesterday, however, Sophie had shown Henry the paints he had been given for Christmas. She had strapped him into his highchair, taken the tray off and pushed the chair up to the kitchen table, so he couldn't escape, and then started painting. To her delight, Henry had taken the proffered paint brush and joined in. Sophie had decided to use Henry's new skill to her advantage and had positioned him at the kitchen table in time for Lucy's knock at the door.

Sophie was very pleased to see her friend. She took her coat and ushered her into the kitchen.

'Henry's going to do some painting, so we can talk. What would you like to drink?'

'A cup of coffee would be lovely please, Sophie. Nice paints, Henry. Were they a Christmas present?' Lucy sat down at the table and picked up a piece of paper to join in.

'Dominic's parents sent them from France. Probably cost more to post them than buy them, but they like to choose their own presents rather than sending money,' said Sophie, as she poured three cups of coffee and took one into the study for Dominic. She came back and sat down at the table. 'How was Christmas?'

'Lovely, thanks,' said Lucy. 'It was just the three of us, but Mum and Dad were on good form. How about you?'

'Great, thanks. It was just the three of us too, and then we had a good weekend in Eastbourne. Sometimes I wish we lived a bit closer to my family, but we are where we are. It must be very nice for you living so close to your parents.'

'It is, but I only moved back to Oxley two years ago, you know. I lived in London after my physiotherapy degree, thinking it would be a good career move to work in one of the teaching hospitals. Mum and Dad were a bit shocked. They would never have said anything to stop me, but I think they had hoped I'd find a job closer to home. I'm an only child, and I think they missed me.'

'I'm sure they did. But *was* it a good career move to go to London?'

'Yes, I don't regret it. I learned a lot at work, joined a great church and had some lovely flatmates, but then friends started getting married and moving away and I found myself coming home more frequently and then feeling sad when it was time to go back to London. Mum saw a job being advertised at a physiotherapy clinic in town, so I applied and got it. I moved back in with Mum and Dad for a while and then found my flat. I could never have afforded to buy somewhere of my own in London.'

'It's a lovely flat.'

'Thank you. It's small, but it's just right for me. My only regret is that I can't fit a piano in.'

'I didn't know you played!'

'Don't get excited – I only play for my own amusement. I don't think I could ever play in front of other people. I'm not Hayley!'

'I'm glad you're here,' said Sophie, looking up from her painting and smiling at Lucy. A sparkle coming from Lucy's neck caught her eye. 'That's a pretty necklace. Present from your parents?'

'Present from a patient, actually,' said Lucy, grimacing slightly.

'Oh,' said Sophie, noticing the look on Lucy's face. 'Male, by any chance? Does he like you?'

'I kind of got that impression,' said Lucy. 'Not my type, though, and even if he was, it wouldn't be allowed. Nice to be noticed, though. Gives one hope.'

Sophie hadn't known Lucy to be involved with anyone romantically in the time she had known her, but this was the first time Lucy had admitted that it would be something she would like. 'Is there anyone you're interested in, in that way?'

'Not really. There's no one at church is there?'

'No,' agreed Sophie. 'Not really.'

'I am praying for the right man,' said Lucy. 'I've been praying for eight years now. I've always known, since I was a little girl, that I wanted to get married and have children. I do love my job, but I never really wanted to be a career girl. I had a couple of dates with boys from school when I was a teenager, but nothing serious. Then, when I was twenty, I realised that if I was going to get married, it would have to be to a Christian. I mean, I'm trying to live my life dedicated to God. I want to be married to someone who feels the same way, not someone pulling me in another direction.'

'I know,' said Sophie, 'but some people don't have that choice. I mean, take Hayley, for example; it's difficult if you become a Christian after you get married.'

'Well, I *have* got a choice,' said Lucy. 'But what I'm trying to say is, eight years of praying with absolutely nothing happening is a very long time. Maybe I have to accept that it just isn't going to happen, but it's not really the way I imagined my life working out.'

'Never say never!'

'No, but maybe God just isn't listening to that particular prayer, or maybe He's saying no. He made me the way I am, so perhaps it just isn't important to God whether I get married or not. He's not here to grant our wishes, is He? Perhaps He just made me unattractive to men.'

'Lucy, you're not unattractive; you're lovely.'

'That's kind of you to say, but... realistically... there were single men and women at the church I went to when I was at university and at the church I went to in London. Other people paired up and I went to lots of weddings, but I never had one of my own. There must be a reason for it. It feels as if my prayers are falling on deaf ears. I know Mum and Dad are round the corner and you are here and everyone at church is here but, sometimes, to be honest, I feel lonely.'

'You're still young.'

'I'm twenty-eight.'

'That is young!'

'OK, but it's still eight years of waiting. Sometimes it feels as if God just doesn't care!'

'He cared enough to die for you.'

'I knew you'd say that... and I know you're right, of course I do, it's just... I won't stop praying for the right man, but I'm getting tired of waiting.'

Sophie marvelled at her friend's commitment and silently thanked God that Dominic had come along when she was quite young. 'Right, let's think about this. Describe your ideal man,' she said, mentally going through a rather short list of single Christian men of her acquaintance.

'Well,' said Lucy. 'Godly, upright and holy, obviously!'

'Obviously!'

'Brainy – I do need a man who I can look up to intellectually. Reasonable dress sense – I suppose that narrows the choice down a bit in Christian circles,' Lucy smiled. 'No anoraks or sandals.'

'Tricky,' agreed Sophie. 'What else?'

'I would have to be able to find him attractive – tall, dark, handsome.'

'Mmmm, yes,' said Sophie, gazing into the distance.

'No beards.'

'Definitely not.'

'And a nice hairy chest is essential.'

'Couldn't have put it better myself.'

They both started giggling just as Dominic walked into the kitchen with his empty cup. 'What are you laughing at?'

'Nothing,' they said together. Sophie noticed Dominic checking himself in the hall mirror as he walked back to the study.

'Thinking about it, though,' said Sophie, after Dominic had shut the study door, 'don't get too worried about dress sense. When I first started going out with Dominic, he had no idea. He dressed a bit like a 1970s throwback. For our first date he wore a pair of jeans with a matching denim shirt and no belt. He looked as if he was wearing a denim jumpsuit. He had this old pair of trainers that he wore everywhere, except o the office. They smelled a bit, actually.'

'When you say "office"...?'

'Oh, yes, it was before he trained for the ministry. We were both working in business when we met and when we got married.'

'So, you didn't know you were going to end up married to a vicar, then?'

'No, but it was a decision we made together. I carried on working to see him through theological college and then gave up when he was ordained. We had to move away anyway and there seemed to be plenty to do in the church when we arrived, so I never went back to paid work. Then Henry came along.'

'Going back to Dominic, though,' said Lucy, 'he dresses quite well now.'

'Ah, that's because I took him shopping to sort him out. He isn't allowed to go clothes shopping unsupervised any more.'

Sophie and Lucy passed the rest of the morning happily chatting and painting. Eventually Henry tired of the paints and Sophie began to wipe him and the table down.

'I'd better be going,' said Lucy.

'OK. Are you doing anything special later, to welcome in the New Year?'

'Just going round to Mum and Dad's for the evening. I used to party when I lived in London, but not so much these days. You?'

'The thought of voluntarily staying awake past midnight when you know you are going to get an early wake-up call from a toddler in the morning kind of puts one off, to be honest.'

'I can imagine. Oh, I know what I was going to say to you… Is Hayley OK? I haven't seen her for a while. She wasn't at church on Sunday or on Christmas Day.'

Sophie hadn't been given permission to share Hayley and Paul's problem, so she skirted the question. 'They were at Paul's work Christmas bash on Saturday and they stayed at the hotel overnight. I don't think she wanted to come back early for church on Sunday. I'm intending to meet up with her this week. I'll give her a call this afternoon.'

'OK,' Lucy seemed satisfied. 'Thanks for the coffee and chat. Thanks for sharing your paints with me, Henry. I'll see you on Sunday.'

After lunch, Sophie realised that Henry wasn't going to be easily distracted so she decided to message Hayley rather than try to speak on the phone. 'Hi Hayley, hope you're OK. Wondered if you wanted to meet up before you go back to work? x'

Half an hour later, she got a message back. 'Hi Sophie, all OK thanks. Bit busy this week, but I'll see you on Sunday. Paul said he would come too! x'

'Everything OK?' asked Dominic, as he came into the room and saw Sophie looking at her phone.

'Yes, just a message from Hayley. I asked her if she wanted to meet up before she goes back to school, but she said she was busy.'

'Is that a problem?'

'No, I'm just a bit surprised. I thought she might want to talk. Still, she said she would see us on Sunday. And guess what?'

'Paul said he would come?'

'Exactly.'

'Let's see, shall we?' said Dominic, as he began to walk out of the room.

'Dominic, before you go, can I just ask you something?'

'Go ahead,' he said, from the doorway.

'Lucy…'

'What about her?'

'This isn't a trick question, but do you think she's attractive?'

'Why do you ask?'

'I told you it's not a trick question. It's just that she thinks men don't find her attractive, but that's not true, is it?'

'Oh, I see, no… Lucy's great. Any man would be lucky to have her.'

'Good, that's what I thought. I think she's finding it hard that she hasn't met anyone yet.'

'Better to have no man than the wrong man.'

'I know, but that's easy for us to say – we're already married. She is praying for the right man.'

'Well, perhaps you should be praying for her too.'

'You're right and I will.'

Hayley was at home, alone. Paul had taken the whole of the previous Sunday to get over his hangover. Guilt for getting drunk and passing out at the hotel had driven him to agree to accompany Hayley to church the following Sunday. Hayley knew he was trying to make up for his terrible behaviour.

Hayley was struggling with feelings of guilt stronger than Paul's, but Paul didn't know this and Hayley didn't want him to find out. She had concentrated on maintaining the appearance of normality and waited for Paul to leave for work each morning. On the Tuesday morning the guilt had so overcome her that, after Paul had left, she had gone back to bed, wrapped herself up in the duvet and let the tears flow. What had she done? What on earth had she been thinking? She lay in bed until two o'clock, allowing the full horror of her own actions to wash over her. She was disgusted with herself. She had broken her marriage vows. How could she ever make this right? She tried to work out how she had arrived at this point; she tried to justify herself, but she couldn't.

In the early afternoon, when she received the message from Sophie asking if she was free to meet up, she said she was busy. At that moment she could face no one.

She had to know how to move on from this point. She couldn't tell Paul; she couldn't tell her mum, her sister, Sophie, any of her friends. No one must know… But no one did know, except herself, God and one other person. That other person had promised, promised faithfully, never to tell a living soul. That person knew she was sorry. He had said he was sorry too. She needed to say sorry to God. 'God can forgive anything,' she reminded herself. She shut her eyes and began to pray.

A little later, she got out of bed and went to the shower. She dressed herself, arranged her hair and put on her make-up. Then she started to tidy and clean the flat. She would have everything arranged for when Paul got home. She would make his favourite dinner and pamper him. Later they would meet friends in the pub to see the New Year in, as planned. As long as Paul didn't find out what she had done, everything would be all right.

Five

The following Sunday, Dominic and Sophie were pleasantly surprised when Paul really did accompany Hayley to church. He didn't look too happy to be there, thought Sophie, as she took her seat at the back of church with Henry. In fact, there was quite a good turnout for a cold January morning. Belinda and John were sitting near the front with their boys, and the two other families with young children were also in church. Sophie felt relieved that the Henderson boys wouldn't be sitting in Sunday school by themselves. She didn't want John and Belinda to regret their decision to join All Saints. She checked to see who was leading the children's group and was pleased to see that it was Lucy, helped by Sarah, wife of Mike, the guitarist. The children liked Lucy and Sarah. The Henderson boys would have a good morning.

Sophie and Henry went through their normal Sunday morning routine – the service started, everyone went quiet, Henry started shouting, Sophie took him into the back room. Much as she always hoped that one day Henry would let her stay in the service for a little while, she didn't really mind. From behind the glass doors she could see everything that was going on in church and there was a speaker on the wall which allowed her to hear everything that was going on too. There were some old toys that had been stored in church for the crèche, but Sophie knew that Henry wasn't really interested in playing with them. He did, however, like to watch Sophie play with a wooden train set, which Sophie kept in a box in the corner of the back room. She started putting the train set together and pushing the trains around the track, while listening to the service and glancing up every so often to watch through the door.

Dominic was trying his hardest to make the service accessible to all. He spoke to the children before they left for their group. He included modern worship songs and traditional hymns. Then he preached his sermon. Sophie knew that Dominic always spent a long time preparing his sermons, making sure he fully understood the Bible passage and could explain it in its context. This could often take him a whole day during the week, but Dominic saw the Bible as God's words to His people and teaching it as a responsibility that he must take very seriously. Sophie never underestimated the privilege she enjoyed in being married to a man whom she could always come to with her faith questions.

From her position behind the glass doors, Sophie could see virtually everyone in church from behind. She noticed that people's reactions to the sermon were very variable. Some people seemed to sit with their Bibles open, listening intently, some seemed to be staring into space, one or two had nodded off. Sophie noticed Doris, an extremely large lady in the choir, who seemed to be going through a routine of falling asleep, gradually sliding sideways down the pew, waking with a start just in time to stop herself from toppling to the floor, sitting up and then falling asleep again. Sophie smiled to herself.

During the closing hymn, Sophie packed the train set away and picked Henry up. She wanted to catch Hayley and Paul before they left, but that turned out to be easy. They were approaching her. They exchanged pleasantries, and then: 'Actually, Sophie, we were wondering whether you and Dominic would pray for us before we go, weren't we, Paul?' said Hayley. Sophie noticed that Paul didn't look enthusiastic about this. In fact, he looked extremely awkward, but she wasn't going to refuse to pray for anyone.

'Of course. We might just have to wait a few minutes, until it's a bit less busy in here.'

'Sure,' said Hayley. 'Let's get a cup of tea and chat to a few people.' They all walked towards the kitchen hatch, where drinks were being served. Sophie put Henry down to pick up a cup of tea. That was her mistake. Henry seized the moment. Quick as a flash he was off, running between the many pairs of legs to get out into the main part of the church. Then, in and out of the pews he ran, screaming in delight, Sophie in hot pursuit.

'Please, God, don't let him knock any old ladies over,' Sophie silently pleaded. Finally, he ran between two pews with a stone pillar at the end. Sophie had him cornered. She scooped him up and turned around. Some people averted their eyes. Others continued to stare, frowns of disapproval on their faces.

Sophie went to find Dominic. He was talking to John Henderson by the door and had his diary out. Belinda Henderson was talking to Audrey. Audrey glanced at Henry, then Sophie, then spoke to Belinda.

'I must say, your boys sit beautifully in church,' she said.

Belinda glanced at Sophie, awkwardly. 'Thank you,' she mumbled.

Audrey turned to John. 'I was just saying to your wife, your boys are so well behaved.'

'That's because they've got a lovely mummy, who's bringing them up so well,' said John, smiling at Belinda, completely oblivious to Sophie's embarrassment.

Dominic leaned towards Sophie. 'You OK?' he asked.

'Yes, except that everyone obviously thinks I'm a terrible mother,' said Sophie, sulkily.

'No, they don't, because you aren't.'

Sophie didn't argue. She knew she needed to put her own feelings to one side for the moment. 'Anyway, Hayley and Paul would like us to pray with them, when it's quietened down a bit in here. I'll see if Catherine will mind Henry for a few minutes.'

Sophie went to find the retired vicar's wife. 'Dominic and I need to pray with someone before they go. Would you mind looking after Henry, please?'

'Of course,' said Catherine. 'You're doing a great job with him,' she added, seeming to know how Sophie was feeling. 'Come along, Henry, let's go and see what the big children have been doing in Sunday school.' She walked off with Henry obediently holding her hand. Sophie wondered for a moment how Catherine managed to make looking after Henry so easy. The main thing was that she was free to pray for her friends, though. She wanted to use the Henry-free moments well.

Dominic, Sophie, Paul and Hayley found a spare pew away from the people left chatting at the back of church. Paul still looked uncomfortable, but they talked for a while and then Dominic led them all in a prayer, committing them to God, asking for God's help and guidance for the way forward and for His peace and blessing on them. At the end, Sophie gave Hayley a hug and Dominic turned to Paul. Hayley began talking about the new school term, but Sophie was only half listening. She was aware of Dominic telling Paul that he had been in his situation and knew how he felt. When they got up to go, she noticed that Paul's attitude seemed to have softened and he looked a lot happier.

'Thanks,' he said, looking first at Dominic and then at Sophie.

Church was emptying. Sophie collected Henry from Catherine. Robert, her husband, was with her. 'Your husband did a very good job this morning. Lovely service,' he said.

'Thank you, I'll tell him. And thanks for minding Henry, Catherine. I really appreciate it.'

'No trouble,' said Catherine.

'I'll see you back at home,' Sophie said to Dominic as she left.

Over lunch, Dominic and Sophie talked about their morning. Henry was busy eating, which gave them plenty of time.

'Robert and Catherine were kind,' said Sophie. 'Robert said he thought it was a lovely service and that you did a good job.'

'That helps,' said Dominic. 'Geoffrey had a bit of a grumble about the modern worship songs. He said that some people don't like them.'

'That's a shame,' said Sophie. 'I thought they were lovely and Mike and Hayley did really well. I suppose you're never going to please all of the people all of the time. Anyway, I've got a plan to help me with Sunday mornings.'

'Go on.'

'Ridiculous as it sounds, given that we live next to the church, if I take Henry to church in the pushchair and bribe him to get into it at the end of the service...'

'Bribe him with...?'

'A drink and a biscuit, probably. Then I can strap him in and talk to people without worrying about him running round the church, tripping people up or escaping out of the door.'

'Excellent plan.'

'Good, I'm glad you agree. Did you make a date with John? I saw you with your diary out.'

'Yes, he wants to pop round this afternoon to talk about a few ideas he's had. Is that OK?'

'Yes, of course. I'll do you a deal. You look after Henry while I wash up and I'll take Henry to the park when John comes round, so you can talk in peace.'

A bit later on Sophie bundled Henry into the pushchair in his coat and hat and started to walk towards the park in the middle of the village. It was dry and bright, but cold, and Sophie was glad of her warm mittens. Something about pushing the pushchair seemed to make her hands extra cold. She walked quickly to stay warm.

Oxley was built on a slight incline, so she was walking uphill on the way to the park. Most of the houses on the church side of the village were older and larger than the newer ones on the other side. A few of them were worth quite a lot of money, Sophie thought. Unfortunately, a lot of the roads were quite narrow and didn't have pavements, so Sophie zigzagged her way through the village, sticking to the roads where she knew they would be safe.

Towards the centre of the village were the few shops and the school that Henry would attend in a couple of years. Dominic enjoyed taking assemblies there. Often, when they were out together, Sophie would see children waving at Dominic because they recognised him from his visits to school.

Sophie knew where most of their church members lived, having visited them when she and Dominic had first arrived in Oxley, in the pre-Henry days. She turned into the road where Geoffrey and Audrey Bickerstaff lived in a very large house, which had been in Geoffrey's family for many generations. As she passed the end of the long drive, the front door opened and Doris emerged. Sophie stopped to wave to Audrey in the doorway and then waited for Doris to walk down the drive. She waddled slowly towards them.

'Hello, Doris, how are you?' Sophie asked.

'Fine, thank you,' said Doris, a little breathlessly. 'The Bickerstaffs invited me for a sandwich after church,' she said, proudly. 'They had something they wanted to talk to me about,' she went on. Sophie noticed that Doris didn't seem to want to meet her eye. Doris changed the subject. 'Their kitchen is as big as my house. I'm sure the whole house is very grand, not that I've seen the rest of it. I'm going home to feed my rabbits now.'

'We're walking towards the park,' said Sophie. 'We can walk along with you for a bit.' The pavement was narrow, so they had to walk in single file. Doris was in front. Sophie couldn't help glancing at her enormous bottom as it swayed from side to side. Doris seemed almost as wide as she was tall. Walking seemed to be quite an effort and she looked rather uncomfortable. She stopped for a moment. 'Are you OK, Doris?' Sophie asked.

'Oh, I have such pains in my legs,' said Doris. 'I've told my doctor, but he just doesn't listen. All he says is that I must lose weight – he just doesn't listen.'

Sophie, who privately thought that it was Doris who wasn't listening to the doctor, decided it was her turn to change the subject. 'How many rabbits do you have?'

'Just two now, but I've had seventeen altogether, over the years. They're very special. They have all been house-trained, you know. I train them myself.'

'Mmm,' said Sophie. Having been to Doris's house, she seriously doubted that the rabbits were as house-trained as Doris liked to think. There had definitely been more than a hint of eau-de-rabbit in the air and there were bald patches in the carpets where the rabbits appeared to have been nibbling.

'But they need a lot of looking after,' Doris went on. 'They're angora rabbits, so their wool keeps growing. They have to be groomed and trimmed regularly, but I can sell the wool for quite a bit of money! I have photos of them all and I keep them with me always.' She stopped, blocking the pavement with her bulk and, to Sophie's dismay, rummaged in her handbag. She brought out a small photo album. 'This is Wally, my first rabbit. Then there was Cedric and Geraldine.'

'Mmm,' said Sophie again, trying to sound enthusiastic. Doris didn't seem to feel the cold in the same way as other people.

'This is Peter, he was quite mischievous.' On and on she went. Sophie jiggled the pushchair backwards and forwards, hoping Henry wasn't too cold. He looked all right. Finally, they got to the last rabbit.

'Very beautiful rabbits. Thank you for showing me. I'd better get moving, otherwise Henry will start to get cold.'

'Oh, yes,' said Doris. She put the album back into her bag and waddled on. She stopped at the corner where she would go one way and Sophie the other, and blocked the pavement again. 'I must just say that your husband's sermon was far too long this morning.'

'Oh,' said Sophie, somewhat lamely. She wanted to follow it up with, 'How would you know? You were asleep.' But she didn't want to offend Doris, so she merely said goodbye and walked away. She felt quite downcast while she pushed Henry on the swings and supervised him on the slide.

When Henry was tired of the play park, she tucked him back into the pushchair and began the walk home. The days were still short and it was starting to get dark, even as she reached the vicarage. John's car was still in the drive. She opened the front door to see that he was just leaving.

'Sophie,' said Dominic, 'it's all right if John, Belinda and the boys come for lunch the last Sunday in January, isn't it? There's nothing in the diary after church that week.'

'Oh, yes, of course,' said Sophie, turning to John. 'Is there anything you don't eat?'

'No, we eat anything. Thank you, that's very kind,' said John. 'See you next Sunday, then.'

When she was sure he was driving away, she turned to Dominic. 'You might have asked me first, instead of springing it on me in front of him. I could hardly say no, could I?'

Dominic looked crestfallen. 'Oh, sorry. Isn't it all right, then? I thought you wouldn't mind. We always used to have people for Sunday lunch.'

'Yes, but that was before Henry,' snapped Sophie. She knew she was being unreasonable and that she had been thinking about inviting the Hendersons at some point. She was just feeling a little got at, what with Doris's comment and Audrey that morning.

'Sorry, you're right. I really should have checked with you first. It was just a really good meeting. He's got some great ideas and I thought it was the right thing to do.'

Sophie breathed in slowly. 'Sorry. I mean, you should have asked me first, but I did want to invite them and it is the right thing to do. I'm just feeling a bit flat at the moment. And the Hendersons are a bit, well, perfect, aren't they?'

'No one's perfect, but I know what you mean. Go and sit down and I'll make you a cup of tea.'

Later that evening, when Henry had been put to bed, Sophie asked Dominic about his meeting with John. 'John has an idea about having an event at church, probably Easter Saturday, when we invite people into church and just offer them hospitality. We have crafts and games for children and things for adults to do (that bit needs a bit more thought) and a café with free drinks and cakes. We have a prayer corner for anyone who wants to be prayed for and we give people an invitation to come to church on Easter Sunday. What do you think?'

'Sounds like a great idea,' said Sophie, truthfully. 'The only thing is, it might be expensive to run and there are some people in the church who only want to get involved with events like that if it raises money for the church.' Then she added, 'And we have to admit, we do need to raise money for the church if we're going to survive.'

'True,' said Dominic. 'It is only an idea and we would have to take it to the church council before deciding anything. But it's good to offer something to the community, and inviting people into a place where they can hear the Christian message is what we are about. I just think it's great when people have ideas and enthusiasm.'

'So do I. I'm glad he came round.'

'Now, tell me why you were feeling so flat when you came back from the park? Did something happen?'

'Oh, it was just Doris. I saw her coming out of Audrey's and she stopped in the middle of the pavement to show me photos of all her rabbits and then said your sermon was too long this morning. But she wouldn't know because she was asleep – I could see her. And I'd already had that comment from Audrey, about how the Henderson children sat so nicely in church, because she knows Henry didn't.'

To Sophie's surprise, Dominic laughed. 'Well, don't take too much notice of Doris,' he said. 'She only comes to church because she's lonely. She has no interest in the sermons, so she goes to sleep. As for Audrey, if she can't understand that Henry is a handful and we are doing our best, that's her problem, not ours. Anyway, going back to Sunday lunch, here's an idea. I know it means cooking for one more person, but how about inviting Lucy for lunch that Sunday? It would be good for her to get to know the Hendersons a bit better and she's great with the children.'

'I don't want her to think I'm inviting her to help with the children,' said Sophie. 'Two families might be a bit overwhelming for a single lady. She might feel a bit funny.'

'You could ask her,' said Dominic. 'See what she thinks.'

Sophie went to ring Lucy. 'She seemed really pleased to be asked,' she reported when she came back into the living room. 'She would love to come.'

By the time she went to bed, Sophie was feeling a lot better.

Six

The weather turned colder as January wore on. Then, on a Friday morning at the end of January, Oxley woke up to a layer of snow. Sophie was excited. She wanted to build a snowman with Henry.

'Don't be too ambitious,' said Dominic. 'Maybe just take him for a walk in the snow first and see how he likes it.'

Sophie showed Henry the vicarage garden from the bedroom window. Henry looked surprised to see the garden looking white instead of green. Sophie didn't know if he had seen snow before but, if he had, he would have been too young to remember.

After breakfast, Sophie rang some of the less-mobile members of the congregation to see if they needed anything, but they all seemed fine. Later, she dressed Henry in his coat, hat and mittens and put two pairs of socks on his feet before pushing them into his shiny, blue Wellington boots. She put him in the pushchair and ventured out down the drive. Quickly she realised that the small wheels of the pushchair weren't able to cope with snow. 'Henry, this isn't going to work,' she said, feeling foolish. She dragged the pushchair back towards the front door.

'No, no, no,' shouted Henry. 'Walk, Mummy, walk.'

'Yes,' said Sophie, quickly, 'just not with the pushchair today.' Picking him up, she cautiously stood him on his feet. The snow wasn't too thick and didn't come up above his boots.

'OK,' said Sophie. She needed to go to the post office, but had never walked Henry that far before. 'Let's see how we get on.' She took Henry's hand in hers and began to walk down the drive. Henry took his first few steps hesitantly and then seemed to gain confidence. By the time they reached the end of the drive he was laughing. He loved it.

It was going to be a slow process. Henry wanted to tread on as much snow as possible, but Sophie didn't mind. Snow had stopped falling and the air was still. They would be fine as long as they kept walking to stay warm. If Henry was enjoying it, she wasn't going to stop him.

It took almost an hour to reach the centre of the village, a journey that would have normally taken them fifteen minutes at most. There was very little traffic on the roads, but they were already looking grey and slushy. They approached the small parade of shops near the primary school. From a distance it appeared that the school was closed. She could see a lady, wearing bright pink boots, going into the pharmacy. She then noticed someone coming out of the post office. They must both be open, she thought. They continued their slow walk. By the time they reached the post office, the lady in pink boots was coming back out of the pharmacy, clutching a small bag. Sophie recognised her at once. 'Hi, Hayley,' she called. 'How are you?'

'Hi, Sophie. Hello, Henry. Fine, thanks. School's closed because of the weather, but I'm not complaining. Paul drove into work, though. How are you both?'

'We're fine, thanks. I realised the pushchair wouldn't go in the snow, but Henry walked all the way.'

'Well done, Henry. Are you going to build a snowman?'

'Maybe tomorrow. It took us an hour to walk here. If it takes us another hour to walk back, I think that might be enough snow for one day.'

'Fair enough. I'd better let you keep going. I'll see you on Sunday.'

'See you on Sunday,' said Sophie as she opened the door to the post office.

It did take them another hour to walk back. Sophie began to worry that Henry would get cold, but he seemed happy and the novelty of walking in the snow hadn't worn off by the time they arrived back at the vicarage. Sophie took Henry's mittens and boots off and felt his hands and feet. She was both surprised and relieved to find that they were as warm as toast. It must have been quite an effort for him to keep walking for so long, she thought.

Dominic came out of the study. 'I'd almost given you up for lost,' he said.

'Sorry,' said Sophie. 'Henry walked all the way to the post office and back. He loved it, but it took ages. He wanted to tread in as much snow as possible. I think I might leave the snowman until tomorrow.'

'Good plan,' said Dominic. 'Maybe I could take an hour off in the afternoon and join in.'

Sophie sat Henry in the highchair at the kitchen table and began to get lunch ready. As they ate, they discussed plans for Sunday lunch with the Hendersons and Lucy.

'You know, I find it so hard to do anything with Henry awake, so I think I need to be very organised,' said Sophie. 'I did the shopping yesterday. I've got a leg of lamb in the freezer. I'll set the table and chop the vegetables the night before. The lamb can go into the oven on a timer before we go to church. I'll make an apple crumble on Saturday. Custard will come out of a tin and mint sauce will come out of a jar. Oh, and I've also got some different ice creams in the freezer, in case the children don't like crumble.'

'Excellent! You seem to have it all under control,' Dominic reassured her.

'I do hope so. Anyway, although Lucy's on coffee duty on Sunday, she's going to come straight over when she's finished to look after Henry while I finish the cooking. She can talk to the Hendersons at the same time. Come and help me when you get back from church, though, won't you?'

'Of course I will. What are you and Henry going to do this afternoon?' Dominic turned his attention to Henry. 'Oh, Henry... is he OK?'

Sophie looked at Henry. He had almost finished his lunch. A carrot stick was dangling from his mouth, but he was fast asleep in the highchair. Sophie took the carrot out of his mouth, wiped him down and lifted him out, but he didn't wake. 'He must have exhausted himself walking in the snow,' she said. She carried him into the living room and laid him on the rug, then went back to the kitchen and put the kettle on. Dominic was still sitting at the kitchen table.

'Did you see anyone when you went out?' he asked.

'Just Hayley,' Sophie replied. 'School's closed because of the weather. She was coming out of the pharmacy.'

'Oh, is she unwell?'

'She said she was fine.' Sophie thought for a moment. 'She did look a bit pale, though. I hope she's OK. She said Paul had driven into work. I wouldn't fancy driving in this weather.'

'No, it's on days like this that I'm glad I only have to commute down the stairs in the morning.'

Hayley was back at home, but she wasn't having lunch. She was too frightened to think about food. The anxiety was also making her feel a little nauseous. She was very glad she hadn't had to go into school that morning.

Hayley and Paul's two-bedroomed flat was a homely space on the third and uppermost floor, which meant no one lived above them and they had a loft space for storage. There was also a lift, which Hayley had always hoped would be useful if she had a pram one day. The flat had been new when they had bought it and had a modern kitchen and bathroom suite. The pale-coloured walls and cream carpets made it feel light and spacious and they had taken great pleasure in choosing furniture and decorating. Leading from the patio doors in the living room was a balcony, with black railings, overlooking the communal garden and car park below. The balcony was cleverly built at an angle and shielded from the neighbouring one by a screen, but Paul and Hayley were sometimes aware that their conversations could be overheard by Mrs Solomons, next door, when she was sitting on her balcony. Paul had planted pots, which flowered in the spring and summer, making it feel like their own little garden. There was also a small wooden table and chairs which had been a wedding present from Paul's parents. They had left the wooden furniture out throughout the year and it was starting to become a little weathered, but Hayley hoped it would last one more summer. The flat had been a labour of love and now there was only one thing missing – the longed-for baby.

Hayley sat on the sofa and stared at the small paper bag on the coffee table. She had imagined this point in her life many, many times over, but this was not how she had meant it to feel. She felt sick and she felt scared. She had expected to feel anxious, anxious in case of a negative result, fear of a disappointment. Now, however, she felt more than anxious. She felt terrified, terrified of a positive result. She also felt another emotion – sadness. She felt sad that she had spoilt what should have been one of the most exciting moments in her life. She had ruined everything. But had she? She didn't know. Maybe it would be a negative result. There was only one way to find out. She needed to know her fate. She picked up the bag and walked to the bathroom.

Henry slept for an hour after lunch. Dominic put his boots on and went out to make some house calls, so Sophie decided to use the time while Henry was asleep to her advantage. With Sunday's lunch in mind, she set out to make the house spic and span. She got the vacuum cleaner out and started work.

Henry woke up in a grumpy mood. Sophie couldn't blame him. On the odd occasions in her life when she had fallen asleep in the daytime herself, she had always felt ghastly upon waking. She picked him up and sat on the sofa with him on her lap. There was a large, wooden toy box in the living room, under the window that looked out over the vicarage garden. Sophie had filled it with lovely toys, some of which had been Christmas presents and none of which Henry had shown any interest in so far. Maybe it was time for another try, thought Sophie. She carried Henry over, sat on the carpet with him on her lap and opened the box.

There was a wooden train set near the top, which had been Henry's Christmas present from Sophie and Dominic. She took it out and began to build the track. Henry had watched Sophie do this with the train set at church. The tears stopped as he watched intently what she was doing now. She talked to him as she put the track together, told him the names of the trains and pushed them around the track. Then she picked up a train and put it in his hands. 'Can you do it, Henry?' she asked. With immense pleasure, she watched him get up from her lap, bend down and put the train on the track and begin to push it round. Gradually Henry began to examine each train, one by one, and push it along the track. When Dominic came in, they were still playing. 'Come and see what Henry's doing,' called Sophie, happily. Whatever Dominic had been intending to do after his house calls, he abandoned, and they all played with the trains until teatime. It was the first time that Henry had sat down to play, rather than throwing the toys across the room, and nothing was going to stop them from encouraging him and enjoying the moment.

On Saturday morning, Sophie woke up to find Dominic's side of the bed empty. Henry was shouting, 'Out, out, out,' so she went to fetch him from his cot. Together they went downstairs to look for Dominic. He was in his study.

'Hello, early bird,' she said.

'I woke up early and thought I'd get on,' said Dominic. 'I need to make up for spending time playing with Henry and the trains yesterday. I wouldn't have missed it for the world, but I'm not quite as organised as I need to be for tomorrow. I don't think we'll be making a snowman today, though. Look outside.'

He was right. Sophie looked out of the window to see that it was raining heavily and the beautiful white snow that had covered the garden the day before was disappearing rapidly.

'Never mind,' said Sophie, sadly. 'At least we went out in it yesterday. And it means people can travel much more easily. No one will have trouble getting to church tomorrow either.'

She took Henry into the kitchen and sat him in the highchair while she prepared his breakfast. Then, while he was busy eating, she double-checked that she had everything she needed for Sunday lunch. She took the leg of lamb out of the freezer to defrost. She needed to make an apple crumble. If she was quick, she could chop and cook the apples while Henry was eating breakfast. She went to get the four large cooking apples she had bought earlier in the week. She thought she had left them on the worktop, but they weren't there. Where, she wondered, had she put them? In the larder? No, not there. Sometimes, when she was anxious, she got distracted and put things in odd places. She had once found a bottle of ketchup in the cupboard under the sink. She checked all the kitchen cupboards, the broom cupboard, the cupboard under the stairs. Still no sign of the apples, and then the phone rang. Sophie let Dominic answer it; it was invariably for him, anyway.

A couple of minutes later, Dominic came out of the study holding the phone towards Sophie. 'It's Lucy,' he said, 'about tomorrow.'

'Hi, Lucy, how are you?' said Sophie, silently praying that she wasn't ringing to say she couldn't make Sunday lunch. She was depending on her help.

'Fine, thanks. I just wondered if there was anything you wanted me to do for tomorrow. Would you like me to make a pudding?'

'Oh,' said Sophie, feeling relieved. 'No, that's OK… although… actually, would you mind making a pudding? I had intended to make an apple crumble, but I seem to have lost the cooking apples.'

'No, problem,' said Lucy. 'I'm going into town this morning, so I can shop for ingredients and make something this afternoon.'

'Thanks,' said Sophie, 'that's a real help.'

Lucy put the phone down at her end and went to look through her recipes. She didn't so much have a recipe book as a recipe pile. Over the years she had collected lots of different recipes from various sources. Eventually she had ended up with a kitchen drawer full of bits of paper. Chocolate cheesecake, thought Lucy. She made a shopping list and then put the rest of the recipe pile back into the drawer in the well-organised kitchen.

Lucy's one-bedroomed flat was smart and neat and situated on the ground floor. Lucy glanced out of the kitchen window as Chloe, Hayley's sister, walked past. Maybe, thought Lucy, she had been visiting Hayley, just up the road.

Lucy wasn't a driver, not because she didn't want to drive, but she had simply never learned. She hadn't had the money as a student and she hadn't needed to drive when she lived in London. Now she had her flat to pay for and she could get to work by bus, something she had been very glad about when it had snowed the day before. Lucy put her coat on and walked to the bus stop outside the pharmacy.

By Sunday morning the snow had completely cleared, it had stopped raining and the sun was shining weakly over Oxley. Sophie walked up the drive to church, steering the pushchair along the familiar route around the potholes. Her plan of taking Henry to church in the pushchair had been working well and she had found herself more able to talk to people at the end of the service, something she felt was important. Sophie was feeling reasonably well organised and Lucy had already dropped a large chocolate cheesecake off at the vicarage on her way to church.

The first person she saw as she pushed the church door open was Geoffrey, obviously on welcoming duty this morning.

'Good morning, Sophie,' Geoffrey said, looking glum. It would be so much nicer if he could just smile sometimes, thought Sophie.

She parked the pushchair in the back room and walked Henry to their usual position in one of the back pews. As the service started, Henry started shouting so Sophie took him out. She looked at the congregation through the glass doors. Somehow, the knowledge of who had and who hadn't come to church each Sunday governed Sophie's mood for the rest of the week. She knew it was wrong and that church attendance was between those people and God, but as it seemed such a make or break situation for All Saints, she couldn't help herself. She looked first for families. The Hendersons were down at the front. That was good. The Starkies, with six-year-old Eleanor, were there too, but the Browns with their two children were missing, which was disappointing. These were the only other families with children at All Saints. At least the Henderson boys wouldn't be entirely alone in Sunday school.

Mike was there with his guitar, but Hayley was missing. That was disappointing too. Perhaps, as Dominic had suggested, she wasn't very well. All the usual suspects were present in their usual places. 'Why,' wondered Sophie, 'do people always sit in the same place at church?' Doris was already looking sleepy.

There was a man sitting halfway down the church on the right-hand side, whom Sophie didn't recognise. As the congregation stood to sing, Sophie could see that he was quite tall and slim, with fair hair and glasses. Sophie was sure he hadn't been before. She felt the sudden feeling of elation she always felt with the idea that someone new might be coming to join them. He turned his head at one point. She could see that he had a beard, but that he looked quite young, maybe early thirties. Was he alone? Yes, there didn't seem to be anyone with him. She made a mental note to try to talk to him before he left. She wanted him to feel welcome.

At the end of the service, as Mrs Fowler-Watt started to play the familiar tune of the last hymn, Sophie noticed Lucy get up from her place and walk to the kitchen to prepare tea and coffee. She also saw Audrey get up. She must be on coffee duty with Lucy, Sophie thought. She hurriedly put the trains away and went to the kitchen hatch. The kitchen was full of steam from the enormous metal urn full of boiling water. Sophie could make out the trays of institutional-style blue and green cups and saucers, set out regimentally in rows. 'Lucy, can you let me have a biscuit for Henry, please? I need to get him back into the pushchair.'

Lucy passed a chocolate digestive through the hatch. 'No problem.'

'Thanks,' said Sophie.

'You need to give him a biscuit to put him into a pushchair?' remarked Audrey, frowning.

'I need to give him a biscuit to put him into a pushchair without starting World War Three in the middle of church,' said Sophie.

Audrey rolled her eyes. 'Lucy, if I pour the drinks, can you manage the washing-up?' she said, pushing in front of her.

'Sure,' said Lucy. Standing behind Audrey, she winked at Sophie and smiled. Audrey had a very strict routine for tea and coffee. Tea must be poured into the blue cups from a giant metal teapot, whereas the green cups each had a spoonful of instant coffee in them, ready to have hot water added as and when required.

Sophie walked into the main part of church, Henry in the pushchair, biscuit in hand. She found the fair-haired man walking towards the door. 'Hello,' she said. 'I don't think we've met before. I'm Sophie and this is Henry.'

'Pleased to meet you both,' said the young man, beaming at her and looking delighted. 'I'm Rufus.'

'Welcome to All Saints. Are you just visiting or local?'

'I'm just visiting at the moment, but hoping to move to the area,' said Rufus, happily. 'I moved up from Surrey just after Christmas. I've been staying in a hotel in town, courtesy of my company, but I've had an offer accepted on a house in Oxley and I thought I would try the local church. I've tried a few of the churches in town over the last couple of weeks and they were very good, but I met a lady called Hayley when I first moved up and she spoke highly of the church here, so I thought I'd give it a go.'

'Oh,' said Sophie. 'How do you know Hayley?'

'Her husband, Paul, works for me. I met Hayley at our work Christmas party, but I can't see her here.'

'No,' said Sophie, feeling disappointed that Hayley wasn't with them. 'She does usually come. She plays the piano with Mike the guitarist, for our more contemporary songs, I mean. Mrs Fowler-Watt plays the organ for the hymns. I don't know why Hayley isn't here this morning. Have you got time for a cup of coffee?'

'Lovely,' said Rufus, smiling again.

'Come this way and I can introduce you to a few people.' She led him through to the back room and the kitchen hatch. 'Audrey, this is Rufus. He's hoping to move to Oxley.'

'Lovely to meet you, Rufus,' said Audrey. 'What would you like to drink?'

'A cup of tea, thank you very much,' said Rufus, beaming again. Audrey poured the tea and Rufus took the proffered green cup and saucer.

Sophie saw Shirley and Clive, Lucy's parents, walking towards them. Sophie knew Shirley and Clive would make Rufus feel welcome. They chatted for a little while but, as Rufus drank his tea, an odd look came over his face. For a moment he looked as if he might be sick, then he seemed to recover himself and was smiling again.

Catherine and Robert came up to join in the introductions. Sophie extracted herself and left them to it. She needed to get home to put the potatoes in the oven to roast. She passed Dominic at his station by the church door. 'I'm going home to cook,' she told him. 'Send Belinda and John across whenever they are ready. There's a new man called Rufus you might like to catch before he leaves.' She turned round to point Rufus out and noticed Lucy collecting cups to wash up. She could see her approach Rufus and join the conversation. 'He's there, talking to Lucy,' she said. Lucy started walking back to the kitchen holding the green cup and saucer. 'Green cup,' said Sophie to Dominic.

'Pardon?' said Dominic.

'Green cup, green cup, green cup,' repeated Sophie, looking horrified. 'The new man. No wonder he was looking a bit funny. He asked for tea. Audrey poured tea… into a green cup… green cups already have instant coffee in them. Audrey broke her own rules. Bless him, he drank it and he didn't say a word.'

'Oh dear,' said Dominic, looking anxious. 'That wasn't very welcoming. I hope it doesn't put him off coming back.'

Sophie walked back to the vicarage with Henry and was soon joined by Lucy and the Henderson family.

In the end, with Sophie's forward thinking and Lucy's help, Sunday lunch went rather well. Lucy enjoyed chatting to Belinda and John, while helping Henry with his train set. Sophie finished cooking and serving the meal. With Henry being entertained by Lucy, she found she didn't really need Dominic's help when he returned from church after all.

Noah, Jonah and Boaz Henderson all came armed with little backpacks containing books, puzzles, crayons and paper and amused themselves quietly, only speaking when they were spoken to and being very polite. This was, Sophie mused, both pleasing and ever so slightly irritating at the same time. The only tricky moments were when Belinda called to the boys, 'No, Joe, Bo,' and Dominic had to leave the room quickly to stop himself laughing, and when Boaz tried to join in with the train set and Henry hit him over the head with a piece of wooden train track. There were many apologies and Henry got a telling-off, which didn't seem to bother him, but Boaz soon stopped crying and Belinda and John didn't seem too worried.

Over lunch the conversation inevitably turned to church matters. John and Belinda were both very enthusiastic. Belinda seemed keen to join the women's Bible study group on

Thursday mornings and John offered to lead one of the evening groups. The church had two evening study groups and, up until that point, Dominic had been leading both of them, so this was going to be very helpful. They also seemed to have lots of ideas for church improvements. 'The church has been improved over the years,' said Dominic. 'About twenty years ago someone left a legacy to the church and the back pews were removed to make room for the meeting room, the Sunday school room, the kitchen and the toilets.'

'That was very fortunate,' said Belinda. 'My aunt goes to an Anglican church that doesn't have running water or electricity. But people in her village are determined to keep it that way, because it's historical!'

'Needless to say, those people aren't actually members of the church,' added John. 'But what about our church drive? It's full of potholes!'

'The trouble is,' explained Dominic, 'it will cost money to repair properly, money we haven't got at the moment, but you're right – it's unpleasant, it's dangerous and it gives a terrible first impression. I really would like to get it sorted.'

After lunch, they all went back to the living room and Sophie brought a tray of teas and coffees in. 'I'll just put these up on the shelf, where Henry can't reach them, while they're a bit too hot to drink,' she said. Belinda and John looked a bit surprised, but didn't comment. Clearly the Henderson children had never had to have things put out of their reach.

Eventually the Hendersons said their goodbyes and left, but Lucy stayed behind for a while to help clear up.

'Do you mind?' asked Sophie. 'You've already helped me so much. Just knowing someone was minding Henry so I could think about what I was doing in the kitchen made such a difference. And the cheesecake was delicious.'

'I don't mind at all,' said Lucy. 'It was a pleasure to get to know Belinda and John, and I always like being with you. Besides, anything I can do to help with your ministry here is something I want to be part of.'

Later that evening, when Henry was in bed and they were talking over the day, Sophie said to Dominic, 'You could go a long way to find a friend like Lucy. I'll get her some flowers when I go shopping next week.'

'Yes,' said Dominic. Then as an afterthought he added, 'Oh, speaking of shopping, I've been meaning to say to you. Sorry to complain, but those apples you bought last week, I didn't really like them and they were absolutely enormous.'

'Ahh,' said Sophie, finally putting two and two together. 'Now I know what happened to my cooking apples.'

Seven

Hayley had been on an emotional roller coaster since the previous Friday. With the pregnancy test stick held in front of her, like a time bomb, she had walked the few feet from the bathroom to the living room. In two minutes she would know. She set it down on the coffee table and sat on the sofa, her eyes fixed on the little window that would tell her yes or no. She could feel her heart beating in her chest, as if it might explode. 'Please let it be negative, please let it be negative,' she pleaded silently to God. 'I promise I'll never do anything like that ever again, even if it means I'll never have a baby.'

Positive. It was positive. That was it. Peeing on a stick had changed her whole life. She was pregnant with another man's baby. She was horrified. Her heart was beating so fast she felt as if she might die, then her ears began to buzz and her head began to spin. She felt sickness rising and she ran to the bathroom, just in time to vomit into the toilet bowl. Then she collapsed onto the bathroom floor and lay cold, clammy, sweating and gasping for air.

After what seemed like half an hour, when her heart rate began to slow and she no longer felt sick, just exhausted, she crawled to the bedroom and pulled herself up onto the bed. She dragged the duvet over her and rested her head on the cool pillow.

The one thing she did have, she told herself, was time to think. No one knew yet and no one had to know for a while.

Time was on her side. What were her options? She could just tell Paul the truth. She could explain that she had been so desperate for a baby, so shocked about the test results from the doctor that when another man had made a pass at her, she had taken the opportunity. She had had sex with another man, in a hotel room after the Christmas party, while her husband had been drunk and unconscious on the bed in a room along the corridor.

Could she really tell Paul that? It hadn't meant anything; it was just sex. She hardly knew the man. She had seized the opportunity in her desperation, hoping she would get pregnant, knowing that it was unlikely that Paul would ever get her pregnant.

She had regretted it instantly. He said he had too. Together they had promised never to tell a soul. She had repented to God and prayed for a child with her husband. But her plan had worked, her desperate plan to use another man to achieve the greatest desire of her heart had worked. She had been unfaithful to her husband and another man's baby was already growing inside her. Could Paul forgive that? If he didn't, she could lose everything – her husband, her home, the respect of her friends and family. Everyone would know her as an adulteress and she would have to carry that shame. She would have to run away, to hide, to start her life again, alone with the baby. Gripped by fear, she began to cry.

What else could she do? There must be another way. She could just get rid of it. She could go to the doctor and ask for a termination. No, apart from the fact that the doctor had referred them to the hospital for fertility tests just a short time ago, she knew that a small human life was growing inside her. That life was not hers to take.

Life, Hayley had always thought, was a gift from God. With that thought, another option began to develop in her head. She reasoned with herself, doesn't it say somewhere in the Bible that all life comes from God? Maybe God had given her this life. They had prayed for a baby, after all. Surely she wouldn't be pregnant unless it was God's will. Maybe this was God's way of giving her a baby. She began to feel a little calmer.

The most important thing was that Paul didn't find out what she had done. But, surely, there was no reason for him to find out. Apart from herself and God, only one person knew what she had done. That person was as guilty as she was. That person, she reminded herself, had promised, promised faithfully, never to tell.

She got out of bed and went to the kitchen. Her head was starting to feel better and her heart rate had slowed to normal. She put the kettle on to make herself a cup of tea. Then she went to the living room and picked up the pregnancy test stick from the coffee table. She looked at it again. Still positive. Definitely positive. She went to the bedroom, opened the drawer of her bedside table, threw the test stick to the back and slammed the drawer shut. The guilt and the horror were still present, but the embryo of a new emotion was starting to rise inside her – excitement. That was the emotion she wanted to nurture. However, she wasn't ready to tell Paul she was pregnant yet. She sipped her tea and then began to clean and tidy the flat. Everything must appear normal.

That weekend was uneventful for Hayley and Paul. Hayley didn't feel like going to church on Sunday, so she didn't go. Telling herself that the baby was God's gift to her was one thing, facing God was another.

On Monday morning Hayley walked to school as usual. She felt a little nauseous, but this was a different type of nausea – not born from shock and fear, but from the pregnancy hormones. Was it her imagination, or were there more babies everywhere, suddenly? At morning break a lady came into the school office to pay some outstanding dinner money. She looked about six months pregnant. 'Sorry,' she said. 'Pregnancy hormones. I'm not quite as organised as usual.'

'That's OK.' Hayley took the money. She wanted to say, 'Me too, I'm pregnant too!' But she didn't, so she just smiled.

Just before home time, Hayley walked out into the playground in search of another parent with a school form to be filled in. The pregnant lady was there again, talking to another mother with a similar-sized bump. Hayley found the woman she was looking for. She had a pram with her. Hayley couldn't help herself – she looked into the pram. A tiny, sleeping baby lay inside, snuggled in a pink blanket and wearing a pink bonnet. 'Ohh,' sighed Hayley, 'what a beautiful baby.'

'Thank you,' said the woman. 'She's called Anna and she's two weeks old. Is that for me?' She took the form from Hayley's hand. Hayley, having forgotten she was holding the form, was momentarily surprised.

As she walked back into the school building, Hayley pushed aside her feelings of guilt. This was what she wanted. This was everything she had dreamed of. She was going to have this wonderful thing. She was going to have her own, perfect, beautiful baby. The baby would be God's gift to them, to her and Paul. It would be born from her own body and they would bring it up together and Paul need never know that it wasn't genetically his baby. What, after all, was a bit of DNA? As long as he was the one to bring the baby up, he would be the father. They would make everything perfect between them. She needed to talk about it; she needed to tell Paul.

By the time Hayley got home, she had made her decision. She went to the bedroom and fished the pregnancy test stick out from the back of her drawer. She found a pretty gift box that had once held a necklace and put the test stick inside. Then she put the kettle on and watched out of the window for Paul's car to come into the car park. This was how she had always planned to tell Paul she was pregnant and it would be no different now. As soon as she saw him coming, she made two cups of tea, put them on a tray with the gift box and set it on the coffee table.

'Hello,' called Paul as he came through the door.

'I'm in here,' said Hayley. 'I've got a surprise for you. Come and sit down.'

Paul took off his coat and shoes and came to sit down beside her. 'What's up?'

Hayley gestured towards the box. 'Look,' she said.

'What's this?' He seemed puzzled. He picked up the box and opened it. He looked inside. 'What's this? Is it...? Is this...? Are you...?' He stared at her in amazement. 'Oh, I can't believe it. You clever girl.' A broad smile spread across his face and tears of happiness leaked down his cheeks. 'Oh, this is wonderful. You clever, clever girl.'

Hayley was smiling too; she couldn't help herself. This felt right. Paul was so happy, how could it possibly be wrong? All feelings of guilt pushed aside, she knew this was going to be perfect. Nothing was going to spoil it for them. She just wouldn't let it.

Sophie, meanwhile, was feeling more positive after the weekend. Leaving aside the episode when Henry had hit Boaz over the head with a piece of toy train track, Sunday lunch had gone well. Lucy had helped enormously. Best of all, Henry was learning to play. He still needed a lot of organising and wasn't able to play without adult help, but it was a start. As well as paints and trains, he had even shown interest in pushing some little cars around on the carpet, as long as Sophie was doing it with him.

With this in mind, Sophie decided her next mission at church was going to be sorting out the toys in the crèche. As far as Sophie could see, the crèche toys seemed to consist of a large jumble of plastic boxes and plastic bags filled with a large jumble of bits of toys and dog-eared books which, for some reason, seemed to live in the entrance to the toilets. As Henry was the only child at church of crèche age and hadn't really played with toys until now, Sophie hadn't bothered to look too far into any of the boxes and bags, save for the train set, but had decided that ignorance was bliss. Perhaps now was the time to tackle them, she thought.

On Wednesday morning, along with Henry and armed with a sit-on car for him and a roll of bin bags and cleaning equipment for herself, she went over to church and into the back room. It was very cold, so she flicked on the switch for the heater, pulled out all the boxes and bags and emptied them over the floor. Henry was wrapped up in his coat and seemed happy to spend some time propelling himself around the church on his little car, so she set to work.

There were a lot of puzzles with bits missing, a lot of mouldy-looking books and some rather ugly dolls with matted hair and grubby faces. There was one good train set, Sophie knew, but also several odd bits of track, none of which seemed to fit with another, and a lot of battery-operated toys with flat batteries. In fact, most of the batteries were so old that they had leaked and ruined what might have been quite nice toys once upon a time. Sophie decided she needed to be ruthless. She filled three large bin bags and then got to work cleaning what was left. A couple of hours later she was left with two nice boxes of reasonably clean cars and books, the train set, and half-a-dozen puzzles without missing pieces. She switched off the heater, put the bin bags into the porch and walked Henry back to the vicarage.

'How did you get on?' asked Dominic.

'Fine,' said Sophie. 'There are some bin bags in the church porch that we'll need to take to the tip, but job done. There are now two boxes of nice toys in the corner of the church room, rather than an enormous heap in the toilet entrance. How about you, how was your morning?'

'OK,' replied Dominic, frowning slightly. 'Didn't get very far with next week's sermon because the phone kept ringing.'

'Anything to report?'

'Well, your mum rang. She asked if you could call back this afternoon. Then Mary Brown rang to say she would call round after lunch to drop something off.'

'Oh, well that doesn't sound too onerous,' said Sophie.

'Yes, but I haven't finished. Then Belinda Henderson rang to say thanks again for Sunday. She also wanted to say that she had found the sermon helpful on Sunday morning but had forgotten to say so at the time. Then Doris rang to complain about the service and say that the sermon was too long and boring. Robert rang to say he thought the sermon and the service went well. Then Audrey rang to say she had some issues with Sunday's service, particularly the sermon, which she wants to come round and discuss at two o'clock.'

'Oh,' said Sophie. 'Two in favour, two against. How do you feel about that?'

'Mixed messages, not sure really,' Dominic replied. 'Let's have lunch, then I'll see what Audrey has to say.'

Sophie lifted Henry into the highchair at the kitchen table, to keep him out of mischief, and Dominic began to put food for lunch onto the table.

'I wonder what Mary Brown wants to drop off?' said Sophie.

'She didn't say. She just said she would pass by on her way into town.'

'OK, well I'll have to wait and see. I'll give Mum a call back this evening, when Henry's in bed. He really doesn't like me being on the phone. I was wondering about inviting Mum and Dad up for Mother's Day weekend in March. What do you think? Did you want to invite your parents, though?'

'No,' said Dominic. 'Mother's Day is later in the year in France and Mum prefers me to send her a card then. Anyway, I forgot to mention, I had an email from my mother at the weekend. They are very busy at the moment and it's such a long way for them to travel to England, but they were hoping that we might go out to stay with them in France for a couple of weeks in the summer, for a holiday. They want to take a couple of weeks off work to take us out. They mentioned spending some time with Henry and giving us a bit of a break too!'

'Ooh,' said Sophie. 'That sounds lovely. Can we do that?'

'Yes, of course,' replied Dominic. 'I just wanted to check with you first. Going on holiday to the in-laws isn't everyone's cup of tea.'

'Oh no, if they want to spend some time with Henry and give us a break, I'm all for it!' said Sophie, then added, 'Oh, and I do like visiting your parents too. They're lovely.'

'Good, I'll talk to Robert and Catherine and see if they can cover us for a couple of Sundays.'

'I'll talk to Mum and Dad about coming up in March.'

After lunch Dominic went out to do a home communion. 'You will be back in time for Audrey, won't you?' said Sophie, remembering Audrey's pointed comments about Henry's behaviour in church.

'I promise,' Dominic assured her, as he went out of the door.

Sophie lifted Henry out of the highchair and over the safety gate into the hall. He might be learning to play with toys, but he was a long way from being safe in a kitchen. Sophie climbed over the safety gate herself and went into the living room. She wanted to give Henry something to play with while she washed up and tidied the kitchen. She opened the toy box. 'What would you like to play with, Henry?' she asked. 'How about these cars?' Henry nodded and she took them out. 'Play with these while Mummy does the washing-up. I'll be back in a moment.'

She went back to the kitchen and began clearing away. Henry, however, followed her and stood at the gate, whingeing. 'I'll be out in a moment,' said Sophie, in her best cheerful voice. She really wanted the kitchen to be tidy before Audrey arrived. It was unlikely that Audrey would go into the kitchen, but just in case... Henry, however, wasn't having it. He started screaming and shaking the gate vigorously. 'Just a moment, darling,' Sophie called, trying to sound calm. She made the decision to ignore the bad behaviour and clear the kitchen. After a few minutes of shaking and screaming and being ignored, Henry went back into the living room.

'Ha,' said Sophie out loud. 'That's the answer. That's just what the books say – ignore the bad behaviour and reward the good.' But thirty seconds later Henry was back, and he was armed. He began throwing the toy cars into the kitchen towards Sophie.

'Or maybe not,' said Sophie. She stepped over the safety gate, scooped Henry up and sat him on the bottom stair. 'That was very naughty,' she said. 'Now you must sit on the naughty step.' Henry, however, had no intention of sitting on the naughty step. In the end, Sophie sat on the step next to him and held him on the naughty step. 'One minute for each year of your life, Henry. That's two minutes and then you can get off.'

Two minutes later, Sophie was about to go back to the kitchen, pick the toy cars up off the floor and have another go at washing up, when the doorbell rang. She held Henry's hand to stop him escaping and opened the front door to find Mary Brown in the porch along with three large bin bags. For a moment Sophie wondered if they were the bags of old toys she had put in the church porch that morning, but surely not. 'Hello, Mary,' she said, holding the door open with one hand and Henry with the other. 'How are you?'

'Hello, Sophie; hello, Henry. I was just passing on my way into town and I wanted to drop these off,' smiled Mary. 'I'm sorry we couldn't get to church on Sunday. We decided to have a morning at home to sort out the children's bedrooms. They had so many new toys for Christmas, we needed to have a clear-out before we could put the new things away. We tried to take these to the charity shop, but the charity shop didn't want them, so we thought the church might like them for the crèche.' Without waiting for an answer, she lifted the bin bags into the hall. 'Anyway, we can't come to church this Sunday because we're going to Alton Towers and the following Sunday we're going on a tour of the Manchester United football stadium, so we can't come then either. Must dash.' Turning her back on Sophie, she trotted back to her car.

'Oh, yes... OK... thank you,' said Sophie, trying really hard to sound grateful. She shut the front door as Mary reversed her car in the drive, and turned to Henry in dismay. 'Oh, Henry,' she sighed, more to herself than him. She looked tentatively into the tops of the bags and saw a jumble of toys and bits of toys, not unlike that which she had so recently removed from the church toilet entrance. 'All that work and now we're back to square one.'

At that moment the house phone rang. Sophie debated whether to answer it. Henry saw the phone as his enemy and now he had three bags of ammunition in the hallway. She made a decision and picked up the receiver.

'Hello, Sophie, it's Mum. Did Dominic tell you I'd called?'

'Oh, hi, Mum, yes he did. I was going to call you back this evening, actually,' said Sophie. Henry was going for the bin bags. 'Henry, leave those alone, please. Mum, could I call you back later? Someone's just dropped off some bags of toys and Henry's getting everything out.'

'Well, if it's only toys, Sophie, I'm sure he can't come to any harm.'

'Yes, no, the thing is…' she began. Henry started throwing toys in all directions. Sophie ducked as a toy fire engine came sailing past. 'The thing is, Henry doesn't like me being on the phone very much, so he throws things.'

'Well, just tell him no, darling. He needs discipline, that's all. Honestly, Sophie, you make him out to be a monster sometimes. He's just a normal little boy with lots of energy.'

Sophie looked at the clock as more toys came flying past. Almost two o'clock. Audrey could be arriving at any moment. She made a lunge for Henry, who saw her coming, made a run for it and tripped over a Humpty Dumpty. Sophie grabbed him by the ankle and ended up lying on the floor holding the phone to her ear with one hand and Henry's ankle in the other.

'Mum, I do want to talk to you, but I'm actually talking to you lying on the floor, holding Henry by one ankle.'

Glenda laughed. 'Oh, Sophie, you are funny.'

Sophie tried another tack. 'Mum, I wanted to invite you and Dad up for Mother's Day. It's just that I can't talk right now.

Can I call you back this evening, please? I can talk to you properly then.'

Eventually she managed to say goodbye and cut the call, just as she heard footsteps on the gravel approaching the front door. She looked up from her position, still lying on the floor, still holding Henry's ankle, toys and bin bags strewn everywhere, just in time to see Dominic come through the door. 'Oh, thank goodness. I thought you were Audrey,' she said with relief, just as Audrey followed Dominic into the hallway. 'Oh, hello, Audrey,' she tried to recover herself. 'Erm, sorry about the mess. Mary Brown came round with some bags of toys and then the phone rang and Henry doesn't like me being on the phone.' She sat up, but didn't let go of Henry.

Audrey stood still for a moment, staring at the strange scene before her. Her face was mask-like, impassive. She didn't make eye contact with Sophie. 'Perhaps we could go into your office, Dominic,' she said, turning and leading the way.

Dominic followed her in. As he turned, he glanced at Sophie, still on the floor. 'Sorry,' she mouthed silently.

'Help,' he mouthed silently back, grimacing as he shut the door.

Sometime later, Sophie had managed to put the toys back into the bin bags and throw them into the kitchen, which was still a mess from earlier. She went into the living room and got the train set out, the one thing she knew Henry would play with nicely, as long as she played with him. After about half an hour she heard Audrey and Dominic coming out of the study. She half-hoped that Audrey would put her head round the door to say goodbye, and see that Henry was playing nicely, but she didn't. She heard Dominic thank Audrey for coming and close the front door. He came into the living room and slumped down onto the sofa, looking drained.

'What was the verdict?' asked Sophie.

'Well,' Dominic considered, 'it wasn't the best conversation. She wanted to let me know that some people aren't happy about the way I'm leading the church. Apparently, they don't like the sermons, because I keep talking about the Bible. What they really want is just a few comforting words, so that they can go home feeling happy. According to Audrey, everyone's saying it behind my back, but Audrey is the only one brave enough to say it to me.

'No, she isn't,' said Sophie, thinking of Doris. 'Anyway, what did you say?'

'I explained that I went to Bible college for three years to get a degree in theology, because the job I'm paid to do is teach the Bible. I told her that I didn't do go to the School of Light Entertainment.'

'Do you think she understood?' asked Sophie.

'Possibly not,' said Dominic, sadly.

'Did you ask her who the "some people" are who feel this way?'

'I did. And she mentioned a few of the flower ladies.'

'There seems to be some sort of law that all vicars must be afraid of the flower ladies.'

'I'm not afraid of the flower ladies,' said Dominic.

'I am,' said Sophie.

Eight

Sophie couldn't get to sleep that night. Normally, when she was unable to sleep, she tried very hard to keep still, so as not to wake Dominic. That night, however, she was aware that he was also awake. Eventually, at two in the morning, she whispered, 'Do you fancy a cup of tea?'

'Yes,' murmured Dominic. 'I'll go, you stay there in the warm.' He slipped out of bed and put his dressing gown on, returning a few minutes later with two steaming mugs of tea. Sophie put the bedside lamp on as Dominic got back into bed beside her.

'Am I getting it all wrong?' he asked. 'Do people really dislike the way I'm leading the church? Perhaps I should just preach a feel-good message on a Sunday morning and leave the Bible to the Bible study groups. At least *they* want to hear what the Bible has to say.'

'I can see why you're saying that,' said Sophie, 'but no, surely not. Just because Audrey assumes authority doesn't make her right.'

'But, apparently, everyone's saying it behind my back,' sighed Dominic, wearily.

'Well, I'm sure some of Audrey's gang are saying things behind both of our backs,' said Sophie, 'but, think about it – church is meant to be for Christians to meet together, to learn together and to worship God together. That's what Christians have been doing since the Church began, 2,000 years ago. Anyway, teaching the Bible is what you're trained to do.'

'I know,' said Dominic. 'It's just... I know we should expect to get opposition to the Bible from outside the church; I never really thought I'd get it from inside the church.'

'But you said it yourself the other day,' said Sophie, 'you know, when I met Doris on the way to the park and she complained about the sermon, even though she was asleep. You said she comes to church because she's lonely. People come to church for a whole variety of reasons, but that doesn't mean you should stop teaching the people who come for the right reasons. Some people just don't get what church is about, but you mustn't give up doing what's right because of Audrey or Doris.'

'I know,' said Dominic. 'And I won't. It's just hard sometimes.'

After a few hours of fitful sleep, Dominic and Sophie were woken by Henry's shouts. Feeling rather tired and flat, they got up and began their morning. After breakfast Dominic went back to the study to try to finish the sermon, which had been abandoned the day before, and Sophie went to get ready for the women's study group.

Since Dominic and Sophie had adopted Henry, Catherine had offered to host the little group that met on Thursday mornings. The ladies sat around Catherine's kitchen table and Catherine herself led most of the studies. The crèche was Sophie's responsibility, and was situated in the living room, clearly visible from the kitchen through the adjoining glass double doors. Although the group was an All Saints group, several other young mums from the village, who were members of the bigger churches in town, also attended. It was a lively group and Sophie missed sitting with the other women around the table, but at this point she felt she needed to supervise Henry herself.

Apart from Henry, there were two little girls in the crèche that morning. It was to be Belinda's first time at the group and

Sophie had wondered if she might bring Boaz, but he was at nursery. Sophie was anxious for Belinda to enjoy the group, and she managed to catch her in the hallway at the end to ask her how she had found it.

'It's a lovely group,' said Belinda, smiling. 'I've told Catherine that I would be happy to lead some of the studies, if she would like me to. I've done that sort of thing before.'

'Oh, thank you,' said Sophie. 'I'm sure Catherine would be delighted. She's very kind and she never complains, but she's been leading the studies by herself every week since Henry came along. I know she would appreciate sharing the workload.'

'I'm really happy to help,' said Belinda. 'I'd better get a move on, though. Boaz needs picking up from nursery. I'll see you on Sunday.'

When the other ladies had left and Sophie was struggling to get Henry into his coat (he kept jumping up and down and taking his arms out of the sleeves), Catherine asked, 'Are you all right, Sophie? You look a bit peaky, if you don't mind my saying so.'

'Oh, I'm fine really,' said Sophie. 'We didn't sleep too well last night. Just church stuff on our minds.'

Catherine gave Sophie a knowing look. 'Robert and I were talking last night. We wondered if we could come round this evening, if you're free? Just for a chat and a cup of tea, after you've got Henry to bed.'

'Oh, yes, that would be lovely. Belinda's husband has just taken over leading the Thursday night study group, so we've got a free evening.'

'We won't stay too long,' said Catherine. 'We just wondered if you might like to get a bit of that "church stuff" off your chests. Remember, we've been where you are.'

Sophie smiled gratefully. 'It would be good to talk,' she agreed.

Robert and Catherine knocked quietly at the door at about half past seven. They came in with a nice-looking bottle of red wine, so Sophie switched off the kettle and took four wine glasses out of the cabinet in the kitchen. They settled down in the living room.

'How did you know?' asked Sophie.

'Know what?' asked Catherine.

'Well, you said you and Robert were wondering about coming round to see us, before I said anything about not sleeping and church stuff.'

'Ah,' said Catherine, 'I had a message from God in a dream… No, not really. I was passing when Audrey came out of your house yesterday afternoon, looking quite pleased with herself. Then I bumped into her again in the post office, talking to Doris. When I went up to say hello, they both stopped talking abruptly, but not before I'd heard a little of what they were saying. You don't have to say anything about that, of course. We just wanted to come round and tell you that we think you're doing a great job and to ask how we can help you.'

Sophie felt some of the tension she had been carrying easing and she was aware of Dominic starting to relax beside her. It was amazing how healing a few words of reassurance could be.

In the end, Dominic and Sophie told Robert and Catherine about their horrid day. Sophie explained how she had sorted out the crèche toys just before Mary dropped three bags of old toys into the vicarage, then about Glenda ringing and Henry's behaviour and Audrey turning up in the middle of the mess. Then Dominic told them about Audrey's and Doris's opinions on the sermons and how he had doubted himself.

'The thing is,' said Robert, leaning forwards earnestly, 'in every church in the country you will get people who come for different reasons. Lots come to worship God, learn and pray together, which is good and right, but some come for company, some for reasons of nostalgia and tradition, and some because churchgoing makes them feel like good people. Some of those people might also be interested in the message of the Bible, but many aren't.

'Your job is to preach and teach. That's what you were trained to do, just as I was. That's your responsibility before God and you mustn't let anyone tell you any different. You're doing a good job, you know.'

'Thanks,' said Dominic. 'I do know what I'm here to do, but it helps to have it confirmed by other people.'

Robert smiled. 'You know,' he continued, 'I had opposition too, in my time, but a retired minister in my congregation was always there to encourage me and keep me on track. I want to do the same for you.'

'Thanks,' said Dominic again. Sophie thought he looked a little close to tears.

Catherine seemed to be thinking along the same lines. She changed the subject quickly. 'And as for the bags of toys Mary dropped off, why don't you just take out one or two of the better ones and add them to your boxes, then ditch the rest? If the charity shop won't take them, take them to the tip. Mary's children are too old for crèche, so she won't notice if the toys aren't there. But if she does say anything, you can say you sorted out what you wanted and let the rest go because you didn't have space for all of them. That wouldn't be a lie.'

'Thanks, that's a good idea,' said Sophie, feeling much cheered by the conversation and a little by the glass of wine.

'We used to get some funny things dropped at the vicarage in our old parish,' said Robert, crossing his legs. 'Someone left two threadbare armchairs in the front garden when we were out once, with a note saying, "For the poor". We had to pay someone to take them to the tip in a van.'

Catherine laughed. 'I remember, they smelled of cats. Whoever it was must have thought we were pleased because a couple of days later we found a dilapidated dining table with chairs, a kitchen bin, a broom and a framed photograph of Margaret Thatcher in the garden, with another note in the same handwriting. We had to pay the van man to come back again!'

'Anyway, you must take a holiday this year. We'll make it our priority to cover you, if you give us some dates,' said Robert.

'Oh, that is kind,' said Dominic. 'Actually, since you mention it…' and he told them about the holiday they hoped to have in France with his parents.

'That sounds perfect,' said Catherine, getting her diary out of her handbag and writing the dates down. 'Have your parents lived in France very long, Dominic? I've never asked you.'

'Yes, they met when they were both studying French at university, got married and then Dad got offered a job at a firm in Tours, exporting goods to the UK. Mum obviously went with him and then got offered a job at the same firm. I don't think they intended to stay forever, but they fell in love with the country and never came back. I'm not sure they ever will now. I was born there.'

'I imagine you speak French fluently, then?' asked Robert.

'I'm bilingual. I did all my schooling in France, but then came to the UK for university, met Sophie and never went back.'

'You've got a brother, haven't you? Does he still live in France?'

'Yes, Nicholas, he's fifteen years younger than me. He was a bit of a surprise to Mum and Dad – a happy surprise – but he's only just eighteen. He's studying maths in Paris.'

'Do you speak French, Sophie?' Catherine asked.

'No, I did it at school, passed the exam and then forgot pretty much all of it!'

'A bit like me,' laughed Catherine. 'Now, the other thing I wanted to say to you, Sophie, was, when you feel ready, why don't you let me look after Henry in the crèche on a Thursday morning? I know he has his issues. He can't help it,' she added, quickly, 'he had a difficult start in life, but I think I can cope. You rejoin the group and share leading the studies with Belinda. It will do you good.'

'I don't know what to say,' said Sophie, and she really did shed a few tears. 'What would we do without you both?'

The rest of the week passed much more productively. Buoyed up by Robert and Catherine's timely encouragement, Dominic and Sophie were feeling much stronger by the following Sunday. Sophie felt even more pleased when she noticed that the visitor, Rufus, had returned to church. She spotted him sitting near the front, next to Lucy. At the end of the service he sat for a while in the pew, chatting with Lucy and looking as happy as he had the week before. Clearly, thought Sophie, his experience of church beverages had not put him off.

Sophie went to chat with some other members of the congregation, meaning to catch Rufus when he had finished speaking to Lucy. However, when he got up, Rufus made for the door, leaving Lucy to come into the back room for coffee alone.

Sophie went to speak to her. 'Hi, Lucy, how are you?'

'Fine, thanks. You? I was just talking to that new man, Rufus.'

'Yes, we're fine, thanks. Rufus, yes… Do you think he likes it here?'

'He seemed very enthusiastic, although he comes across as one of those people who are very enthusiastic about everything. He seemed disappointed not to see Hayley, though. Apparently, Paul works for Rufus and he met her at the Christmas party,' said Lucy. 'I asked him if he wanted a cup of tea, but he seemed anxious to get away at that point.'

'Ah, I think there may be a reason for that,' explained Sophie. She told Lucy about Audrey's mistake and the tea/coffee combination and they both had a giggle.

'Poor man,' remarked Lucy. 'No wonder he didn't fancy risking it again. If he comes back next week, we can apologise discreetly. It's a shame Hayley isn't here, though. Is she OK?'

'I don't know,' said Sophie, truthfully. 'Perhaps I had better try to catch up with her this week.'

Later, over a quiet Sunday lunch in the kitchen with Dominic and Henry, Sophie mentioned Hayley's absence at church to Dominic. 'I wonder if I ought to call on her one day after school,' said Sophie. 'I'm worried she's taking this infertility thing very badly. I know I can't make that any better for her, but at least I can honestly say I know how she feels. Sometimes that helps. School finishes just after three, so she's usually home alone for a little while before Paul gets in. It's tricky to talk with Henry about, though.'

'Let me look at my diary,' said Dominic. 'Audrey and Geoffrey probably wouldn't agree, but I think it would be a good use of my time if I look after Henry so you can visit Hayley for an hour.'

The following Wednesday, Sophie went to call on Hayley after school, leaving Dominic and Henry at the kitchen table with the paints. She went up to the top floor of the block of flats and knocked with some trepidation. Hayley opened the door, and seemed pleased to see her; she invited her in.

Sophie thought Hayley looked quite unwell. Her concern increased.

'How are you?' she asked, as Hayley took her coat and hung it up.

'Fine,' said Hayley. 'Well, a bit nauseous, actually.'

'Oh no,' said Sophie, instantly thinking that she didn't want to catch a tummy bug and then feeling selfish for thinking it. 'When did it start?'

'I've been feeling sick on and off for a week or so,' Hayley replied. She couldn't suppress a smile. 'Actually, we aren't really telling anyone yet, but I have some news.' She told Sophie all about the baby, how she had been buying a pregnancy test when she had met Sophie and Henry walking in the snow that day and how it had been positive and how pleased Paul was. 'You see, it must have been an answer to prayer. That's what I told Paul, anyway. He's so happy he said he'll come to church. I'm sorry I haven't been for a while. It's just this morning sickness and I've been feeling very tired. I will come back again, I promise.'

'I'm so happy for you,' said Sophie, as she got up to leave. 'But I promise not to tell anyone.'

'Except Dominic,' said Hayley, as she stood up. 'Tell Dominic those prayers worked.'

'Except Dominic,' agreed Sophie.

An odd look came over Hayley's face. 'Are you OK?' asked Sophie, feeling concerned.

Hayley rushed out of the room, in the direction of the bathroom. A moment later, Sophie could hear her being sick. Sophie sat back down and picked up a magazine from the coffee table, while she waited for Hayley to recover herself. It was a mother-and-baby catalogue. Sophie noticed that the corners of several of the pages had been folded down.

Half an hour later Sophie was walking back to the vicarage. She had left Hayley's before Paul had returned from work, but it was already getting dark and it was cold. She hurried, glad to be by herself for a little while, but looking forward to the warmth of her home. She felt a mixture of emotions and she tried to examine her own thoughts. She felt very happy for Hayley and Paul, but also vaguely concerned. Hayley was obviously very excited, but she must be very early on in her pregnancy and, from the looks of things, she was already making a lot of plans. There was another emotion in the mix too, a sadness which Sophie couldn't completely account for.

She opened the front door and went inside, deciding to keep conversation light for the moment.

Later on, when Henry had been put to bed, Sophie was finishing some washing-up when she heard Dominic come into the kitchen behind her. 'Cup of tea?' he asked.

'Yes, please,' Sophie replied. 'I have news,' she added, not looking at her husband as she spoke.

'What news?'

'About Hayley and Paul. Hayley's pregnant. Her prayers have been answered. She's going to have a baby in September. She didn't want to say anything too early, but I'm allowed to tell you.'

'Well, that's wonderful,' said Dominic. He put his arm around her and kissed the top of her head. 'Are you OK?'

'Yes,' she said, peering down into the sink, 'and no. I don't know. Yes, I'm really happy for them both. Really, I am. To be honest, whenever anyone says they are pregnant I'm always happy for them and I'm always relieved. I'm relieved to know that any couple can have a baby, that they won't have to go through... this... won't have to feel like this. Really, I'm delighted for them.' She looked at him directly now. 'But why do I feel so awful at the same time? I'm genuinely happy for them. I never stop being sad that I can't have a baby, and someone else being pregnant doesn't make that any worse. It doesn't change our situation, so why do I feel so much more miserable about it now? I don't understand my own feelings.'

Dominic looked thoughtful for a moment. 'I think,' he said, slowly, 'it's just always hard watching somebody else living your dream.'

'It is,' admitted Sophie. 'It really is, and I don't know why God has done this to me. Having a baby has always been so important to me. Ever since I was ten and we had that lesson at school, you know, the one about the birds and the bees? Did you have that one in France?' She didn't wait for him to answer. 'Anyway, we had that lesson about where babies come from and a girl sitting in front of me put her hand up and said that her auntie couldn't have babies. The teacher asked her if her aunt was very upset about it and I can't even remember what the girl said. I was just so horrified to find out that there were people in the world who couldn't have babies. Ever since that day I've dreaded it happening to me. I was always more scared of not being able to have a baby than I was of having a life-threatening disease. I know that sounds ridiculous, but it's true. And yet, that is what God did to me. That's what God allowed to happen to me. Why? Is it because I'm a rubbish mother? Maybe I should never have been a mother, perhaps God intended me to be childless and we should never have adopted Henry.'

'You're not a rubbish mother. What are you talking about?'

'I am. Look at the way Henry behaves. Belinda's children don't behave like that.'

'Belinda's children didn't have Henry's start in life.'

'No, I know, but even Henry doesn't behave like that when Catherine looks after him. I must be doing something wrong. There must be a reason why God didn't let me have a baby, because that's the truth – God didn't let me have a baby.'

'Sophie, God didn't do this to you out of spite. But, yes, He allowed it to happen. We live in a world that's in rebellion against its creator; of course bad things are going to happen, right up until the end of time. But He's in it with us, God is in it with us, He feels our pain with us. He brings good things out of bad things if we trust Him and, yes, Sophie you are meant to be Henry's mother.'

'I know,' said Sophie. 'I know it in my head; it's just hard to feel it in my heart sometimes. We prayed and prayed for a baby and it didn't happen, but then, no one ever promised us a baby. I do know I'm meant to be Henry's mum, I just wish I could come to terms with infertility, that's all. I still feel so sad about it.'

'I have one idea,' suggested Dominic.

'Go on.'

'You know we're having a healing service after Easter? Well, why don't you come?'

'But I'm not ill; I'm not depressed.'

'No, no, I know you're not. But why don't you come and ask for prayer to come to terms with infertility? Prayer to stop feeling sad.'

'Oh, I don't know,' said Sophie. 'It would seem weird, unnatural, wrong, even, not to feel sad about it. It would be like asking God to stop me feeling a normal feeling. Do you see what I'm trying to say?'

'I do see what you are saying,' Dominic replied, 'but I think you should come.'

'Let me think about it,' said Sophie, uncertainly. Then, to change the subject, 'Oh, and guess what else.'

'Paul said he'll come to church?' said Dominic, raising his eyebrows.

'Exactly,' said Sophie.

As it happened, Paul was as good as Hayley's word and did turn up for church with Hayley the following Sunday. They arrived late and sat near the back. Sophie thought Hayley still looked quite ill.

Sophie was also pleased to see that Rufus had come to church again. He arrived early and sat near the front, next to Lucy. Sophie couldn't help feeling that Paul and Rufus meeting at church would be a positive thing for both of them. She fully expected Paul and Hayley to greet Rufus at the end of the service. However, as Mrs Fowler-Watt struck the opening chords of the final hymn, Hayley and Paul crept quietly to the door and slipped away. Sophie felt quite cross for a moment, then she remembered Hayley's morning sickness and admonished herself.

As Lucy also got up during the final hymn and went to the kitchen with Audrey to make the tea and coffee, Sophie decided to go to speak to Rufus herself.

'Hello, Rufus,' she said. 'It's lovely to have you with us again this morning. How are you? How are your plans for the new house?'

'Ah, Sophie,' he beamed. 'I'm very well, thank you. The house plans are going smoothly; should be moving out of the hotel in a couple of weeks, all being well.'

'Great,' said Sophie. 'Then you really will be part of Oxley. I hope you're starting to feel part of church too?' she ventured.

Rufus smiled again. 'Absolutely. People have been very friendly and welcoming. Still no sign of the elusive Hayley, though.'

'I'm glad you feel welcome. I must just tell you, though…' and she went on to explain about the tea/coffee. 'Also, Hayley was here this morning, with Paul, but I don't think she was feeling too well and she left during the last hymn. Sorry.'

'Oh, that's a shame,' said Rufus, 'but I'm sure there will be other occasions.' He glanced towards the church kitchen. 'Maybe I could risk another cup of church tea.'

Sophie walked to the back of church with Rufus, meaning to introduce him to some other members of the congregation, but was intercepted by Doris before she got there. 'Now, Sophie, I must say your husband does preach a very long sermon,' began Doris. Sophie glanced towards Rufus. He seemed to be confidently introducing himself to people, so she turned back to Doris, wondering if she dared point out that Doris had, as usual, been asleep during the sermon and, therefore, couldn't know how long it was. She decided she didn't dare, so she changed the subject by enquiring after the health of Doris's rabbits. Doris seemed happy with the change of subject and Sophie listened and nodded, chancing the odd glance around church as she did. Belinda was talking to Catherine, her three boys sitting quietly together on the back pew, looking at books. John was talking to Geoffrey. John seemed quite animated, but Geoffrey looked rather cross. Sophie wasn't sure whether he looked more cross than usual.

As the church gradually emptied out, Sophie managed to extract herself from Doris and make her way towards the door. Rufus was among the last to leave. Sophie couldn't help noticing that he made a point of putting his head into the kitchen before leaving, to thank Lucy for the tea. Was it her imagination, or did he glance at Lucy more often than was natural? Sophie wasn't sure. She went to say goodbye herself and then walked back to the vicarage with Henry, leaving Dominic talking to Geoffrey in the doorway.

Ten minutes later, Dominic came through the vicarage door. 'Everything OK?' Sophie called from the kitchen.

'Sort of,' Dominic answered. 'I think everything went reasonably well this morning. It was just Geoffrey who didn't seem happy. He wants to come and see me when they come back from their holiday.'

'Oh, when are they going on holiday?'

'Tomorrow, I think. They're off on a cruise for a couple of weeks. I'm not going to let it get to me, though. I'm doing my best and that's all I can do.'

'Good,' said Sophie.

Sophie rang Hayley later.

'Sorry, Sophie, it's just this wretched morning sickness,' Hayley explained. 'Don't tell anyone, but I was sick behind one of the gravestones outside church. It looked about 100 years old, so I don't think anyone will be visiting it. Hopefully no one will find out.'

'Poor you,' Sophie sympathised. 'It must be ghastly.'

'Oh, it's not too bad really,' said Hayley. 'In a way I don't mind – it kind of makes it more real somehow. Paul thinks he's being funny. He told me to cut out the middleman and just tip my breakfast straight down the toilet in the mornings. Anyway, seriously, I will do my best to come to church when I can, but I think I'm going to have to step back from the music for a while. Do you mind?'

'Of course not,' said Sophie. 'I'll mention it to Dominic and he can speak to Mike, but Mike won't mind playing on his own for a while. You just look after yourself for the moment.'

That night, Sophie lay in bed thinking about all of them. Audrey, Geoffrey and Doris, so negative. Catherine and Robert, John and Belinda, so positive. Lucy and Rufus... Had Rufus noticed Lucy, or was it Sophie's wishful thinking? How might Lucy feel about that? Paul and Hayley and the baby they would be bringing into the world... She drifted into sleep.

Sophie's labour pains were becoming more intense. She looked down at her pregnant abdomen. Dominic was beside the hospital bed, holding her hand. The years of sadness and yearning were behind them and soon, very soon, she would be holding her own newborn baby. Another contraction was building... she awoke with a start to find herself in her bed at home. Period pains. She got up and went to the bathroom, tears of disappointment running down her face.

Over the next couple of weeks, the atmosphere at church seemed somehow lighter, with the absence of Audrey and

Geoffrey. Rufus moved into his new house in the village and seemed to have become a church regular. However, Hayley and Paul were not to be seen. Sophie and Dominic put this down to the pregnancy and decided not to be too anxious for the moment. The music wasn't quite the same without Hayley, but Mike seemed to be coping well leading on his guitar, and there was always Mrs Fowler-Watt with the organ.

Then, on the Sunday before Audrey and Geoffrey were due back from holiday, Lucy approached Sophie, looking as if she needed to say something.

'What's happened?' asked Sophie.

'Rufus asked me to go to the zoo with him next Saturday,' said Lucy.

'Oh,' Sophie smiled. 'That's exciting... isn't it?'

'I think so... I mean, yes, but I don't know whether he's asked me as a friend or a date.'

'Oh, well, would you like it to be as a friend or as a date?' asked Sophie.

'I don't know. He's a really nice person, but I don't know whether I find him attractive,' said Lucy, truthfully.

'OK,' said Sophie, feeling slightly disappointed, but trying to stay positive. 'Go as a friend – and see what happens.'

Nine

On Monday morning Lucy took the bus to work. As usual, she mulled over a list of patients she knew were coming to see her. She liked to be prepared, as much as possible. The majority of her patients were referred with joint, nerve or muscle pain and Lucy enjoyed using careful questioning and examination to locate the source of a problem and treat it.

Then she found her thoughts turning towards Rufus. She was looking forward to the zoo trip on Saturday, despite its uncertainties – zoo trip, so early on in the year? It seemed a bit strange.

She had been gradually getting to know Rufus at church and enjoyed his company. He seemed a kind and positive person, but Lucy still wasn't sure whether she found him attractive, or whether he was attracted to her.

On Saturday morning, Rufus arrived promptly, in a long, sleek, black car. Lucy got in and sank into the upholstery. 'Hello, thank you for coming to pick me up. Nice car!'

'Morning! Thank you, but actually, the car belongs to my company. We own a fleet of them!'

They chatted as he drove. Rufus had, at last, moved into his new house.

'Have you unpacked everything already?' she asked.

'There wasn't an awful lot to unpack,' Rufus replied, laughing. 'What I really need to do is buy some furniture. I've got my bed, a wardrobe, one armchair and a television, but that's pretty much it, so far.'

They parked easily when they arrived at the zoo. As expected, it wasn't as busy as it would be in the summer months. Rufus insisted on paying for Lucy's ticket. 'Shall we get some hot drinks?' he suggested. 'We can take them with us. Where would you like to start?'

Lucy thought. 'How about the elephants?'

Rufus bought them each a hot chocolate from a kiosk, then, 'Elephants it is,' he said, looking at the zoo map and leading the way. They walked at a fairly brisk pace, both wrapped up warmly in coats and scarves.

Rufus seemed to be a mine of information when it came to the animals. 'You know,' he said, as they watched the elephants and sipped their drinks, 'a baby elephant has no control over its trunk.'

'I didn't know,' admitted Lucy.

'For their first year of life, they tend to trip over them.'

It was the same with the porcupines. 'Did you know, a porcupine can kill a predator with its quills?'

'Really?' said Lucy, intrigued.

'Yes, the quills have hundreds of barbs on them, which make them sink into the predator's flesh easily, but also make it very difficult to get them out.'

'Goodness!' exclaimed Lucy. Some people, she thought, might describe Rufus as a 'know-it-all', but she found his knowledge rather interesting.

To warm up, they went to the zoo restaurant for an early lunch. Once again Rufus insisted on paying. Really, thought Lucy, it was starting to feel quite a lot like a date. It dawned on her that this thought was a pleasant one.

After lunch, the sun came out and they strolled at a more leisurely pace, stopping for hot drinks mid-afternoon, which Lucy persuaded Rufus to let her pay for this time.

They walked towards the giraffe enclosure. 'A giraffe's neck,' began Rufus, 'is six feet long and its tongue is between eighteen and twenty inches long.'

'Do you know everything about animals?' enquired Lucy.

'Oh… no… I was reading that from the wall behind you.'

Lucy turned round to look at the board. 'Oh yes… You do seem to know quite a lot about animals, though.'

'Well, you see, my brother, Monty, is actually a zookeeper here. I was hoping we might meet up with him for lunch today, but he had to go off to escort some monkeys to another zoo at short notice.'

'Oh, I see.'

At last it was time to leave and they walked towards the zoo exit. They passed the rhino enclosure on the way. The rhinos, which had been spread out across their spacious paddock earlier, were standing by their gates, waiting patiently. Two zookeepers approached the rhino house, wheeling barrows of food for the animals. The gates were lifted and the rhinos went inside.

'They're obviously familiar with the evening routine,' commented Rufus.

'I quite like a rhino,' said Lucy, 'but I think that might be a minority viewpoint.'

'Oh no, I quite agree,' said Rufus. 'They aren't the most handsome of creatures, but I think they're rather sweet.' Then he added, 'A rhino's horn is made of hair.'

'You're doing it again,' said Lucy, and he laughed.

'I've been invited to have supper with my boss, Mr Wainwright, and his wife this evening,' said Rufus, on the way home. 'I'll drop you home first, obviously, then I'd better get going. I'll see you tomorrow at church, though.'

'Thank you for a lovely day,' said Lucy. 'I'm sorry you didn't see your brother, but I had a nice time.'

'I had a lovely day too,' said Rufus, as he pulled up outside Lucy's block of flats. 'I was wondering, if you're not doing anything next Saturday, how would you feel about coming furniture shopping with me?'

'I'd love too,' said Lucy, smiling. Just as she was about to get out of the car, Rufus leaned across and kissed her gently on the lips. She flinched.

'Oh, sorry,' said Rufus, blushing and looking embarrassed.

'No,' said Lucy. 'It's fine! Everything's fine. It's just... just... I'm sorry, I don't like beards,' she finished, lamely.

'Just the beard that's the problem? Not me?'

'Definitely just the beard, not you.'

'Right, right,' he said, stroking his beard thoughtfully. 'No problem, then,' he smiled. 'I'll see you in the morning.'

'Thanks again, see you tomorrow,' said Lucy. She got out of the car and gave him a wave as he pulled away.

Really, she thought, he was very nice... and he wasn't an unattractive man. It was just the beard, but she was sure she could get used to it. She was a little worried that she had offended him, but he seemed to be a pretty confident character. However, his reaction when he thought his kiss was unwanted betrayed a vulnerability that she found rather endearing.

The next morning Lucy arrived early at church. She was leading Sunday school with Sarah, but had prepared well in advance, so she went into the Sunday school room to get organised. The craft activity took a little longer to set out than she had planned and the first hymn had started as she entered the main body of the church, so she found a seat on the back pew and sat down. She could see Rufus from behind, sitting near her parents. She would have to catch him at the end, she thought, as she watched Sophie taking Henry out to the back room.

'How did it go?' mouthed Sophie, as she passed. Lucy gave her a thumbs up; details would have to wait until after the service.

Sunday school went well, although Lucy was disappointed that only the Henderson brothers were there. The other families were rather sporadic attenders. At least, with Belinda and John attending regularly, she knew she should invariably have some children to teach. There had been times in the past when she had spent hours preparing for Sunday school and no one had turned up.

At the end of the service the children left and Lucy began to clear up. Sophie put her head around the door. 'So you had a nice time yesterday?'

'It was lovely, thank you,' said Lucy, smiling.

'And was it…' she waited a moment, as Sarah left the room to get a cup of coffee, '… was it a date?'

'I think it was. At least, he kissed me before I got out of the car.' Lucy failed to hide an embarrassed smile, which made them both giggle. 'The only trouble was… I flinched. Then I said…' Lucy looked down the church to check Rufus wasn't near, but he was talking to her parents. 'I ended up saying…' Rufus turned around. Lucy gasped, 'I ended up saying that I don't like beards!'

Sophie put her hands to her mouth. 'Oh, Lucy, he must really like you!' she laughed. Rufus gave Lucy a wave, running his other hand across his clean-shaven jaw.

'I didn't really like it that much myself,' he explained to Lucy later. 'It was just that some people in the office thought I looked too young to be the IT manager. I thought it might make me look older.'

The following Saturday morning Lucy walked to Rufus's house.

It was a small terraced cottage near the centre of the village, probably built in Victorian times, thought Lucy, as she walked through the front door straight into the living room. The house had obviously been recently decorated, with plain walls and carpets. It was small, one room wide, with a kitchen behind the living room and a small, square garden behind that. The kitchen looked as if it had been recently updated.

'Do sit down,' said Rufus, gesturing towards the only chair in the room. He sat on the carpet. 'I've made a list,' he added, taking a piece of paper and a pen from his pocket, 'but I thought you might have a better idea of which shops to visit than I do; you're much more familiar with the area.'

'What's on the list?' asked Lucy.

'Well, another chair wouldn't go amiss,' said Rufus, 'or maybe a little sofa. I think there would still be room for a small dining table and chairs. A little table for the television would be good, and a small bookcase would be a bonus.'

'I'm sure we could manage that,' said Lucy, already planning a route around Stafford. 'What about upstairs?'

'All sorted.'

Lucy followed Rufus up the stairs onto a small, square landing. The landing was quite quaint, with a step up on one side into a bedroom, just big enough for Rufus's bed and wardrobe, and another step on the other side, where a tiny corridor led to an empty box room and the bathroom. There was also an odd-looking door halfway up the stairs which Lucy couldn't account for. The bathroom, like the kitchen, appeared to have been recently updated. Lucy couldn't help noticing that that there was only one curtain at the window in the bedroom and a matching one at the window of the box room. Together they obviously made a pair. She smiled to herself and made a mental note to take Rufus curtain shopping at some point.

Rufus seemed very pleased with his first house and Lucy was happy to encourage him with her enthusiasm. After a quick cup of tea they set off in the car, Rufus driving and Lucy directing. They visited all the shops Lucy could think of and Rufus seemed grateful for Lucy's advice and opinions on what might go where. They stopped for lunch in one of the department stores at midday and reviewed the shopping list. Really, Lucy thought, Rufus was very fortunate. When she had bought her flat, money for furniture had been scarce and she had had to rely on hand-me-downs.

After lunch they finalised their choices (Rufus seemed to think it important that Lucy be included in the choosing) and Rufus paid and arranged to have the furniture delivered during the week.

'Thank you so much for your help today,' he said, as he dropped Lucy off later that afternoon. 'I really appreciate your coming with me. I wonder, could I take you out for dinner this evening, as a thank you?'

'That would be lovely,' said Lucy.

'I'll book a table somewhere and pick you up at about half past seven, if that's convenient?'

Lucy felt rather tired following the shopping expedition and was glad of a rest and a hot bath before she got ready to go out that evening. Rufus picked her up on the dot of half past seven and drove to a restaurant on the outskirts of Stafford.

While they were waiting for their meals to arrive, Rufus again thanked Lucy for her help that day. 'We've talked a lot about me today,' he said. 'Tell me about you and your family.'

'You've met Mum and Dad at church,' said Lucy. 'I'm an only child, so there isn't much more to tell. I was born and brought up in Oxley. I went away to study, then I worked in London for a while, but I've ended up back in the village and I'm quite happy about that. I love my church, I'm close to my parents and I have a lovely job and a lovely flat. I consider myself very fortunate, really.' She didn't add that the only thing missing was a lovely man to share it with, or that she had already wondered whether Rufus might turn out to be that man.

'Where did you go to school?' asked Rufus.

'The local primary school and then the local comprehensive,' Lucy replied. Rufus looked down. For a split second Lucy thought she had seen an odd look on his face – disappointment, perhaps? It passed quickly. 'Why do you ask?' she ventured. 'Where did you go to school?'

'My brother and I went to Montgomery School,' he said. From his tone of voice, Lucy could tell that this was a school she should have heard of, but she hadn't and she decided not to betray her ignorance, so she kept quiet for a moment.

'You've heard of Montgomery School, haven't you?' asked Rufus, frowning slightly.

'Actually, no. You probably think I should have, but I haven't.'

'No problem. It's an independent boarding school for boys. It has a very good reputation.'

'Oh, well, I'm state educated.' Lucy tried not to sound as if she was apologising for the fact. 'Is that a problem?'

'No, of course not. At least, not to me. Mother and Father place quite a high emphasis on that sort of thing, but my parents' values are not my values.'

'Tell me about your parents.

'They live in Surrey. They have a house on an estate in the country. Father's a merchant banker in London, although sometimes he works from home, too. Mother used to write children's books, but she gave up work when she had me. Then, two years after I was born, she had Monty and she was rather busy for a while. Mother spends most of her time looking after Father and the dogs and running the house now.' Rufus looked at Lucy and she felt he was trying to read her expression. 'I expect you think it's funny that I call my parents Mother and Father.'

'I don't really know anybody else of our age who doesn't just say Mum and Dad,' said Lucy. 'Not that I know how old you are,' she added.

'I'm twenty-nine,' answered Rufus, then, 'I know, it is a bit Enid Blyton, isn't it? Mother and Father prefer it, though.'

'I'm coming up for twenty-nine, too. Have you got any other brothers or sisters? Tell me more about Monty.'

'Just the two of us. Monty always wanted to be a zookeeper. Mother and Father weren't really very keen. They wanted us both to be successful in business. It's very important to them that we both do well, but Monty insisted that he had to work with animals. Mother and Father said he had to go to university first, so he did a degree in zoology, then got a job at the zoo. My parents are still not that keen, but they are encouraging him to work his way up the ladder. I think they would like to see him managing the zoo, really, but Monty likes being hands-on.'

'Is Monty married?'

'No, he has a girlfriend called Helen. She works at the zoo too. He met her at work. Mother and Father preferred his previous girlfriend, because she was a high-flying lawyer.'

Lucy's heart sank. Rufus appeared to notice the change in her expression. 'How did you become a Christian?' he asked.

'Brought up with it, really. We've always gone to All Saints as a family. I went to other churches when I was at university and when I worked in London, and I think my faith got stronger then. I learned to rely on God when I didn't have my parents to look after me. What about you?'

'I became a Christian at university. I made friends with some chaps in the Christian Union and we had some long talks, right through the night sometimes. I had a lot of questions, but gradually it all started to make sense. My parents don't approve. They think it's a phase that I'm going to grow out of, and I'm not sure what Monty thinks. He probably just feels relieved it isn't only him who isn't toeing the party line.'

'I was wondering whether you might like to join one of the Bible study groups at church,' said Lucy. 'I go to the one on Tuesday evenings at the vicarage.'

'That would be nice,' said Rufus.

At the end of the evening, Rufus drove back to Oxley and pulled up outside Lucy's home.

'Thank you for a lovely evening,' she said.

'Thank you for a lovely day and evening,' said Rufus, and he leaned across and kissed her goodnight. This time she didn't flinch.

Over the coming weeks Rufus and Lucy spent most of their free time together and people became accustomed to seeing them sitting together at church on Sundays. Rufus also became a regular member of the Tuesday night study group at the vicarage.

During March, the days started growing noticeably longer and there was less of a chill in the air. Mother's Day approached and preparations were well underway. Hayley had still not made it back to church, but Dominic had called in at school and asked Hayley to put invitations to the service into the children's school bags which, with the Head's permission, she was happy to do.

Every lady in the church was to receive a posy of daffodils. The previous year a patch of the vicarage garden, which was quite large, had been put aside to grow daffodils. Bulbs had been donated by members of the congregation and planted in time to come up ready for the special Sunday service. Arnold Smith, a retired man who didn't like to come to church but liked to keep the churchyard tidy, had volunteered to harvest the daffodils at the appropriate time. Audrey, as chief of the flower ladies, had volunteered to organise the actual assembling of the posies.

As it was hoped that the Sunday service would attract people from the village who might not regularly come to church, Dominic had arranged a special prayer meeting to take place in the church on the Saturday morning at nine o'clock. This had been announced in the Sunday morning notices.

One week before Mother's Day Audrey caught Dominic just as the service was about to start. 'I need a slot in the notices this morning,' she said, and hurried off to sit down. It was a statement rather than a request.

'Oh, right,' said Dominic to Audrey's retreating back.

The notices were always given after the first hymn. Dominic reminded everyone about the nine o'clock prayer meeting the following Saturday. 'And I think Audrey has a notice,' he finished.

Audrey got up and bustled to the front. 'We will be assembling the Mothering Sunday posies at nine o'clock in the church next Saturday morning,' she boomed. 'Please do come along and support us. There is a lot of work to be done.' She flapped back to her seat in the choir importantly.

Later, over lunch, Dominic said, 'I'm sure she did that on purpose. If she had only told me that she wanted to organise the flowers at nine o'clock, I could have arranged the prayers so that they didn't clash, but I suppose I'm just meant to know these things. Never mind. Geoffrey finally made a date for the meeting he's been threatening me with, so I can't say anything in case I make things worse.'

'Geoffrey might be coming round to say something nice or helpful,' suggested Sophie hopefully.

'I don't think so, somehow. He wouldn't say what he wanted to talk about, just that it had resulted from a conversation with John Henderson. We'll see.'

Preparations for Mother's Day were also underway at the vicarage. The guest room had been prepared, meals planned and shopping bought. Glenda and Patrick arrived on the preceding Friday evening and Sophie, Dominic and Henry were all pleased to see them.

Henry was much more manageable in his own home, where he could be contained, and Sophie felt able to chat more freely with her parents than she had done at Christmas. Glenda agreed to mind Henry on Saturday morning so that Sophie could go to the prayer meeting and then join in with making the posies. This, Sophie hoped, would please Audrey.

Dominic had planned to have the prayer meeting in the room at the back of church, but they realised this was not going to be possible as soon as they entered. Tables had been set up with stations for daffodil assembly, foliage trimming, foliage wrapping and ribbon tying, and Audrey's gang had been organised into a production line.

'Morning,' said Dominic, but no one acknowledged his presence and Audrey didn't even turn around. 'Let's retreat to the kitchen,' Dominic said to Sophie, picking up a stack of chairs and exiting hurriedly. Soon they were joined by a prayerful few, Catherine, Robert, Lucy and Rufus among them. John Henderson came in a few minutes late, apologising that

Belinda had to stay with the boys, and they committed the following day to God in prayer.

'I'd better go and see if I can help the flower ladies,' Sophie said, after Dominic brought the prayers to a close. She hoped maybe one or two of the others might come with her.

'OK,' said Catherine, putting her coat on.

'Hope it goes well,' encouraged Lucy.

Sophie went into the church room. Be positive, she thought to herself. 'What lovely posies,' she said. 'How can I help?'

'Some of us have been here since nine o'clock, you know,' said Audrey, looking at her watch pointedly.

'So have I,' replied Sophie, hastily. 'I just went to the prayers first.'

Audrey, however, wasn't listening. 'Now, this is what you do,' she instructed, and she explained how the production line worked. Sophie had to admit, it was a slick operation and the results were pretty good.

She returned to the vicarage feeling optimistic about the coming Sunday. As she went through the door, she could hear Glenda and Patrick with Henry in the living room. They all sounded happy and didn't seem to have heard her come in, something she was quick to take advantage of. She went into the study to see what Dominic was doing.

'I'm just printing out some service sheets for tomorrow. I thought it would be nice to have everything on one piece of paper, so any visitors can see where in the service we are and where we are going,' he told her.

'I'll start folding,' offered Sophie. The service sheet was nicely set, with the order of service and the words of all the songs. The front read, 'Mother's Day at All Saints Oxley'. 'You've made these look really nice.'

'Thanks,' said Dominic. 'I just wanted it to seem organised and to help people feel relaxed. Sometimes new people can feel less anxious if they can see what's coming up.'

'True.'

The following morning, Dominic surprised Sophie by bringing her tea in bed with Henry, holding a bunch of tulips. Sophie then took her parents tea and gave her mum some roses. A little later she went to the kitchen to get a head start on lunch preparations while Henry sat in the highchair. She didn't feel the need to be super-organised as she knew her mum would help her after church, but she also wanted Glenda to feel relaxed.

A little later Sophie walked across to church with Henry, Glenda and Patrick. She spotted Lucy sitting with her own parents and went over. 'No Rufus this morning?'

'He's gone down to Surrey to have lunch with his parents,' said Lucy. 'I think he picked his brother up on the way.'

The service went very well and Henry even sat quietly with Glenda and Patrick, at least until the posies had been given out after the first hymn. Then Sophie took him into the back room. There weren't any visitors, but most of the occasional attenders had turned up, making a full church with a happy atmosphere.

Sophie was encouraged to see that Hayley and Paul had come to church that morning. At the end of the service she caught up with them over coffee. 'How are you feeling?' she asked Hayley.

'Fine, thanks. The morning sickness has finally abated and we feel ready to tell people our news.'

'What news?' asked Lucy, coming up behind them.

'Hello, Lucy, guess what? Oh, don't guess, I'll tell you. We're going to have a baby, in September!'

'Oh, congratulations! I'm so happy for you.' Lucy's delight attracted the attention of others around them and soon everyone was asking and being told and congratulating both Hayley and Paul.

'Another little one for the crèche and maybe another mum for the ladies' Bible study on Thursdays,' said Belinda to Sophie. 'You see, God is growing the church.'

Later on, back at the vicarage, they sat down to lunch. Glenda said, 'That was a lovely service, Dominic.'

'Thank you, but it takes a lot of people to run a service. I had lots of positive comments. Except Audrey! I thanked her for organising the Mother's Day posies and she waved the service sheet at me and said that it isn't Mother's Day, it's Mothering Sunday! Still, everyone else seemed happy.'

'Henry was a good boy at the beginning of the service, weren't you, darling?' said Glenda to her grandson. 'You see, Sophie,' she added, 'he's just a normal little boy with lots of energy.'

'He's much better than he was at Christmas. Just needs a bit of discipline,' commented Patrick.

Monday was always Dominic and Sophie's day off (it worked well for them, as they always felt emotionally exhausted after Sunday), and Glenda and Patrick had arranged to travel back to Eastbourne on Monday evening. So they took a trip out to Cannock Chase, a local beauty spot that Dominic and Sophie had discovered not long after arriving in Oxley. It was a place where they often chose to spend their day off, when they had time. It was a lovely day and, before they left, Glenda and Patrick arranged another visit to Oxley for Easter.

Just as they were about to drop off to sleep that night, Sophie said, 'I feel very excited for Lucy. Rufus seems such a nice man. And Hayley and Paul are happy too.'

'And you?' asked Dominic. 'Are you happy, Sophie?'

'I'm just happy that I don't have to worry about Lucy and I don't have to worry about Hayley,' she said, sleepily.

When Sophie awoke to bright sunshine the next morning, she knew what she must do. She got out of bed quietly and went to the bathroom. She took the pregnancy test stick out of its wrapper and read the instructions. A couple of minutes later she was standing still, watching, waiting. Positive, positive at last. The waiting was over. A feeling of the utmost elation filled her. She rushed back to the bedroom to tell Dominic the news but, as she went through the bedroom door, she found herself in her childhood bedroom in Eastbourne. She became aware of a child crying somewhere nearby. She opened her eyes and looked at the bedside clock – two o'clock. Henry was crying. She got out of bed and went to his room, waves of disappointment washing over her.

Ten

On Tuesday morning, when Sophie awoke for the second time, she felt rather groggy and low in spirits. She remembered her dream from the night before and thought about it for a while. She had had a number of similar dreams recently and she knew they had been triggered by Hayley's pregnancy. However happy she was for Hayley, it was, as Dominic said, hard watching someone else living her dream. Henry woke and she got out of bed to begin the day.

Later that morning, as Sophie was giving Henry a drink and a mid-morning snack at the kitchen table, Dominic came in from the study and joined her. Sophie made them both a cup of coffee. After a few minutes of silence, she said, 'You're rather quiet this morning. Are you OK?'

'Geoffrey's coming round in about half an hour.'

'Oh no, I forgot that was this morning,' Sophie sighed.

'I wish you could join us. I could do with a bit of moral support.'

'Bit tricky with Henry,' said Sophie. 'Anyway, I think I'd feel like I was imposing. He's asked for a meeting with you, not us. It wouldn't feel right to butt in.'

'No. No, you're quite right, that wouldn't be fair. I wonder what he wants to say, though.'

'Well, it can't be anything that bad,' Sophie tried to reassure him. 'Let's think about where we are compared to this time last year. We've got a new family and the Sunday school has doubled in size. Hayley's going to have a baby, so we might be able to have a proper crèche soon, not just me and Henry in the back room. Rufus has come. Robert and Catherine are very reassuring and they've actually done the job we're doing. What can he say that's so terrible?'

'Oh, I don't know, it just feels like trouble. Anyway, when I came into the kitchen you were rather quiet too. Are you OK?'

'We-ell, I just had a funny dream last night. I've had a few funny dreams lately. I keep dreaming that I'm pregnant and I'm so happy in the dream… and then I wake up and, well, it's just such a disappointment.'

'Oh,' said Dominic, 'I'm sorry. It's my fault.'

'Don't be sorry. It's not your fault. Nobody did anything wrong – it just happened. If you keep blaming yourself then I can't talk to you, and I need to be able to talk to you about how I feel without worrying about making you feel worse!'

'OK, talk, I'm listening,' said Dominic. 'Really, I'm not blaming myself, I'm just listening.'

'Well, that's it, really. I just feel a bit more sad at the moment, that's all.'

'More sad?'

'Well, I'm always sad that I can't have a baby. It never goes away. I just really want to have a baby,' said Sophie, miserably. But also…' She looked at Henry. He had finished his drink and biscuit and, tired from being up during the night, had decided to have a little nap in the highchair. 'I'm a bit worried about him.'

'Go on,' said Dominic.

'He's just so naughty all the time. I really mean all the time. He's looking for the next naughty thing to do all day. When he knows I'm cross he just gives me that grin and that look that means he knows he's won. He just makes me so angry that I'm worried that… that I don't love him.' Sophie's eyes filled with tears. 'It's just not how I imagined it, not how I imagined being a mum was going to be.'

'But he's getting better,' said Dominic. 'Your parents seem to think he's better than he was at Christmas.'

'Mum and Dad are lovely, but they see what they want to see. Mum just says, "He's a normal little boy with lots of energy," all the time, and Dad says, "He just needs discipline," as if we don't do that,' said Sophie. 'They think he's better because I've arranged the vicarage around Henry. Everything here is Henry-proof and I have strategies for everything. Mum and Dad can't see what hard work he is. I'm scared, scared of how he makes me feel. You love him, but he doesn't push you as hard as he pushes me. I'm frightened that I'll never love him.'

The doorbell rang. Dominic looked at his watch. 'Geoffrey. We'll talk more later. I'll take him into the living room.'

'Ask him what he wants to drink and then come and tell me out here,' said Sophie.

Dominic went to open the front door. A moment later he put his head round the kitchen door, 'Two cups of tea.'

'Coming up,' said Sophie, turning towards the kettle.

'One cup of coffee and I'll have a glass of water,' added Dominic.

Sophie turned around in surprise. 'How many drinks does he want?'

'He brought Audrey and Doris with him,' whispered Dominic, pulling a face, then turning and heading back to the living room.

Really, thought Sophie, it was all very well her not joining the meeting because she didn't think it was fair on Geoffrey, but Geoffrey obviously hadn't felt the same when he'd invited Audrey and Doris. She took a tray, laden with drinks and a plate of biscuits, into the living room. Geoffrey was in full flow, with a sheet of paper in his hand, on which he appeared to have written a long list of notes. 'People want a traditional service with organ music and hymns,' he was saying. 'That's what church is all about.'

'Thanks, Sophie,' said Dominic. Nobody else acknowledged her presence, so she left the room quickly, closing the door behind her.

She felt sorry for Dominic. He worked long hours and tried so hard to keep everyone happy, to keep a balance between the old and the new. It seemed close to impossible to keep the traditionalists happy without making younger people feel alienated. Sophie was sure this wasn't how God intended church to be.

It wasn't until later that night that Dominic finally had time to recount the meeting with Sophie. 'He had a list,' he said.

'I know, I saw,' said Sophie, sympathetically.

'A list of complaints! He started with the worship wars: "Why can't we just sing a few traditional songs?" etc, and then went on to the sermons. "People don't want you to go on and on about the Bible. They have already listened to a Bible reading and they don't need you to tell them what it said. The sermon should be a few uplifting thoughts for them to go home with." Audrey agreed with him. Doris said the sermons were too long, but didn't comment on the content. That was just the warm-up,' said Dominic. 'Geoffrey's very angry because he thinks I'm making decisions behind his back. He'd had a chat with John Henderson. You know what John's like, very enthusiastic and full of ideas. John apparently mentioned his ideas about the Open Day on Easter Saturday and getting the church drive repaired and that he had talked to me about those things. Now Geoffrey thinks I'm organising things without his knowledge.'

'Oh!' said Sophie. 'But surely members of the congregation are allowed to have ideas. That's a good thing.'

'Yes, of course. I told him that John does have a lot of good ideas and I'm always pleased to hear anyone's ideas. I also said that I would like to have a Church Open Day, but that we wouldn't be doing anything without passing it through the church council and that the church council would have to vote in favour before anything could be done. Geoffrey sits on the church council as churchwarden, so he was going to hear about it tomorrow night anyway.'

'Did he calm down after that?'

'No, not really, I think he was enjoying being cross too much. He didn't want to let it go. He went on about money and said we shouldn't have wasted money by printing out service sheets for Mothering Sunday. He said we haven't got enough money to repair the drive and that we shouldn't be organising any church events unless it's to raise money for the church. I think he's one of those people who's been very used to getting his own way by throwing his weight around. He definitely likes to be in charge.'

'But he isn't in charge,' said Sophie. 'You are.'

'Hopefully, God's in charge,' said Dominic. 'But, yes, leading the church forward is the job I've been trained to do and the job I'm paid to do. Anyway, he couldn't really argue his point any further, so then he started asking whether my progress was reviewed and how the Bishop assessed my performance. They all said that they think the Bishop should ask everyone in the church how they think I'm doing and whether they are satisfied with the service I'm providing for them here.'

'The service you're providing? Isn't that missing the point of church? We aren't consumers. We as a church are called to work together as one body for a common cause. Your job is to teach us and lead us in reaching out to our community, but you're not a service provider!'

'I think you'll have trouble getting the likes of Geoffrey, Audrey and Doris to see it that way. Anyway, I'm not going to let them get to me. I'm going to carry on doing the job God has called me to.'

'Has Geoffrey *ever* said anything positive or encouraging to you?'

Dominic thought for a few moments, 'No.'

Despite his pledge not to let Geoffrey, Audrey and Doris get him down, Sophie noticed that Dominic seemed completely unable to concentrate the next morning. She knew he hadn't slept very well and had got up early, but when Sophie came downstairs, she found him not in the study but in the living room, staring out of the window. His eyes looked red and swollen. 'I just feel so useless,' he said. 'I can't concentrate on anything.'

'What have you got to do today that can't be put off?' asked Sophie.

'I was supposed to be meeting Mrs Fowler-Watt this morning, to discuss hymns for next month's services,' said Dominic, 'but she rang last night to say she's come down with a cold, so we've rescheduled. I have some rotas and next week's sermon to work on and there are some people to visit this afternoon, but other than that, there's nothing that can't be put off. Why do you ask?'

'Let's get into the car and take Henry to Cannock Chase again,' said Sophie. 'I know it's not our day off, but you do enough hours the rest of the week and the only person who would complain is Geoffrey and, given the circumstances, he can hardly say anything.'

'I don't really like taking time off on work days.'

'Apart from your one day off a week, you're supposed to be allowed one Saturday off a month. You hardly ever take it and I understand that – pressure of work – but you shouldn't feel guilty about taking one extra morning when you've been made to feel this bad.'

Dominic was quiet for a moment. 'OK,' he said. 'Let's get ready and then get out of here.'

When they got to Cannock Chase, they put Henry in the pushchair, but he wanted to get out and walk. Then he tried his usual tricks to make things difficult – either running away or lying on the ground and refusing to move. However, he soon found that this resulted in him either being put on reins or put back in the pushchair, so he gave up and trotted along with them quite nicely. Spring was in the air and there was a fresh smell of new life around them. Henry had yet to master the art of walking and talking at the same time, so they were able to talk as they walked and pray as they talked. When they returned home for lunch, they both felt calmer and more peaceful.

The church council meeting had been arranged for that evening in one of the rooms at the back of church. Dominic had to chair the meeting and work through the agenda. He was planning to raise John's suggestions for Easter weekend and the repairs to the church drive during the meeting.

Sophie felt quite tired after she had put Henry to bed, but she decided to plough her way through a pile of ironing that evening while she waited for Dominic to return. She had just plugged the iron in when the phone rang. She switched the iron back off again and went to the study to answer it. 'Hello, Oxley Vicarage.'

'Hello,' said a nervous-sounding woman's voice. 'Could I speak to the vicar, please?'

'My husband's out at a meeting at the moment,' said Sophie. 'Can I help?'

'I wanted to arrange a christening for my baby.'

'Let me take your name and number and I'll ask Dominic to get back to you. Are you around during the day?'

'Yes, my name's Melissa Roberts and I'm on maternity leave at the moment.' She gave Sophie her phone number and Sophie promised to get Dominic to give her a call the following morning.

She had just finished the ironing and put everything away when she heard Dominic come in. He took his papers into the study and then joined her in the living room. One glance at his face (tired but hopeful) was enough to tell Sophie that it hadn't been an easy meeting, but that it hadn't been a disaster either.

Dominic didn't bother with any preamble. 'It wasn't easy,' he recounted. 'I gave an outline of the suggestion for Easter. I put forward the idea of a Church Open Day on Easter Saturday, lots of invitations and advertising around the village, everything free and then, on the day, we just give out invitations for the

Sunday morning service, making sure people know it's child-friendly but no pressure.'

'What's not to like?' said Sophie.

'Obviously Geoffrey and chums found lots not to like, mainly because we will have to put a bit of money behind it and it isn't a fund-raising activity but, in the end, we voted in favour!' Dominic smiled. 'John and Belinda have volunteered to do most of the organising, assuming a favourable vote tonight. I think they've been involved in this sort of thing before, in their previous church. We'll announce it in the notices on Sunday and hope for some volunteers to help out.'

'What about the church drive?' asked Sophie.

'Well,' said Dominic, 'we voted to get some quotes for the work and then revisit at the next meeting. I'm happy with that for the time being.'

'Excellent,' said Sophie. 'Oh, someone rang to ask about having their baby baptised. I left her name and number on your desk and said you would ring back tomorrow.'

'Great,' said Dominic. 'And now, let's go to bed.'

That Thursday morning was to be Sophie's first time leading the women's Bible study group since she had had Henry. She was a little nervous, but the study went well and Henry seemed happy to play with Catherine in the crèche. Sophie was also able to let Belinda know that the church council had voted in favour of the Easter Saturday Open Day.

'Brilliant,' said Belinda. 'John and I have lots of ideas. We're really hoping that it will bring lots of families into church on Easter Sunday morning. I've already mentioned it to some of the mums from school.'

When Sophie and Henry returned to the vicarage at lunchtime, they met Dominic in the drive. 'Where have you been?' asked Sophie.

'I had a school assembly, then I called on Melissa, that lady who rang about the baptism. She seems very nice. She and her husband are both maths teachers, but she hasn't got to go back to school until next January. Her husband is called Daniel and it's their first baby, Jessica. She's three months old. I've arranged to see them to talk about baptism and what it means next week, but they said they would try to come to church on Sunday, so that's positive.'

That Sunday morning, Sophie and Henry met Hayley walking up the church drive.

'How are you feeling?' asked Sophie.

'Great, thanks,' replied Hayley. 'I haven't felt sick for a couple of weeks now and I feel really well. It's only when you have felt sick for weeks and then it stops that you really appreciate how lovely not feeling sick is. Anyway, look at this!' She opened her jacket and showed Sophie her tummy, where a small bump was starting to appear. Sophie felt the familiar wistful feelings stirring. 'I'm going to talk to Mike at the end of the service about getting back on board with the music.'

'That's great news. He's been doing a great job on his own, but it will make a big difference to have you playing again.'

At the beginning of the service Dominic gave the notices, but instead of telling the church the plans for the Open Day himself, he invited John and Belinda to do it. The change of voice seemed to catch people's attention. Sophie glanced at Audrey and Geoffrey, sitting in their places in the choir. Audrey looked as if she was doing some quick thinking. Geoffrey appeared to be staring fixedly in another direction.

When Sophie had taken Henry out to the back room and switched the speaker on, she glanced out once more at the church, through the glass doors. She was pleased to see that Rufus was back by Lucy's side. Then her attention was caught by the sight of someone she didn't recognise – a man, youngish, maybe in his thirties, with sandy-coloured hair. He didn't appear to be with anyone and she made a mental note to catch him at the end of the service and make him feel welcome.

Henry was much more easily entertained in the church room, now that he had started to develop an interest in the toys, and

Sophie found she was able to concentrate on the service quite well.

At coffee time, when Henry was safely contained in his pushchair with his biscuit, Sophie began to make her way towards the newcomer. She spotted him walking down the aisle. She was intrigued to see that he was holding a small, carved, wooden box. The way he was holding it struck her as unusual, almost as if he were cradling it, protecting it. However, before she could get to him, she saw that Rufus and Lucy had beaten her to it. She didn't want to swamp him, so she took a detour and chatted to some of the other members of the congregation on the way. She noticed that John and Belinda looked busy with clipboards. Hopefully, lots of volunteers were coming forward. She couldn't help noticing Audrey talking to Belinda, and Belinda scribbling notes furiously as Audrey spoke. She glanced towards Mike, putting his guitar away at the front of church. She had expected to see Hayley talking to him. Hayley, however, surprisingly, had disappeared.

Sophie made her way towards Belinda. 'How's it going?'

'Quite well,' Belinda replied, 'so far. Can I put you down to man one of the children's craft tables, or will you need to look after Henry? I've got Dominic down for the prayer corner, in case people would like to pray with him, or just talk to him, for that matter.'

'My parents will be with us that weekend,' said Sophie. 'I'm sure Mum and Dad can manage Henry between them. Put me down wherever you need me, and let me know what you need me to prepare in advance.'

'Thanks,' said Belinda, then added, 'Audrey was very keen to organise the café. She says she's already got a team together, but they need extra volunteers to make cakes.'

'Great!' said Sophie. 'Put me down for a Victoria sponge and a chocolate cake. But I thought Audrey was dead against the Open Day.'

'I think she is,' said Belinda, trying to suppress a smile, 'but she seemed so anxious at the thought of anybody else

130

interfering with her system in the kitchen… something about green cups and blue cups… that she said she would help out anyway!'

'Oh, well, I'm not complaining.'

More people were approaching Belinda, so Sophie turned to walk towards the area where she had seen Rufus and Lucy talking to the visitor. However, he was no longer there and Rufus and Lucy were walking towards the back room in search of cups of tea. Sophie joined them.

'Morning,' she said. 'I saw you talking to a visitor, but I didn't manage to speak to him myself.'

'Oh, yes,' said Rufus. 'David — he works for me. To be honest, I was a bit surprised to see him here this morning. I've never thought of him as the churchgoing type.'

'What brought him to All Saints?' asked Sophie.

'He said he works with Paul and he'd met Hayley before,' said Lucy. 'A while ago, Christmas, I think. He said that Hayley had spoken highly of All Saints.'

'She did,' said Rufus. 'It was Hayley who first mentioned All Saints to me at the Christmas party. Today is the first time I've seen her here in all the time I've been coming, though.'

Good work, Hayley, thought Sophie. Two plugs for church in one party and two results! 'Did he say anything? He was holding some sort of box.'

'Not really,' said Rufus. 'I've seen that box on his desk at work, now you mention it. I don't know what it is. We asked him if he wanted a cup of tea, but he seemed to want to leave quite quickly.'

It wasn't until they were sitting down to lunch that Dominic remembered that Melissa and Daniel hadn't turned up with baby Jessica.

'Oh, that's a shame,' said Sophie. 'I suppose they only said they would try to come, but even so…'

'Never mind,' said Dominic. 'I'll be seeing them on Wednesday evening anyway.'

'I've made a decision,' said Sophie, remembering her conversation with Hayley before church and changing the subject. 'I'm going to come to the healing service after Easter.'

'Good,' smiled Dominic. 'I hoped you'd say that. We just need to find a babysitter for Henry.'

The following Wednesday evening Sophie glanced out of the window as Dominic was returning from his meeting with Melissa and Daniel. She thought he had a bit more of a spring in his step than she had noticed of late.

'How did it go?' she asked as he came through the door.

'Fine. I explained that when a baby is baptised the parents and godparents are promising to bring the child up in the life and faith of the church. They seemed happy about that and we made another date so I can go through the basics of the Christian faith with them. Then we provisionally booked a date for the baptism to take place during one of the Sunday morning services after Easter. They're aiming to come to church this Sunday.'

'I'll look out for them,' said Sophie.

However, the following Sunday Melissa and Daniel were not at church and neither, to Sophie's surprise, was Hayley. However, David turned up, once again carrying the carved wooden box. At the end of the service, Sophie could see that he was making for the door, so she walked across to where Dominic was stationed, determined to speak to him before he left.

'Hello,' said Dominic. 'Good to have you with us this morning. My name's Dominic and this is my wife, Sophie.'

'Nice to meet you both. Actually, I wanted to talk to you. It's about my mother's ashes.' David glanced at the box in his hands and Sophie realised what it was that he was carrying. 'I wanted to find a nice place to lay Mum to rest and I wondered about burying her in your churchyard. I had intended to ask you last week, but then I changed my mind. I'm not sure that I'm quite in that place yet, but when I am…'

'Ah,' said Dominic, sympathetically. 'I'm sorry to hear that, but there's no rush. Just let me know when you feel the time's right for you and I'm sure we can arrange something. In the meantime, it would be great to get to know you. Do you have time to stay for a cup of tea? It's good to have friendly people around when you're going through a difficult time.'

'Thanks,' said David. 'I'll keep that in mind, but I probably ought to get going.'

'It would be nice to get to know him, but he always seems to be in a bit of a hurry,' observed Dominic as David hurried away.

'To put it mildly,' said Sophie. 'Do people normally bring the ashes with them when they come to talk about burying them?'

'No,' said Dominic, thoughtfully. 'That is quite unusual. Perhaps he thought I'd be able to bury them today.'

'Maybe, but he also said he wasn't sure if he was ready yet.'

'Yes, he did say that, poor man. I suppose we all deal with grief differently. By the way, have you seen Hayley this morning? I was hoping to speak to her. I wondered if she might feel able to help Mike with a little background music at the Open Day.'

'I don't know why she isn't here. Perhaps I should give her a call, but I don't want to sound as if I'm nagging.'

'Why don't I call in at school this week?' suggested Dominic. 'I can ask her to put some invitations for the Open Day in the children's book bags, and ask about the music at the same time.'

However, when he returned from school later that week, Dominic looked disheartened. 'Hayley was happy to give the invitations to the children,' he explained, 'but she doesn't want to be involved in the Open Day. In fact, she said her morning sickness had returned and she wouldn't be able to help out with the music at church on Sundays after all.'

'How disappointing!' said Sophie. 'I didn't know morning sickness could come back again once it had passed. Poor Hayley.'

Hayley, however, didn't have morning sickness at all. There had been other reasons for her wanting to get home quickly the previous Sunday morning. Instead of going to see Mike about helping out with the music again, she had left the church building as soon as the last hymn had ended and gone straight home to find Paul sitting on the balcony with a cup of coffee.

'You're back early,' said Paul.

'I missed you, so I didn't stay for coffee after the service,' lied Hayley.

Paul looked pleased. 'That's sweet. Sit down and I'll make you a cup of coffee.'

Hayley sat down on one of the wooden chairs and looked out across Oxley. It was a beautiful morning. Paul soon returned with a cup of coffee for Hayley and sat down next to her. 'Since you're back early, how about a trip out to Stafford Castle, just the two of us?' he said. 'We should make the most of our time together, before the little one comes along and disturbs the peace!'

'Or, why don't we make a start on the spare room? There's a lot to do before we can turn it into a nursery. We need to clear some things away into the loft and then we'll need to decorate. I've picked out some wallpaper and we'll need new curtains. Then we'll need to buy a cot and a changing table, and I want one of those little baby wardrobes to match. I've been looking in some magazines and I've found some lovely nursery furniture. It's a bit expensive, but look, let me show you.' She got up and went inside, returning moments later with a pile of catalogues.

Paul looked at Hayley and reached for her hand. 'I love you,' he said. 'I'm so excited about the baby and I'm grateful to God that you're pregnant, if indeed God exists, but why don't we just take a bit of time to be together today?'

'We will be together. We'll be together while we're working on the nursery. Paul, I really want to get going on the nursery.'

'OK,' Paul sighed, as she sat down and opened the first catalogue.

Eleven

The plans for the Easter Saturday Church Open Day were going well. John and Belinda were very organised. Geoffrey was studiously ignoring their plans, but Audrey had sprung into action, both to organise the café and to have the church decorated by the flower ladies. Normally this would happen on Easter Saturday morning, after the more solemn services on Maundy Thursday and Good Friday, but before the Easter Sunday celebration. Because of the Open Day, the flower ladies had been asked to prepare arrangements at home to bring into the church early that morning.

Glenda and Patrick were due to arrive on the Wednesday evening before Easter and had agreed to mind Henry on the Saturday, enabling Sophie to sit at a table of Easter children's crafts. This was something she found easy to prepare for, as she often had time alone when Henry had been put to bed and Dominic had evening meetings.

There was to be an Easter egg hunt in the churchyard and Rufus and Lucy, together with some others, had been organised into running some games. Sophie was happy to observe that Rufus and Lucy still seemed to be enjoying spending a lot of time together. Rufus had been invited for Sunday lunch with Shirley and Clive, Lucy's parents, and had got on very well with them. Lucy had shared her hopes with Sophie that a similar invitation might be extended for her to be introduced to Rufus's parents, but so far none had come.

'Mum and Dad really want to get to know Rufus. I can't understand why Rufus's parents don't want to even meet me,' Lucy confided. 'Perhaps they don't approve of me.'

'Why wouldn't they approve of you?' Sophie replied. 'There's nothing not to approve of.'

'But they're very posh and I'm not. I come from a very ordinary family; I'm an ordinary person. I might not be good enough for them.'

'Don't be silly. Is Rufus really that posh? Anyway, it's what he thinks that counts, not what his parents think.'

'He said he loves me,' said Lucy, unable to contain a smile, despite her obvious anxiety. 'And I love him.'

'There you are, then,' said Sophie. 'If he loves you, it won't matter what his parents think. And when they do meet you, they'll love you. Most parents just want their children to be happy. If Rufus loves you, they will be happy for him.'

'Sophie… I think I've found the one I've been waiting for.'

'Oh, Lucy, that's so exciting. I can't tell you how happy I am for you!'

As Easter drew nearer, the vicarage was once again prepared for guests. Glenda and Patrick arrived late Wednesday evening. They were pleased to babysit on Thursday evening, to allow Sophie to go to church with Dominic.

'We brought a recording of *Countdown* that we missed when we were at Bridge Club,' said Patrick. 'We'll catch up while you're out.'

On Friday morning they took Henry to the play park in the pushchair. Sophie was very grateful as she was able to concentrate on the events of Good Friday without any distractions.

'That was helpful,' said Sophie to Dominic, as they walked back to the vicarage after the service.

The Open Day on the Saturday turned out to be a great success, largely thanks to John and Belinda's hard work and preparation.

Sophie realised that, although every child in school had gone home with an invitation, thanks to Hayley, it was largely the families Belinda had invited personally who had come. Among them were church irregulars, the Browns and the Starkies, with their children. Melissa and Daniel came with baby Jessica and Sophie was able to meet them, at last. She had a little chat with Melissa during a quiet moment and found her very easy to talk to. 'We've enjoyed our meetings with Dominic,' said Melissa. 'We'll be at church in the morning.' This pleased Sophie, although she couldn't help thinking that Hayley's Paul often said that he would come to church and then didn't turn up. There seemed to be something rather difficult about walking into a church service for people who weren't used to it, but Sophie wasn't sure what the answer to that was. Maybe, she mused, it was more a question of getting to know people first and then walking into church with them.

There was a very happy atmosphere in the church. People were heard to remark that it was a lovely day and seemed to be genuinely touched that everything had been put on for free, not least the drinks and wonderful cakes.

Sophie watched her parents walking around with Henry. Henry seemed to be behaving rather well. Sophie acknowledged to herself that she had mixed feelings about this. On the one hand, she was delighted that Henry was capable of behaving. On the other hand, why wouldn't he do it for her? She recognised that it made her feel quite jealous and also rather inadequate. Did Henry really dislike Sophie so much that he felt he had to punish her? It was an uncomfortable thought, so she turned her attention back to what she was doing.

Towards the end of the afternoon things quietened down considerably. Belinda approached Sophie at her table. 'Hi, Sophie, how's it been going?'

'Great. All your boys have come and made something this afternoon. I've had a fairly steady stream, but it's quieter now.'

'Why don't you take a break and I'll look after your table for half an hour? Tea's still flowing in the back room and I think Audrey's got quite a lot of cake left.'

'Thanks, that would be lovely.'

Moments later, Sophie was looking for somewhere to sit, with a strong cup of tea and a slice of her own chocolate cake. Lucy and Rufus looked as if they were taking a break too. Lucy waved her over, so she went to join them at their table.

'Everything OK?' Sophie asked as she sat down.

'Great,' said Rufus, enthusiastically. 'It's just gone a bit quiet this last half hour.'

'Good, that's what I thought,' said Sophie. 'I know what I was going to ask you, Rufus,' she went on. 'That man you work with, the one who came to church a couple of times…'

'Oh, yes, David Stubbs, he works for me.'

'Yes, him. He hasn't been back since. I was just wondering, is he OK? I found out what was in that box he was carrying.'

'He seems well – a bit irritable, perhaps, but fine apart from that. He's got a temper; he had a bit of an outburst at work last week. What's in the box? He still puts it on his desk every morning.'

'It's his mother's ashes. It's just that he mentioned burying them in the churchyard…'

'If it's his mother's ashes in the box, perhaps that explains why he got so angry at work,' said Rufus. 'A woman from marketing came in carrying a pile of box files for him and put them on his desk. The top one fell off and landed on his wooden box and he lost it completely, started shouting and screaming at her for not being more careful and not respecting other people's property. The woman ran off in tears and I got a complaint from the marketing manager.'

'Oh dear,' said Sophie. 'It sounds as if he's not coping.'

'Well, maybe not,' said Rufus, 'but I can't have my staff behaving like that. It didn't reflect too well on me when the marketing manager came to see me.'

'Perhaps he needs help,' said Lucy, sadly. 'Could you talk to him, Rufus?'

'Quite right, I will. I can't have that sort of behaviour in the workplace.'

'No, I mean talk to him about how he's feeling.'

'Oh, yes, of course. He really needs to sort himself out.'

Sophie wasn't 100 per cent sure that Rufus really understood what Lucy meant, but at least, she thought, Rufus was planning to talk to the poor man about his difficulties.

Later that evening, when they were having dinner back at the vicarage, Sophie asked Dominic if he had had many people visit him in the prayer corner. 'Not for prayer, no,' said Dominic, 'though several people came over to chat. Mainly church regulars, no visitors.'

'We thought it was a lovely day,' said Glenda. 'And Henry was such a good boy, weren't you, Henry?'

'Yes,' said Sophie. 'I noticed.'

'I don't know why you think he's so difficult,' added Glenda. 'He's just a normal little boy, with...'

'I know,' cut in Sophie, 'lots of energy.'

'Sophie,' said Patrick, 'do you think...' He appeared to be considering his words carefully, '... maybe you overdiscipline him?'

'Unbelievable,' thought Sophie. Her father had done a complete U-turn! But she kept her mouth firmly shut.

The following morning Sophie let Henry walk into church with his grandparents holding his hands, one on each side. Let's see whether you can keep him quiet through a whole church service, she thought to herself. They arrived early to find Dominic hiding six large plastic eggs of different colours around the church.

As everyone who had visited church the day before had been given an invitation for Sunday morning, Dominic had put a lot of thought and preparation into making the service accessible to children and a great celebration. Sophie watched nervously to see whether any newcomers were coming through the door. Melissa and Daniel arrived with Jessica, looking slightly anxious, and Sophie went to welcome them. A lot of church occasional attenders also arrived. Sophie noted the Browns and Starkies among them, so Dominic would definitely have children to help him with his talk. The church felt comfortably full, but by the time the service started she hadn't noticed any other newcomers arrive. After all the effort of the day before, this was very disappointing. Sophie hoped that Belinda and John hadn't noticed, but knew this was unlikely.

Dominic began by thanking everyone who had been involved with the Open Day and saying how lovely the church looked for Easter weekend. When the time came for him to give his talk, he addressed the children and told them that six plastic Easter eggs had been hidden around the church and that they were to find the eggs, but not open them. The children scampered off, although Henry stayed securely on Glenda's lap. Soon they came back holding five of the plastic eggs between them. Dominic asked them to sit down at the front.

'Who has found the brown-coloured egg?' asked Dominic. Noah Henderson brought the brown egg forward. 'Can you open it?' asked Dominic. Noah did so, revealing a small wooden cross hidden inside. 'Who can tell me why I have a cross in this egg? I'll give you a clue – what special thing did we remember two days ago?'

'Jesus died on the cross,' said Noah, immediately.

'That's right. On Good Friday we remember how Jesus died on a cross and, although it was horrible for Jesus, we call the day Good Friday because it was good for us. It's good for us, because if we trust in Jesus, He pays for every bad thing we have ever done, by taking the punishment we deserve in our place. But how do we know Jesus really did die? Who has the white egg?'

Emma Brown came forward with the white egg and duly opened it. Inside was a folded piece of white cloth. 'What do you think this is?' asked Dominic. This time there was a silence. 'After Jesus died, a man called Joseph and his friend Nicodemus took Jesus's dead body and prepared it to be buried. As they could see that He really was dead, they wrapped up His body in linen cloth, a bit like an Egyptian mummy. Who can tell me where they took it?' All the children put their hands up. This time Dominic chose Emma Brown.

'To the tomb,' she said.

'That's quite right, to Joseph's tomb,' said Dominic. 'And can you remember who else was there, watching all this take place?' After a short period of silence, he said, 'Some women who were followers of Jesus were watching and they followed and saw where the body of Jesus was laid. Now, who has the pink egg?'

Jonah had the pink egg. 'I know, I know, I know,' said Jonah, opening it before he had quite been asked. 'It's the stone.' He held a large round pebble up.

'Well done, Jonah,' said Dominic. 'That's exactly what it is. Jesus's body was put in the tomb, and where did the stone go?'

'In the doorway!' shouted Jonah.

'Yes,' said Dominic, 'and then it was sealed and guarded by soldiers and nothing happened at all during the next day, Saturday, because that's the day when the Jewish people rest.'

'I know, that's called the Sabbath,' put in Noah, apparently not wishing to be outsmarted by his younger brother.

'The next egg is the yellow egg,' said Dominic. 'Euan, I can see you have that one. Can you open it?'

Euan Brown opened the egg to find a bright yellow marble. 'A marble? Why have I got a marble?'

'This represents something big, round and yellow up in the sky. It's the…?'

'Sun!' shouted out Henry, to everyone's surprise.

'Excellent, Henry,' said Dominic, looking proud. 'The sun was just rising on Sunday morning, and do you remember the women who saw where Jesus was buried? They set out on their way to the tomb, but why were they going back there? This brings us to our next egg. Let's find out what the women took with them. Who has the orange egg?'

'Me!' shouted Eleanor Starkie. 'I've got it.' She opened the orange egg. 'Ooh, it's a little packet of powder.'

'That sounds dodgy,' called out Rufus from the congregation. Audrey looked scandalised, but there were a number of chuckles from some of the other adults.

'It's a packet of spices,' said Dominic, 'because the women wanted to go and anoint Jesus's body with spices. You see, although Jesus had told people that He was going to rise from the dead on the third day, people didn't seem to understand Him when he said that. Now, who has the final egg? It should be green.'

The children all looked at each other. The final egg was missing. 'Ahh,' said Dominic. 'Can everybody please have a look under the pews, by their feet or next to them on the pews? It should be around somewhere.' After a moment or two of shuffling, the egg had not appeared. Dominic decided not to lose the momentum. 'Never mind,' he said. 'It doesn't really matter, because do you know what? There was nothing in the last egg. In fact, the last egg was completely empty, to remind us that the tomb was empty! Jesus was no longer there! Well, actually, the tomb was not completely empty. The linen cloths were still there, but the body had gone!'

'And the angel!' shouted Noah, clearly wanting to show how clever he was.

'Yes,' said Dominic. 'Our Bible reading tells us that there was a young man there and he explained what had happened. Can you remember the Bible reading? This young man said they wouldn't find Jesus there, because He had been raised from the dead, and that they'd soon see Him. And do you know what? Later that day, they did. And this is why we celebrate Easter. Easter tells us three things: Jesus did die for the sins of the world, Jesus really did rise again, and anyone who puts their trust in Him will be forgiven and live forever.'

The service closed with a traditional Easter hymn. Dominic whispered thanks to the children for their help and told them that they could go and sit with their parents. However, Boaz Henderson seemed to have spotted something. He started running towards the choir stalls. He reached his hand behind Doris, who had risen to her feet, and withdrew it triumphantly. 'I've got the green egg!' he shouted, as he ran back to Dominic. The green egg had indeed been under Doris's bottom all the time.

At the end of the service Sophie took Henry to meet Melissa and Daniel, who were looking much more relaxed than they had at the beginning.

'Church wasn't a bit like I thought,' said Melissa. 'It was interesting. It really helped me understand about Jesus.' Sophie managed to introduce them to Belinda and John and wished she could have introduced them to Hayley too, but Hayley, once again, was missing.

Hayley and Paul were busy decorating the nursery. The second bedroom had now been cleared and the ceiling and woodwork painted. Paul got up on Easter Sunday morning to begin hanging wallpaper. Hayley walked into the room, still in her dressing gown. Paul looked at his watch. 'Aren't you going to church? You're cutting it fine!'

'No, I don't want to leave all the work to you!'

'I don't mind. I know church is important to you, especially at Easter. This time last year you went about three times! Not that I'm complaining about having your help, of course.'

'No, we really need to get the nursery finished and the long weekend is the best time to do it. Besides, I've ordered the nursery furniture to be delivered next week, while school is still closed for the holidays, and I really want the decorating to be finished before it arrives.'

Hayley pushed away any feelings of guilt about missing church. After all, she told herself, she didn't have to go to church to be a Christian. Her faith was between her and God and she could be a Christian at home. She was sure God would understand how important the decorating was.

Glenda and Patrick were not due to return to Eastbourne until Tuesday morning. The weather was nice on Easter Monday, so they all went for a walk around the village in the morning and then sat in the garden in the afternoon. Henry was happy playing with his ride-on cars. Dominic got some garden chairs out of the shed and the adults chatted over a cup of tea and some leftover cake from Saturday that had been given to Glenda by Audrey.

'It was nice to see the Browns and the Starkies in church for Easter,' said Sophie. 'It makes such a difference to have families in the service.'

'It was nice,' Dominic agreed, 'although, unfortunately, both Mary Brown and Gerald Starkie gave me a list of reasons why they can't come for the next few weeks.'

'Such as?'

'Football, swimming, parties, you name it.' Dominic suddenly looked downcast.

'Interesting use of the word "can't",' murmured Sophie. She tried to think of a way to raise Dominic's spirits. 'I spoke to Melissa and Daniel and they seemed to have enjoyed church.'

A bit later, when Dominic had gone inside, Sophie turned to her mother. 'How did you find the talk yesterday, Mum?'

'Oh, yes, very good,' replied Glenda. 'I think what Dominic was trying to say was that we must all be nice to each other.'

Sophie was momentarily stunned into silence. It wasn't that people shouldn't be nice to each other. Of course they should. But how on earth did Glenda get that message from Sunday? 'Yes, but it was also about how Jesus died for us on the cross.'

'Yes, well, if that's what you think is true. That's fine, if that's what makes you happy. People can choose to believe whatever they want to believe, and if that's what you want to believe, then it's true for you.'

Sophie wasn't sure how to answer that, so she didn't, but she mentioned it to Lucy when she came to the vicarage for study group with Rufus on Tuesday evening. The house phone had rung just as people were arriving and Dominic had gone into the study to answer it, so Lucy was helping Sophie with the cups of tea.

'Did your parents enjoy Easter weekend?' asked Lucy.

'Yes, thanks. But Mum said something funny when I asked her what she thought of the talk. She said something like, "If that's what you think is true," and "People can choose what they want to believe and that makes it true for them." I mean, if you look at it like that, I could choose to believe in the fairies at the bottom of the garden and that would make it true. I didn't know what to say.'

'Oh. Well, I suppose that it *is* kind of true. If you want to believe in God and Jesus and the Bible, you'll find out about it and then you'll find enough evidence to realise it's true. If you don't want to believe, you won't find out and that will leave you with enough questions to hide behind. So, in a way, it *is* about what you choose to believe.'

'Hmm,' pondered Sophie. 'I think I can see where you're coming from. Anyway, did you have a nice Easter?'

'Yes, great,' answered Lucy, stopping and lowering her voice before going into the living room. 'Just one snag – somehow in all the conversations on Saturday, it came out that Rufus and Geoffrey went to the same school, and now Geoffrey is all over Rufus and we've been invited for dinner.'

Later that night, when people had gone home, Sophie told Dominic about Lucy and Rufus being invited to Audrey and Geoffrey's.

'We've never been invited to Audrey and Geoffrey's for dinner,' she pointed out.

'Well, keep quiet about it and hopefully we never will be,' laughed Dominic. Then, looking more serious, he added, 'Anyway, that reminds me, it was Audrey on the phone just as people were arriving. Apparently, I didn't thank the flower ladies for the Easter decorations.'

'I'm sure you did.'

'No, Audrey said I thanked everyone who took part on Saturday and I said that the church looked lovely, but I didn't actually thank the flower ladies specifically and now they are all put out and feel as if I'm not grateful for all they do for me.'

'But,' said Sophie, 'they aren't doing it to be thanked by you, are they? Surely, they're doing it to honour God.'

'I'm not sure that's entirely true,' said Dominic, and they went upstairs to bed.

Twelve

Several things happened in the weeks after Easter. The first was the long-planned-for healing service. This was something that All Saints held every so often and it took place on the Sunday evening following Easter. Sophie was still having mixed feelings about attending. Partly she still struggled with the idea of asking God to help her with her sadness. It still seemed wrong to ask God to take away those feelings which were, after all, very natural. She also didn't want anyone to think that she wasn't content with being Henry's mum or that she didn't love him. She was, of course, struggling with her feelings towards Henry too, but she didn't want other people to know this. There was always the fear that other people were thinking she wasn't meant to be a mum and that was why God hadn't allowed her to have a baby. And there was always the fear that she might end up convinced of that herself.

However, one thing she did know: she couldn't carry on the way she was. She was continuing to have to deal with the disappointment of waking from those dreams where she was pregnant. Recently the dreams had gone one step further. Now she was aware that she could be dreaming, but she had somehow managed to prove to herself that, this time, it was real. Of course, every time she woke up again to disappointment. She carried her sadness with her always and there were days when it so overwhelmed her that she had difficulty functioning normally. Everyday tasks, looking after Henry and managing the vicarage, became mechanical. On some days she felt she was speaking to people from behind a mask.

It was time to tackle the problem.

Lucy had agreed to come and babysit for Henry. Sophie looked out of the window when she came downstairs, having settled him to sleep, to see Lucy walking up the drive. As she looked, Rufus bounced up behind her and took her hand. It pleased Sophie to see the smile on Lucy's face as she turned to look at him. They continued up the drive and Sophie opened the door before they got there, to ensure that the doorbell didn't wake Henry.

'Thanks for doing this,' said Sophie, as they settled themselves on the sofa together, with a cup of tea. 'I really appreciate it.'

'No problem,' said Lucy. 'Hope it goes well.'

The service itself was very calming. At the end there was an opportunity to go forward to be prayed for privately, either with Dominic and Sarah in one corner or with Robert and Catherine in another. When Sophie looked back, she could remember a very relaxed atmosphere, but she couldn't recall exactly what it was that made her stand up and walk to the corner of the church where Catherine and Robert were sitting, waiting to pray with anyone who came to them. Somehow she just became aware that she was walking in that direction. She sat down with her back to the rest of the congregation, well out of earshot.

'Sophie,' said Catherine kindly, 'what can we pray for you?'

Sophie hesitated for a moment. 'I just wish I could come to terms with not being able to have a baby. It's on my mind all the time. Sometimes the sadness takes over in my head and makes me feel as if I can't think about anything else rationally but, at the same time, I don't think it would be normal not to feel sad. I don't really know what to ask for.'

'Sophie,' said Catherine, 'I'm sure God doesn't want you to feel like this.' Robert nodded in agreement. They prayed. Sophie listened.

'Amen,' said Sophie at the end. Amen – please God, let it be so.

From the moment Sophie opened her eyes she knew that she felt different. She wasn't exactly sure how, at first, but she knew something had changed. 'Thank you,' she said, and she got up and walked back to her seat. Something had happened to her at that moment, sitting in the corner of the church with Robert and Catherine praying for her. When she walked back to the vicarage with Dominic later that evening, she felt definitely different.

Over the next few days Sophie tried to analyse how she felt. 'The sadness hasn't gone,' she explained to Dominic, 'but it's changed. It's as if there is a box in my head and all the sad feelings have gone into the box. If I choose to open the box, the sad feelings are there, very much as they always were, which is right and natural. The difference is that I'm in control of the box – it no longer controls me. I don't have to open the box. I no longer have to wake up in the morning to feel that immense wave of sadness, the knowledge that I will never have a baby, wash over me. I only have to think about those feelings if I choose to. I'm functional again.'

Sophie felt sure that a small miracle had happened that day.

A week later, baby Jessica was baptised during the morning service. Melissa and Daniel had continued to attend church and had started to get to know members of the congregation. Sophie and Dominic were well aware that couples often attended church leading up to the baptism of a baby, but then stopped. However, they were cautiously optimistic that Melissa and Daniel were going to be different. The church was filled with their family and friends and they both looked very proud of their baby daughter as they made their promises to bring her up in the Christian faith.

The thing that happened the following weekend was less agreeable, at least from Lucy's point of view. The time came for

Lucy and Rufus to dine with Audrey and Geoffrey Bickerstaff. Lucy wasn't exactly sure why this had become such a big issue for her. Maybe it was the fact that Audrey and Geoffrey lived in a very big house or perhaps that Audrey had always seemed a little patronising in the way she talked to Lucy when they were on the church coffee rota together. Perhaps it was because Geoffrey spoke to Rufus as if Lucy was somehow in the background, although he had known Lucy since she was a child.

Possibly it was even that Rufus had started telling Lucy how to behave.

No, she thought, not exactly telling her how to behave, Rufus wouldn't go that far. It was more that he was telling her how he knew she would behave in certain situations, in a way that made her feel he was stating his expectations. 'Lucy, I'm sure you are always polite in company,' or, 'Lucy, I know you wouldn't ask personal questions,' or even, 'Lucy, I'm sure you're good at keeping your opinions to yourself.' That was what was happening and it made Lucy feel uncomfortable.

Whatever the cause, she had become nervous about the occasion. She woke up very early on the Saturday morning and couldn't get back to sleep. Eventually she gave up trying, made herself a cup of tea and took it back to bed. What, she wondered, could she do to boost her confidence? She checked her bank balance and made a few calculations in her head. Then she reached for the phone and made an appointment at the hairdressers. When she got up, she had a plan formed in her head. She would catch the early bus into town and shop for a new dress, then go to the hairdressers on her way back.

On the evening of the dinner, Lucy and Rufus had arranged to walk over to Audrey and Geoffrey's, so that Rufus didn't need to worry about driving. As Lucy would pass close to Rufus's house on her way to the Bickerstaffs', she arranged to call there first so they could walk together. She checked herself for the umpteenth time in her bedroom mirror before she left – her hair, expertly blow-dried into its dark, shiny bob, felt nice; her dress looked lovely (it should do, it cost enough), and shoes and jewellery set it off nicely; her make-up had been done carefully – and now she was a little tight for time. However, she needed to make a good impression, especially on Rufus. She very much hoped that he, at least, would say something nice to give her confidence a boost.

She left the house, walking briskly. It was a little breezy and she hoped the wind wouldn't ruin her hair. She knocked at Rufus's door and he opened it, holding a bottle of wine, ready to step outside.

'Can I just visit your bathroom?' she asked, meaning to check her hair in the bathroom mirror.

'Oh… really? OK, then, but you had better hurry up. We don't want to be late,' he said, stepping back into the house.

Lucy ran up the stairs, taking her hairbrush out of her handbag as she went. She noticed again the small door halfway up the staircase which appeared to go nowhere. It made her curious and she thought she would ask Rufus about it when she came down. She checked herself in the mirror over the washbasin. Everything, including her hair, was still in place. As she put her hairbrush away she noticed a bottle of aftershave on the shelf under the mirror. It was almost empty. She looked at the name on the bottle and made a mental note. It was Rufus's thirtieth birthday the following week, just a couple of weeks before her own twenty-ninth birthday. A new bottle of his favourite aftershave would make a nice present. Rufus's birthday fell on a Saturday and she was planning to take him out to dinner as a surprise. She could give him the present at the table, she thought.

'Are you coming?' called Rufus. She could almost hear him looking at his watch.

'I am,' she called back, as she ran down the stairs. She still felt anxious and she hoped Rufus might pay her a compliment to make her feel better, but as she approached the front door, he was stepping out of it and putting his key into the lock, ready to leave. 'Let's not be late,' he said, and he set off down the drive, Lucy following at a bit of a jog, trying to keep up with his long strides. She really wished Rufus didn't have to be quite so punctual.

They walked up the gravel drive to Audrey and Geoffrey's house bang on time, Lucy a little breathless. Really, thought Lucy, this house was rather grand. It was on the older side of the village, closer to the church. A large, red-brick building, it was obviously quite old, but had been very well maintained. There were garages to one side and, through the space between the garages and the house, Lucy could see a spacious garden with well-kept lawns and flowerbeds and some quite large trees. At the end there appeared to be a tennis court. She couldn't help thinking that Audrey and Geoffrey must be very well off.

Rufus knocked on the door. Lucy noticed that the large, brass door knocker was in the shape of a bull with enormous horns and a ring through its nose. It didn't feel very welcoming.

Audrey opened the door and ushered them inside. Lucy stepped into the large, oak-panelled entrance hall, feeling slightly intimidated. 'Come into the drawing room. Geoffrey will get you some drinks. That's a pretty dress, Lucy.' Lucy felt a little better – Audrey liked her dress!

'Ah, Rufus,' said Geoffrey, as they walked into a large room to the left of the hallway. He shook Rufus by the hand and gave him one of his rare smiles. 'And Lucy, welcome. A glass of wine?'

'Thank you, that would be lovely,' said Rufus, beaming in his usual way.

'Thank you, yes, please,' said Lucy, finding her voice. 'What a lovely home you have.'

It was, indeed, a beautiful room they were standing in. It had a high, ornate ceiling and ran the width of the house, with a large bay window to the front and glass doors overlooking the garden at the back. Lucy couldn't help wondering how much it must cost to heat. Most of the furniture looked antique and there were paintings on the walls that appeared to be originals. Everything looked very polished.

'Shall I show you around?' said Geoffrey and, without waiting for a reply, he began what felt to Lucy like their own personal tour of a small stately home.

The house was built over three floors with attic rooms, in addition to a basement with a wine cellar and a safe. Lucy could only guess what might be in there. She was very impressed, but felt as if she had walked into somewhere she didn't quite belong. Rufus, on the other hand, seemed very at home and bounced along in his usual happy way, chatting knowledgeably about the antiques and paintings. Lucy knew very little about such things. The little boost she had felt after Audrey's compliment about her dress was diminishing rapidly.

Lucy felt relieved when Audrey called them to the table, but the relief was short-lived. As they sat down at the long dining table, Lucy noticed the many sets of cutlery and different plates and glasses. How was she to know which ones to use when? She decided just to watch what everyone else did and do likewise.

At dinner, which was four courses and, Lucy had to admit, very good, the conversation turned to school. Geoffrey began to talk at length about people he had been to school with and their various achievements.

'Humphrey Brassington was headmaster in my Montgomery days, wife was a minor royal, three boys of his own at school. Brassington Major was two years above me, head boy, went to Cambridge, ended up as chairman of McArthur Bank – branches all over the world, you know. Brassington Minor was in my year, rugger captain, went on to play for England in his time. Brassington Minimus was three years younger. He was the arty one. The painting in the hallway where you came in is one of his.'

'He married a friend of my cousin,' Audrey added. 'That family are very big in antiques, you know. They have shops in five counties now. They send us a Christmas card every year.'

'Sir Hugo Jankells was the head in my day,' said Rufus. 'The masters called him "Sir Hugh" and the boys found it rather comical because that made him Hugh Jankells.' Audrey tittered.

'I went to school with a boy called Sean Head,' said Lucy. 'Everyone thought it sounded like a very short haircut.' There was a pause where everyone should have laughed, but no one did. Lucy felt crushed.

Rufus appeared to be thinking. He obviously didn't want to be outsmarted by the Bickerstaffs.

'I went to school with Damian Brownley-Stevenson,' he went on, 'the one who does those home improvement programmes for the BBC. Damian always took a lead role in the school plays. His father was a TV producer and he knew a lot of people at the BBC. I think Damian was destined to be famous, but he wanted to be in front of the cameras, unlike his father.'

Lucy found it hard to think of very much to say. Her school friends weren't in the same league as Audrey's, Geoffrey's or Rufus's. She felt quite out of her depth. The best thing she could do, she thought, was to show that she was listening and look interested. So she smiled and nodded a lot, but inside she felt as if she was shrivelling up.

At the end of the evening Rufus held Lucy's hand. 'I'll walk you home,' he said.

'Thanks,' said Lucy.

'You were very quiet this evening.' Was it a criticism? Perhaps she hadn't fulfilled Rufus's expectations. She didn't want him to be disappointed with her.

'I just don't know a lot about art and antiques or all those people you seem to know.'

'No... no, perhaps not.'

Lucy decided she needed to make amends. 'I was just thinking about your birthday,' she said, trying to sound cheerful. 'How about I take you out to dinner on Saturday?' Rufus was quiet. 'Unless there is something else you would like to do?'

'That's very sweet of you, but the thing is,' said Rufus, sounding awkward, 'Mother and Father are organising a bit of a family celebration at their home. I'm going down to Surrey for the weekend.' Lucy waited for an invitation to go with him, but none came. 'Father has invited some of his business associates. There will be a number of fairly influential people there and it will be good for me to get to know them.'

'Oh,' said Lucy. For some reason she couldn't quite fathom, she didn't want to admit to Rufus how disappointed she felt. 'Well, perhaps I could take you out on the Friday evening instead, or cook for you at home if you prefer?'

'You're very kind, but I need to leave straight from work on Friday night to pick Monty up.'

Lucy decided to throw caution to the wind. 'I just thought you might have wanted to celebrate your birthday with me.'

'It's not that I don't want to be with you, it's just that... well, it could be important for my career, and my parents have gone to a lot of trouble, so I don't want to upset them. You want me to do well, don't you? You understand?'

'Yes, of course I understand. What if...' She didn't have the nerve to actually invite herself for the weekend. 'What about if I came down by train, for the day, just so I can give you your birthday present on your birthday?'

'Leave it with me,' said Rufus. 'I'll speak to Mother and see what she says.'

Lucy felt very downcast. As they approached Rufus's house, she said, 'Don't worry about walking me home. I'll be fine. I'll see you at church in the morning.'

'If you're sure,' he replied. 'See you in the morning.'

He kissed her goodnight and she walked on. Lucy felt very sad. The combination of not being included in Rufus's birthday plans and the evening at the Bickerstaffs' had made her feel very small and insignificant. Really, she thought, she hadn't done very well, but it would have been so nice if Rufus could have just noticed her new dress or said she looked nice. But Rufus didn't really do that sort of thing.

Sleep didn't come easily to Lucy that night. The evening had left her feeling inadequate and stupid. Audrey and Geoffrey obviously thought very highly of themselves, but the more she thought about it, she realised that she didn't really care too much about what they thought of her. The thing that bothered her was that she knew she had let Rufus down. She hadn't been the type of girlfriend that Rufus would have wanted to take to that type of social occasion. She felt as if she had had an interview for a job and left knowing she was going to be turned down. She had failed.

Something else was niggling at her. She hadn't wanted to acknowledge it to herself up until this point, but it bothered her that Rufus never seemed to pay her any compliments. She knew she ought not to be looking for such things, but it was just that she had always imagined that, if she had a boyfriend, she would have someone to say nice things to her, to make her feel special, attractive and wanted. But one thing she did know about Rufus, he was nothing if not honest. If Rufus didn't pay compliments it would be because she hadn't earned them.

Lucy gave herself a stern talking to. She loved Rufus and she mustn't lose him. She must do better. She needed a plan. She would pay much more attention to her appearance when she was with Rufus. Maybe she would be able to go to Surrey and meet his parents and be sweet and lovely.

The following morning at church Lucy was leading Sunday school, so she arrived early. Rufus arrived just before the start of the service, rushing in just as the first hymn began, so Lucy didn't manage to speak to him until the end. She caught up with him near the doorway, where Geoffrey was chatting animatedly. Really, thought Lucy, hadn't they seen enough of each other the night before?

'Morning,' said Rufus, smiling at Lucy in his usual happy way. 'I was a bit late, so I had to drive to church. I'll drop you home to save you walking.'

They walked down the church drive together. It had been dry for a while now and the potholes were less of a hazard. They slipped into Rufus's sleek, black car and were outside Lucy's flat in minutes. 'Come in for some lunch, if you like,' said Lucy.

'Thanks, but no thanks. I have to catch up with some work. I just needed to tell you, I rang Mother this morning. That was why I ended up late for church, actually. I mentioned you coming down at the weekend.' He looked down then said, in a business-like voice, 'Mother said maybe not this time. She said you could come down some other time.'

'Oh... OK,' said Lucy. She didn't know what else she could say. 'I'll see you on Tuesday, then, for study group. Shall I call round on my way to the vicarage?'

'I might need to come straight from work,' said Rufus. 'I've got a lot on at the moment. I'll see you there and then I'll drive you home afterwards.'

Lucy tried to cheer herself up by reasoning that there was one positive thing. Rufus had asked his mother if she could come to Surrey, so he must have wanted her to come. Also, his mother had said that she could come some other time, so it wasn't all bad.

The following Tuesday she arrived at the vicarage early. She wanted to talk to Sophie.

'How did Saturday evening go?' asked Sophie.

'I was hoping to talk to you about that,' said Lucy. 'They live in an amazing house, don't they? I've walked past it hundreds of times, but that was the first time I've ever been inside.'

'I've only ever been inside once,' said Sophie. 'When we first arrived in Oxley we went around visiting people from church... It is very nice.'

'Yes, well, Geoffrey showed us round and it was very interesting, and Audrey is a really good cook. The meal was lovely and she said she makes all sorts of jams and preserves from fruit she grows in the garden. It was just that I found it really hard to join in with the conversation. They talked about art and antiques and all these people in high places. Rufus is fine with all that, but I don't really know about that sort of thing. I don't know those sorts of people. I think I was too quiet. I felt like I'd let Rufus down.'

'Well, you were a guest in Audrey and Geoffrey's house,' said Sophie. 'Really, they should have made the effort to include you in the conversation. You know, talked to you about things that interest you.'

'I didn't think of it like that. I just don't want Rufus to think I'm...'

The doorbell rang and people began arriving. Sophie went to answer the door. 'Just remember,' she affirmed, 'you are a lovely, kind person, and that's all that matters.'

Lucy appreciated Sophie's words and she felt a little better. Rufus arrived at the last minute, sat down next to Lucy and squeezed her hand affectionately. He just had time to whisper, 'I've got some good news,' as Dominic began the study. Lucy's spirits rose a little more. Maybe Mother had changed her mind and she had been invited to Surrey for Rufus's birthday after all.

At the end of the meeting people said their goodbyes and started to leave. It was drizzling and there was a chill in the air. Lucy was glad of a lift home and she sank back into the comfortable upholstery of Rufus's car gratefully. 'Come in for a moment when you drop me off,' said Lucy.

'OK, just for a few minutes. I've got to be up early for work.'

They went into Lucy's living room and sat down. Lucy had planned to give Rufus his birthday present, but she wouldn't have to if she was going to be with him on his birthday after all.

'What was your good news?'

'I've got a promotion,' he said, happily. Not quite the good news she was hoping for, but Lucy was pleased for him. 'I'm going to be managing marketing as well as IT. It means more responsibility and I'll probably have to work late sometimes, but it's a real step in the right direction career-wise.'

'Well done! You've only been at the company for such a short time, you must be doing well,' said Lucy, brightly.

'Also, Mr and Mrs Wainwright, the boss and his wife, have invited us to have dinner with them Saturday week.'

'Oh.' Another social occasion with people above her station. Just what she needed.

'Is that OK? You're not doing anything, are you?'

'No, no, that will be lovely,' Lucy enthused, overcompensating.

'Great, that's settled. Well, I'd better be off, got to be up early for work.'

'Oh, wait, just a minute. I wanted to give you your birthday present,' said Lucy, picking up a small wrapped box and a card from the table. 'You can open it now, if you like.'

He did. 'Thank you, that's lovely, just the one I like. How very thoughtful of you.'

'Would you mind, I mean, shall I ring you on your birthday? Just to say happy birthday on the day.' Rufus seemed to hesitate. 'Or not?'

'No, yes, do ring,' said Rufus. 'It's just there's very little mobile signal in the area. You'll need to use the landline. Here, I'll write it down for you. And I haven't forgotten that it's your birthday soon too. What would you like to do?'

'Surprise me,' she said. 'But can it be just the two of us?'

'Of course.' Rufus kissed her goodnight and she waved as the black car purred around the corner and out of sight. As long as she played her cards right, all was not lost.

The following Saturday Lucy picked up the phone and dialled the number Rufus had given her. She decided the best time to call would be in the morning, before guests arrived and the celebrations got started.

'Hello.' A woman's voice.

'Hello, is that Mrs Parsons?'

'Speaking.'

'Hello, Mrs Parsons, this is Lucy. I just rang to wish Rufus a happy birthday.'

There was a short silence. 'One moment,' said the voice, coldly.

After a few moments Lucy heard Rufus's voice.

'Hello.'

'Happy birthday, Rufus! How are you?' Lucy kept her tone light. She was determined not to let Rufus know his mother had upset her.

'Very well, thank you. It was nice of you to call.' He didn't sound his normal self. It was as if he was being overheard and was uncomfortable about it.

'What have you been doing?'

'Oh, this and that, helping Mother get things ready for this afternoon. I'll catch up with you soon. Thanks for calling. Goodbye.'

She felt as if someone had punched her in the stomach. For a little while she stared into space. What had happened? Where had her lovely Rufus gone?

Thirteen

The following morning Sophie and Henry met Lucy walking up the drive to church. Sophie thought Lucy looked a little down in the dumps. 'Hi, Lucy, how're you?' she called.

'OK, thanks,' responded Lucy, unconvincingly. 'Rufus went to Surrey to see his parents for his birthday.'

'Oh… OK… didn't he… didn't you…'

Lucy relieved her of her awkwardness. 'I wasn't invited. I rang to wish him a happy birthday yesterday, but his mum was a bit strange on the phone. She obviously didn't want me to intrude.'

'That's not very nice, you're his girlfriend. What did she say?'

'Nothing, really, that was the problem. With very few words she managed to let me know that I shouldn't have rung.'

'How unkind! Well, perhaps you should tell Rufus how she made you feel.'

'Perhaps I should,' said Lucy, doubtfully, as they walked into church.

At the end of the service Sophie had wanted to speak to Lucy again, but she saw Melissa coming towards her and decided she ought to speak to her first.

'Hi, Sophie, I wanted to ask you something. I'm a bit confused,' said Melissa. Daniel came up behind her, with Jessica asleep in the pram.

'Of course,' said Sophie. 'Anything.' She hoped fervently that she would have a suitable answer.

'Well, Dominic has explained about Jesus and I get that bit, how Jesus is the Son of God and how He died to pay for our sins. It's just like a giant – well, cosmic, really – maths equation. God is perfect and He created humanity in his image, that's a positive. Humanity rebelled against God. That's obvious; you don't have to look very far to see that. That's a negative. Jesus died to take away the sin – so that's removing the negative and leaving us with the positive again! So, as long as we trust in Jesus, we're back where we started, forgiven and made perfect.'

'You summed that up really well,' said Sophie, then clapped her hand over her mouth as she realised what she had said, but Melissa and Daniel both laughed.

'It's OK, we're used to maths jokes. The thing is, though,' said Melissa, seriously, 'I've been reading bits of the Bible. Like I said, I get the bits about Jesus and I believe that. I mean, when I read it, I just know I'm reading about a real person who said those things and did those things. It's too...' she searched for the right word, 'too unpredictable to be made up. The thing is though,' Melissa continued, 'I just find some bits of the Bible hard to believe. How can I believe some parts of the Bible so much more easily than other parts?'

Sophie paused before she answered. 'I still find parts of it hard to understand myself. Can I tell you something that helped me when I was first thinking about becoming a Christian?'

'Yes, of course.'

'I had a teacher at school, my English teacher. He was called Mr Wheeler. He was a Roman Catholic and a lovely man and he came to the school Christian Union. I had a similar problem with the Bible to the one you've described and I told Mr Wheeler about it. He told me to remember that the Bible is not one book, but a library of sixty-six books. In that library are books of history, books of poetry and songs, and books of prophecy. Some of it can seem strange at first, although I believe it's all there for a reason. The thing to remember is that the parts about Jesus are history books. It's reliable, eyewitness history. Start with understanding Jesus and other things will fall into place in the light of that later on.'

'That does help,' said Melissa. 'Perhaps we can talk about things like this another time.'

'If you're still on maternity leave, you might be interested in coming to the women's Bible study group on Thursday mornings? That would probably help. We have a crèche for the little ones. There aren't that many of us, but they're really nice ladies. I'm sure you would like them.'

Sophie realised she had been talking to Melissa for a while and church had almost emptied. She hadn't managed to talk to many people but, she reasoned, sometimes you just had to give your attention to one person, especially a newcomer with a question. Unfortunately, she couldn't see Lucy. Audrey was about to leave.

'Audrey, has Lucy gone?' she asked.

'Yes, most people have. I'm sorry to have to say this to you, Sophie, but Doris was most offended. She said you hadn't even said hello to her today.'

'Sorry,' said Sophie, wondering why she was apologising to Audrey. 'Someone needed to talk.'

'Yes, well, the elderly people like to be acknowledged,' said Audrey, and she huffed out of the church and down the drive.

Lucy decided not to follow Sophie's advice and tell Rufus that his mother had upset her. That, she reasoned, might upset him and be counterproductive. She would just enquire after his weekend and only talk about the phone call if he said anything to her. The best way forward would be to concentrate on making a really good impression when she and Rufus went to dinner with Mr and Mrs Wainwright. She started to make a list of what she needed to do. She could wear her new dress. Another trip to the hairdresser was a little extravagant, but maybe it would be money well spent in the big scheme of things, so she made an appointment for Saturday morning. Then she sat down with her laptop to research the company Rufus worked for – that should help her with the conversation. She made herself a fact sheet to learn before Saturday night.

Lucy didn't see Rufus again until the following Saturday. He had started his new job within the company the Monday after his birthday weekend in Surrey and seemed to be late home from work every night. He didn't even make it to the Bible study group on Tuesday. On Saturday afternoon, however, he picked Lucy up to go shopping. 'I want to buy your birthday present,' he said, 'but I'm not sure what you would like.'

'How was your weekend?' Lucy tried to sound light and casual.

'Yes, yes, very nice thanks,' Rufus replied, keeping his eyes on the road.

It was no good. She had to say something. 'Your mother was very off-hand with me on the phone.' She immediately regretted speaking. Why had she said that? Why couldn't she have just kept her mouth shut? Now he would be cross with her.

'Was she?'

'Yes, she was.' Please say something nice, she thought. Please show you are sorry that your mother hurt my feelings. Tell me you'll stand up for me. Tell me that you'll tell her not to speak to me like that.

'Perhaps you just misinterpreted her,' said Rufus.

'No, I don't think so,' insisted Lucy. 'Why? Did she say anything to you about me?' Why had she started this? Rufus stared ahead in silence. 'Rufus, what did she say?'

'She said…' Rufus always told the truth.

'What?'

'Mother said you had a funny accent.'

The rest of the journey passed in silence.

They parked and started walking towards the shops. Rufus held Lucy's hand and broke the silence.

'What would you like?' he asked, as if nothing had happened. 'A new dress? A piece of jewellery? Some perfume? You say.'

Lucy had no way of undoing what she had said. The little cloud that she felt she had been carrying around with her recently had got a bit darker. She didn't feel like shopping, but she knew she had to move forwards, not backwards. Try to think positively, Lucy, she told herself. Rufus wanted to buy her a birthday present, so that was a positive. There might be other social occasions with Rufus where she needed to make a good impression. 'A new dress would be lovely, if that's all right?'

'Lead on,' said Rufus. She did.

When Rufus dropped Lucy home at teatime, a pretty new dress was sitting in a carrier bag on the back seat of his car. 'We need to be at Mr Wainwright's by half past seven,' said Rufus. 'I'll pick you up at a quarter past seven, OK?'

'Yes, I'll be ready,' she replied.

'Good,' he said. Then, as if he were reading her mind, he added, 'You just need to be more confident and you'll be fine.'

Lucy had her hand on the handle of the car door, about to get out. She stopped. 'But I'm not confident. I don't feel confident.' If he would just say something to buoy her up a little, it would be a lot easier to feel confident.

'You'll be fine. Just be more confident,' he repeated. 'I'll see you at a quarter past seven.'

'See you later.' She got out of the car. It was all very well Rufus telling her to be more confident, she thought, but if you weren't born with confidence, as Rufus seemed to have been, it had to come from somewhere. She went into her flat and toyed with the idea of telling him that she needed him to affirm her; but no, she knew that would never work. If Rufus said nice things to her because she had asked him to, it wouldn't count. She needed him to affirm her because he wanted to, to say nice things to her because he meant them.

She started to run a bath and picked up the company fact sheet she had made. As she passed the phone, another part of their conversation came back to her. She pressed the button on the answer machine and listened to her outgoing message: 'Hello, this is Lucy. I'm sorry I can't take your call right now. Please leave a message after the tone and I'll get back to you.' Did she really have a funny accent? Maybe Mother thought she sounded *common*. Perhaps she should think about getting some elocution lessons.

Lucy was ready before quarter past seven. Her hair still looked nice from her trip to the hairdresser that morning, despite having tried on clothes in the shops. She had on the dress she had worn to the Bickerstaffs' and her make-up and accessories were in place. She watched out of the window for Rufus to arrive. The black car came round the corner at quarter past seven precisely.

The Wainwrights lived near the centre of Stafford. When they arrived, Lucy was dismayed to see another large house, not dissimilar in size to the Bickerstaffs' home. Only natural, she thought, for a man in his position. She supposed these were going to be very grand people too.

'Ready?' asked Rufus, opening the car door for her. 'Just be confident.'

The Wainwrights turned out to be nothing like the Bickerstaffs. They welcomed Rufus and Lucy warmly and told them to call them Christopher and Andrea. Their house, though large, had a homely, lived-in feel about it. There were family photographs scattered around the windowsills and mantelpieces. Lucy noted some quite young children in the photos, whom she supposed to be Christopher and Andrea's grandchildren. There were also birthday cards on display with '60' on them. One of the cards said, 'Happy Birthday Grandad'.

Andrea took Lucy into the kitchen, where she was putting the finishing touches to the Beef Wellington. Lucy noted some children's artwork stuck to the refrigerator. 'How many grandchildren do you have?'

'Soon to be four,' said Andrea. 'Our daughter has twin boys, just turned five. Our son has a daughter of three and a new baby on the way.'

Lucy smiled. 'So… What can I do to help?'

'If you could help me carry some of this through to the dining room, that would be helpful. It's a bit hot, so use these oven gloves. Then I'll ask Christopher to get you some drinks.'

Perhaps, thought Lucy, this wasn't going to be such an ordeal after all. Indeed, it all seemed to be going quite well until they sat down at the table. It wasn't that the conversation turned to work – Christopher and Andrea seemed determined to avoid the subject and Lucy forgot her fact sheet altogether – it was just that Lucy seemed to find it very difficult to talk to either of them in front of Rufus. She was so anxious to do well in front of him that she became very aware of him watching her. She kept thinking about her accent and her need to be more confident, but the more she worried, the harder it became to speak. In the end she shrank back into herself and became very quiet again.

On the drive back home later that evening, Lucy felt Rufus was rather cool towards her. He said very little and she felt she had, once again, disappointed him. Please still love me, she thought.

'I'll see you in the morning,' he said. 'Oh, and I've booked a table at a nice restaurant in town for your birthday on Thursday.' He smiled and kissed her goodnight. Still, she thought, all was not lost. When they went out on Thursday, it would be just the two of them. It was only when she felt she had to perform to others in front of him that she struggled. Thursday would be a good evening.

Although Lucy saw Rufus at church on Sunday, he was missing again on Tuesday evening. Lucy hoped this wasn't going to become a habit. The new job certainly seemed to be taking more of his time, and he often took work home with him too. She looked forward to Thursday evening very much. Rufus was due to pick her up at half past seven.

At seven o'clock on Thursday evening the phone rang.

'Lucy, it's me. I'm so sorry, I'm still at work,' said Rufus. 'I'm not going to make it for dinner. I really am sorry to let you down. Can I call round later, maybe about nine o'clock? We'll go out at the weekend.'

Lucy put the phone down, feeling very upset. It rang again almost immediately.

'Hello,' said Lucy, in a small voice.

'Hi, it's Sophie. Just wanted to catch you before you go out to say happy birthday, but I won't hold you up.'

Lucy felt embarrassed to tell Sophie that her birthday celebration had been cancelled because of Rufus's work, but she couldn't hold it in. Rufus had put work before her, and it hurt.

'Actually, we're not going.' She began to cry. 'Rufus got held up at work. He said he would call round at about nine o'clock and we're going out at the weekend instead.'

'Oh! How disappointing! What are you going to do? See your parents instead?'

'No, I don't really want Mum and Dad to know Rufus isn't taking me out after all. They would have taken me out themselves, but it's too late now.'

Sophie felt a plan forming in her head. 'I'll see you soon,' she said.

At half past seven Lucy heard a knock at the front door. Sophie was standing outside, holding a bottle of wine and a cake. Hayley was standing just behind her, holding a carton of orange juice. 'Happy birthday,' said Sophie.

'Happy birthday, Lucy,' said Hayley, 'and let's be glad for late-night opening at the corner shop, which has everything you need for a birthday.' She put her hand in her pocket and pulled out a packet of birthday candles and a box of matches.

They put the candles on the cake, lit them and sang 'Happy Birthday', then ate it with a glass of wine for Sophie and Lucy and a glass of orange juice for Hayley. Lucy cheered up a bit and they chatted about life, Hayley's baby, Rufus and his new job, Hayley's baby, Henry and his potty training and Hayley's baby. Hayley talked at length about the new nursery. 'We've decorated it in neutral colours, because we want the sex of the baby to be a surprise!' She then went on to talk about the new furniture and all the little clothes she had bought.

Just before nine o'clock, Hayley got up. 'Come on, Sophie, Rufus will be here any minute. Let's leave Lucy in peace.'

Sophie and Hayley walked towards Hayley's block of flats.

'It's nice to see you,' Sophie said. 'We do miss you.'

'I know,' said Hayley, 'but I've been so busy getting ready for the baby.'

'There's a new couple at church,' said Sophie. 'Melissa and Daniel. They've got a baby called Jessica, who has just been baptised. I'd love you to meet them. She came to Bible study for the first time this morning. I was hoping you might come too when you finish work.'

'I'll stop work when school finishes for the summer holidays and then I won't go back. I was planning to come to the Thursday group.'

'That would be great,' said Sophie brightly. 'But do come back to church as well, Hayley. You're a Christian, you're meant to be with us in church. We don't just need God; we also need each other. That's what Sundays are for.'

'But I don't think you have to go to church to be a Christian. You can be a Christian in the community.'

'Hayley, when you become a Christian you become part of the church. Not being involved is like being a duck and not being in the pond.'

'Some ducks sit on the edge of the pond.'

'A duck is a duck, it belongs in a pond. You're part of a team and the team misses you.' They had reached Hayley's block. Sophie didn't want to end the evening on a bad note, so she said, 'Thank you so much for coming with me this evening. I'm sorry it was such short notice, but Lucy seemed so disappointed and I didn't want her to be on her own. It was just handy Dominic didn't have to go anywhere this evening, so I could leave him with Henry.'

'I'm glad you asked me… it was lovely to spend a bit of time with you and Lucy.'

Neither of them noticed the man sitting in the sleek, black car parked on the other side of the road. The man had been watching them approach the block of flats. He raised his newspaper to hide his face.

Hayley and Sophie said goodbye to each other and Hayley went inside. Sophie continued her walk across to the other side of the village. The black car pulled away and disappeared around the corner.

Lucy tidied up the living room and put the plates and glasses in the sink. Looking out of the window at a quarter past nine, she was just in time to see a black car arrive outside. A moment later, Rufus stepped out of it. She walked into the hall to open the door.

'I'm so sorry about this evening.'

'Don't worry, sit down. I had a good time anyway. Sophie and Hayley came round with a bottle of wine and a cake.'

'Oh, really? The elusive Hayley!' said Rufus. 'How is she?'

'Hayley's doing well, thanks.'

'Good! I'm glad you had a nice time and I promise we'll go out at the weekend. It's just work at the moment. I needed to speak to Mr Wainwright about one of my men who's causing a few problems.' Rufus leaned back on the sofa, looking tired. 'You remember David, the one with the wooden box and the temper?'

'Oh, yes, how is he?'

'Well, he's stopped bringing his wooden box to work, but he's been coming in late. A couple of times he's smelled of alcohol first thing in the morning and his work isn't up to scratch.'

'Oh dear, did you talk to him? Is he getting help? Perhaps he needs someone to talk to.'

'Yes, he mentioned friends in Shrewsbury who he talks to. But he's making mistakes at work that are unacceptable and I've had to speak to Mr Wainwright about disciplinary procedure. He's letting the company down and I can't afford to take risks.

I may have to let him go and advertise for a replacement. I've worked hard to get where I am and I don't want him to ruin it for me.'

'What did Mr Wainwright say?'

'Mr Wainwright said he trusted my judgement and he'd leave it to me. He's been impressed with my work. He said I'm doing a lot better than my predecessor!' he smiled. 'Anyway, let's not talk about that. Happy birthday!' He passed her the dress. It was still in the carrier bag from the shop.

'Thank you,' said Lucy. She took the dress out of the bag and the receipt fluttered down to the floor. Lucy felt disappointed to see that there was no birthday card. She had hoped for some loving words, some expression of his feelings towards her. The dress was lovely, though. It was on a shop hanger, so she hung it on the back of the door. She picked up the receipt from the floor and handed it to Rufus. 'I think this belongs to you,' she said.

Fourteen

As Sophie walked home across the village she reflected on her evening. Lucy seemed to be very devoted to Rufus. Sophie liked Rufus, but just lately she hadn't felt entirely comfortable about Lucy's relationship with him. Lucy may be in love, but she didn't seem quite as happy at the moment as she had been when she first became attached to Rufus.

Hayley was definitely happy. In fact, Sophie mused, positively euphoric might be a better description. She really didn't seem to be thinking about anything other than the baby due in September.

As she walked, Sophie thought about her own emotions. There had been a time, up until very recently, when an evening like this would have sent her spiralling into a negative thought bog. She could very easily have been walking home revisiting her own hopes and dreams of a baby and driving herself to despair. However, she gratefully acknowledged that those feelings were safely sealed in the metaphorical box in her head – very real, but securely tucked away unless she chose to open the box. She prayed a silent prayer of thanks as she walked.

The sun had set, but it wasn't completely dark. As Sophie walked past the play park and the school, her thoughts moved on to Henry. She may be coping with her emotions regarding infertility, but what about her feelings towards Henry? She was totally committed to doing everything she could to bring Henry up in a secure, nurturing environment, but did she love him as a mother loved her natural child? She wasn't sure. How could she know? Maybe this was to be her next challenge. She walked past the Bickerstaffs' house – a huge black shadow, austere in the semi-darkness – and on towards the vicarage.

Hayley opened her front door and went into her flat. 'I'm back,' she called out to Paul.

Paul was sitting at the kitchen table with some papers in front of him. 'Did you have a nice evening?'

'Yes, thanks. What have you been up to?'

'I was just having a look at our bank statement for the last month. We have been spending a lot of money recently.'

'Babies are expensive,' Hayley stated simply.

'It hasn't even been born yet,' said Paul. 'I'm not complaining,' he added, hastily, 'I just didn't realise we needed quite so much stuff…'

'Some more things arrived today, while I was at work. Mrs Solomons took them in, next door. I didn't have time to tell you before I went out.' Hayley pulled him by the hand towards the nursery and he followed her obediently. In addition to a rather expensive-looking cot with matching wardrobe and changing table, there stood a pram with accessories including a parasol and a detachable car seat. 'We can lift him or her straight from the car into the pram without waking,' said Hayley, happily. 'Also, I bought the Moses basket, baby bath and highchair to match everything else. Oh, and some sun blinds for the car.'

'Lovely,' mumbled Paul, looking at the labels and raising his eyebrows. He pulled some boxes out from under the cot. There were bottles of varying sizes, bottle brushes, a steriliser, an insulated bottle holder, a nursing pillow, a nappy bag which also seemed to match everything else and… 'What's a breast pump for?' he asked. 'No, on second thoughts, tell me another time.'

Next, he opened the wardrobe door. There were piles of nappies, white vests, Babygros, cardigans, coats, jackets and bibs. 'Do we really need snowsuits at this time of year?' he asked. 'And hats, mittens and booties? I didn't think they could walk for about a year.'

'The mittens are scratch mittens and, well, you have to have bonnets and booties, don't you?' It was a statement, not a question. 'Do you like them?'

'Yes, of course, but...' Paul glanced at Hayley's face. 'Yes, it's all lovely. Just... let me know if there's anything else we need and I'll transfer some money from our savings account. I'm glad you had a nice evening with Sophie and Lucy. Now, you've remembered I'm away next Tuesday night, for work, haven't you?'

'Oh, no, I forgot.'

'Well, why don't you invite the girls round for the evening to keep you company?'

As Sophie walked through her own front door she could hear Dominic finishing a phone call in the study. He came out as she was taking her shoes off.

'How was Lucy?'

'She cheered up, I think. It wasn't quite the evening she had planned, but I called round for Hayley on the way and we picked up a birthday cake and some drinks to take with us. Henry OK? Who was on the phone?'

'Haven't heard a sound from Henry and that was John on the phone. He volunteered to get some quotes for the repairs to the church drive. They've come through, but we don't have this sort of money in the funds.' He passed Sophie a piece of paper on which he had scribbled some figures.

'No, I don't suppose we do,' admitted Sophie. 'We need a rich benefactor.'

'Well, we can't really afford to pay from our own savings, especially if we want to go on holiday this summer...'

'You know who's loaded? Audrey and Geoffrey. Perhaps they would like to help out with the drive.'

Dominic looked doubtful. 'We can hardly ask. Perhaps we should just pray about it and see what happens.'

Rufus had arranged to take Lucy out to dinner on Saturday evening, to make up for missing her birthday. He was due to pick her up at half past seven and Lucy had decided to wear the dress he had given her for her birthday. She started getting ready early and was sitting waiting at a quarter past seven. At twenty five to eight she got up and looked out of the window. No sign of the black car coming round the corner. At twenty to eight she started pacing up and down the room.

At quarter to eight the doorbell rang. She went to open it. 'Sorry, I was on the phone,' said Rufus, stepping through the doorway.

'Not to worry,' said Lucy. 'Was it work?'

'No, I was talking to Mother. Are you ready?'

Lucy stepped back and looked down at the dress pointedly. 'What do you think?'

'Yes, yes, fine,' said Rufus, surveying her. 'Shall we go?'

Lucy decided she would have to settle for 'fine' for the moment. 'Fine' was better than nothing, and she didn't want to spoil the evening.

Rufus drove to the restaurant. He told her about the challenges of his new job and his pay rise. Lucy told Rufus about her evening with Sophie and Hayley.

'Are you coming in for coffee?' she asked as he pulled up outside her flat a couple of hours later.

Soon they were sitting on Lucy's sofa together. 'Thank you for a lovely evening,' she murmured, as she leaned back into the cushions.

'You seemed much more relaxed than you have done lately.'

'I know... I am... when it's just us I'm fine...'

'You must be more confident,' said Rufus. He seemed to be studying her quite intensely. This, thought Lucy hopefully, would be a good moment for Rufus to say something complimentary to boost her confidence.

'You're really quite reasonably attractive,' said Rufus.

Lucy took a moment before she could reply. Eventually, 'Reasonably attractive…' she echoed.

There was a silence.

'You've gone quiet,' Rufus observed.

'Well spotted!'

'OK, what have I done?'

'Really quite reasonably attractive?'

'Well, what do you see in me, anyway?' came his reply. 'I'm no oil painting, am I?'

For the first time, Lucy felt angry with Rufus. 'No,' she snapped, unkindly, 'you're not.' Immediately, she felt terrible. 'Sorry. I didn't mean that.'

Later that night, as Lucy lay in bed, thinking, she tried to put things into perspective in her mind. There were many positives about her relationship with Rufus, she reminded herself. Rufus had taken her out for her birthday and they had had a lovely evening. He still seemed to enjoy spending time with her. It wasn't as if they had argued, either. In fact, he had kissed her goodnight and left as if nothing out of the ordinary had happened. So why, she wondered, did she feel so worried? She acknowledged that she was still disappointed that Rufus couldn't bring himself to compliment her properly, but she was sure he hadn't set out to hurt her – it was just his honesty. She would just have to try harder, she decided. Then she thought about what she had said to him. She felt guilty about it. The feeling kept her awake for some time.

Lucy arrived at church the next morning anxious to ensure that things were still amicable between herself and Rufus. She wanted to talk to him away from other people so, at the end of the service, she left him at the church doorway, talking to Audrey and Geoffrey and waited for him at the end of the church drive.

Eventually he left the church and walked towards her. It was a warm day and she stood in the shade of a large tree.

'Sorry to keep you waiting,' he said. 'Would you like to come round for lunch?'

OK, thought Lucy, with relief, she was still in his good books. 'Thanks, that would be lovely.' Audrey and Geoffrey were coming down the drive. Lucy didn't want them to start talking to Rufus again, so she steered him behind the tree while they passed. John Henderson, however, was following them at a bit of a run.

'Geoffrey!' they heard John call out. 'Did Dominic tell you I got those quotes for the drive?'

'No, no he didn't,' said Geoffrey, sounding offended.

'Oh, OK, anyway, perhaps you'd like to have a look?' She heard rustling as John handed some sheets of paper to Geoffrey.

'I don't know where Dominic thinks we're going to get £5,000 from,' stated Geoffrey.

'I've got an idea,' put in Audrey, brightly.

Lucy suppressed a smile and winked at Rufus as they listened to Audrey speak. Then Audrey and Geoffrey walked on up the road and Lucy and Rufus followed at a distance.

On Tuesday Rufus rang Lucy to let her know that he wouldn't be able to make it to Bible study and asked her to give his apologies to the rest of the group. Lucy was ready early and walked down to the vicarage, the first to arrive. Sophie answered the door and Lucy followed her into the kitchen, where she had been boiling the kettle and putting mugs onto a tray.

Dominic joined them from the study.

'I just phoned Geoffrey to let him know that John got the quotes in for the drive. I didn't get round to mentioning it on Sunday, but he said John had already spoken to him and shown him the quotes.'

'Oh, yes,' said Lucy. 'I remember John chasing him down the drive at the end of church.'

'Anyway, I said we would discuss it at the next church council meeting, but the money is obviously going to be an issue,' said Dominic.

'Oh, Audrey had something to say about that,' said Lucy.

'What, really?' said Sophie. 'Well, they are pretty wealthy. Do they want to pay for the drive?'

'That would be brilliant!' exclaimed Dominic.

'No, no,' said Lucy, quickly. 'No, she said she would make some jam to sell at the back of church.'

'Jam?' said Sophie.

'Jam,' said Lucy.

Hayley had settled herself down on her sofa with a cup of herbal tea. Paul was away on business, but Hayley hadn't invited Sophie or Lucy round, as he had suggested. She thought they would be at the vicarage Bible study group anyway. Hayley had more important plans for her evening. She had finally exhausted her many catalogues of baby clothes, equipment and accessories and had decided it was time to work through her book of baby names. Any guilty feelings that Hayley had once had about the conception of this baby were long gone. She had removed herself from the only situation in which she might meet the person who could make her feel uncomfortable and, these days, she gave little thought to her secret. She was going to have her perfect baby, in her perfect nursery, in her perfect home and she was looking forward to a bright future.

She opened the book. She needed two shortlists ready for when Paul came back: one for a boy and one for a girl. Hayley was surprised by a knock at the door. She got up and glanced through the spyhole. There was one heart-stopping moment of recognition, a sharp intake of breath and then she pulled her hand away from the door catch abruptly, as if it had burned her. What was *he* doing here? Why was he knocking on her front door, at this time of the evening, when he must know that Paul was away on business?

Slowly and quietly Hayley sank down onto the floor. She crouched on the doormat, listening. She would keep quiet and wait for him to go away. There was no way he could be sure she was at home.

The knocking came again, louder this time. Hayley jumped, her heart racing. Still she waited. Please go away, please just go away and leave me alone, she thought. He knocked a third time and then she heard a curse, footsteps, and the sound of someone running down the stairs. She steeled herself to stand up and peer through the spyhole once more. He was gone. She crouched back down and crawled into the living room and over to the window. Slowly she knelt up, just enough to be able to raise her eyes above the windowsill and see the parking bays outside, beyond the communal garden. A long black car was reversing out. She stood up, went back to the front door and secured the safety chain.

As May drew to a close the weather got warmer and the days lighter. In June there was a mini heatwave and the smell of summer was definitely in the air. Hayley gradually grew calmer as the weeks went by. There had been no return of the unwelcome visitor and no sign of the long black car anywhere near the flat. Her bump was growing bigger by the day and Hayley was very much looking forward to the end of term, next month, when she would leave school and take things easy until the baby arrived towards the end of September.

When Paul had returned from his business trip, Hayley had presented him with her shortlist of baby names and, between them, they had chosen Alice Hayley for a girl and Alexander Paul for a boy.

Lucy and Rufus saw less of each other during June. Rufus's hours of work apparently only permitted them to meet at weekends. The Tuesday evening study group became a thing of the past for Rufus and he even missed church on Sunday mornings occasionally, citing too much work to get done before Monday morning as his reason. Lucy missed him very much, but she didn't say anything. She didn't want him to feel she was putting any pressure on him.

Lucy had decided, in her heart, that Rufus was the person she wanted to spend the rest of her life with. She knew it was unlikely that he felt the same way yet. After all, they had known each other for such a short time. She planned to sit tight, be there for him when he wanted her and hope things worked out. But Lucy was troubled by an ever-growing fear. Knowing how much she loved Rufus made her feel vulnerable. Being in love came with a cost – the risk of getting badly hurt.

At the vicarage, things were as calm as they ever could be. Henry had mastered the art of using the toilet, although he needed his special step to reach it. Unfortunately, being toilet trained had also given Henry a new weapon to use against Sophie. Just as they were about to leave the house to go shopping, to church, anywhere, really, 'Toilet!' Henry would shout gleefully, the old, familiar glint in his eye.

Dominic took the quotes for the church drive repairs to the church council meeting at the end of June and it was agreed that they would go ahead with the work whenever they felt they had funds to cover it.

'Never, then,' said Sophie, when Dominic came home and reported back.

'Hopefully not "never", but I can't imagine when,' said Dominic. 'I'll give John a ring. I know it's late, but he was the one who found the quotes for us and I promised to let him know how it went.' He went off to the study and closed the door.

Sophie went to make two cups of tea and returned from the kitchen just as Dominic was coming back from the study. They met in the hallway. At that moment there was a loud crash from upstairs. Dominic ran up the stairs two at a time. Sophie put down the tea, spilling some of it on the hall table, and followed close behind. Crying was coming from Henry's room.

Henry was lying on the floor beside the cot. He was wailing loudly and they both rushed over to him. Dominic moved as if to pick him up.

'Don't,' said Sophie, quickly, 'just in case he's hurt.'

She stroked his hair gently and they spoke to him soothingly. 'It's OK, Henry, it's OK. Mummy's here, Daddy's here.'

Gradually the cries died down and Henry started to sit himself up. 'I think he's OK,' said Dominic. But then Henry laid himself back down on the carpet, a rather glazed look on his face.

'I'm not so sure,' said Sophie. 'He would never normally lie himself down after a bump. He doesn't look right, he looks as if he isn't quite with us.'

'Should we take him to the hospital?'

'Yes, I think we should,' said Sophie, with tears in her eyes. 'You pick him up, but be careful.'

There was very little traffic on the roads and they arrived in A&E very quickly.

'You take him in,' said Sophie. 'You can carry him more easily. I'll find somewhere to park.'

When Sophie walked into the hospital a few minutes later, Dominic was walking away from the reception desk, still holding Henry.

'I checked him in. The lady said they won't keep us waiting long.' Henry remained very still in Dominic's arms, but he was awake and quietly taking in his surroundings.

Sophie gently stroked the hair away from his forehead. 'It's OK, Henry,' she said, but her imagination was working furiously. What if he wasn't OK? What if Henry had concussion? What if he had a fracture or brain damage? What if Social Services found out? What if Social Services took him away? She couldn't bear the thought of it.

'It's my fault,' she said, suddenly. 'I should have talked to you about taking the cot down and putting him into a bed. He's nearly three now. If he wasn't sleeping in a cot, he couldn't have fallen out of it.' She started crying. 'But I didn't know he could climb out of the cot – he's never tried to do that before.'

'Don't be silly. How could we know he was going to try to climb out of the cot? Anyway, I'm sure lots of children are still sleeping in a cot at three, aren't they?'

'I don't know,' said Sophie. 'I wanted to keep him in the cot for as long as I could. Putting him into a bed is just giving him another opportunity to be naughty. He'll be able to keep getting up when he's been put to bed and we both know he's going to do it. I was trying to protect us for a little while longer, but now look what's happened.'

They looked up at the sound of footsteps approaching. 'This must be Henry?' said a young-looking woman in a white coat. 'Would you like to bring him over to the cubicle and pop him onto the bed?'

She asked a few questions and examined Henry carefully while Dominic and Sophie looked on anxiously. Henry lay very quiet and still.

'He seems fine,' said the doctor, eventually. 'No damage done, but perhaps it would be wise to put him into a bed, if he can climb out of the cot. I'll give you a checklist of things to watch out for over the next twenty-four hours. Any problems, then come straight back, but I think he'll be fine.'

They drove back to the vicarage feeling much calmer. They put Henry back in the cot and Sophie arranged some cushions around it, just in case, but she was sure Henry wouldn't try to climb out again that night. She sat on the floor until he had fallen asleep, then quietly left. She planned to check Henry at intervals during the night.

Sophie got changed and slipped into bed beside Dominic.

'I learned one thing tonight,' she said.

'What to look out for in a toddler following a bump on the head?'

'Not just that,' said Sophie, tears coming to her eyes again. 'I was so worried. I know he's naughty, but I suddenly thought about Social Services coming and taking him back and saying we couldn't have him any more. I couldn't bear it, I just couldn't bear it. I love him too much.'

Dominic put his arm around her. 'Of course you do, you silly thing.'

Henry's third birthday was at the end of June. Sophie arranged a family party for the afternoon and invited her parents and her brother with his family.

'What a lovely day,' said Sophie, as they walked back through the vicarage door, having waved the merry party off.

'Henry seemed to enjoy being centre of attention!' said Dominic.

'I'm not sure he really knows what a birthday is yet, but he certainly knew that he was special today and he was very proud when he showed everyone his new bed and how he can use the toilet now!'

The phone started ringing.

'I'll get it,' said Dominic, 'then I'll tidy up down here. You take Henry up and get him settled.'

For once, Henry didn't get out of bed after his bath. He was so tired after his exciting day.

Sophie went downstairs to find the washing-up done and Dominic sitting down with two cups of tea.

'Thanks for doing that,' she said, as she sank gratefully onto the sofa. She thought Dominic looked tired. 'You OK?'

'Not really,' Dominic replied. 'That was John Henderson on the phone.'

'And?'

Dominic took a deep breath. 'They're leaving. They feel that All Saints isn't the right church for their family. He said that the boys are often in Sunday school alone and miss having friends at church. They felt they tried really hard with the Church Open Day at Easter. They got families to come and they told them about church, but then none of them turned up on Easter Sunday, or any other Sunday for that matter. I'm sure he also feels frustrated that there's no money to fix the drive, although he didn't specifically say so.'

They sat in silence for a few minutes. Sophie deflated like a balloon.

At last she found her voice. 'But what about us? They were the only other young family that were truly committed to All Saints, the only ones with children who came regularly to the Sunday school. They were our allies. Without them… well, we'll never grow the Sunday school, we'll never attract other young families in. The church will grow older and gradually die out. Without them… we might as well give up.'

'We can't give up… can we?'

'Can't we? I just feel so angry.'

'Don't be angry,' said Dominic, flatly. 'We can be sad and disappointed, but not angry. They haven't exactly done anything wrong. They aren't abandoning their faith, just us, just our church. The only thing they did wrong was pledging their allegiance to us too early… or giving up too quickly.'

It was a long time before either of them spoke again. At last, Dominic said, 'I've been wondering… maybe we aren't really the right people for this job. Perhaps I'm just not very good at being a vicar. No one really likes me, a lot of people seem to think I'm doing things the wrong way. Maybe we should leave and they can advertise for someone else. Another person might be more popular, be able to attract more people, get some younger families in, reach out to the community in a better way.'

Sophie felt her spirits lift a little. Perhaps, she thought, Dominic was right. Perhaps they weren't really meant to be doing this job. Perhaps life didn't really have to be this hard.

'What would we do?' she asked. 'I mean, for money? I don't mind what I do, though,' she added. 'If you could get a job, we could rent somewhere to live. Then, when Henry goes to school, I could get a job too and we could probably get a mortgage. We could still be useful in a church, somewhere. We just wouldn't have to lead one.'

Dominic leaned forward in his chair. 'Do you know, I would be really happy doing something like stacking shelves in a supermarket. To have a job where I could come home and leave work behind me at the end of the day would be so lovely.'

'Me too,' said Sophie, enthusiastically. 'I bet I could get some hours to work around school next year. Maybe we could move down to the coast, near Mum and Dad. I'm sure they would be happy to help out with Henry in an emergency.'

'Let's not get carried away,' said Dominic. 'Look, we should go to bed, try to sleep on it for a while and see how we feel in the morning.'

Fifteen

In July the weather got quite hot. Early one Saturday morning Lucy answered the phone to Rufus.

'I was thinking,' he said. 'I've hardly been out of the office this week and it might be nice to get some fresh air. Shall we go for a walk? There's something I need to talk to you about.'

'Oh, OK. I need to go the shop quickly first to pick up some milk. I'll come round to your house after that. I won't be long.'

Twenty minutes later Lucy was knocking on Rufus's door. 'Come in,' he called. 'I'm almost ready.'

'Can I just leave my milk in your fridge?'

'Sure,' Rufus put his shoes on. 'Let's go and walk by the river.' He led the way over to the car and they drove a couple of miles to a spot outside the village, where a slow river flowed with a footpath alongside it.

Rufus was oddly quiet in the car, giving Lucy time with her thoughts. She wondered what he wanted to talk to her about. She decided not to ask, but she hoped it would be good news. For a fleeting moment she entertained the idea of a proposal. She imagined herself sitting down in a picturesque spot and Rufus getting down on one knee. Really, she knew it was far too soon, but it was a happy daydream.

Rufus parked the car and they got out. 'Let's walk,' he said, as he took her hand. She loved the way he always reached out for her hand when they were walking.

It was still fairly early in the morning and there weren't many people about. Rufus remained unusually quiet. He looked as if he was thinking about something.

Lucy prompted him. 'What was it you wanted to talk to me about?'

'The thing is,' Rufus became very matter of fact, 'work's been going quite well lately. Mr Wainwright… Christopher… has been very good to me. He trusts me, I think. He's given me quite a bit of responsibility, anyway. There's another branch of the company in Maidenhead. There's a more senior management role coming up there quite soon and Christopher is keen for me to take it on.'

'Well, that's great,' said Lucy, immediately wondering how far away Maidenhead was and whether it mattered as much to Rufus as it did to her that they wouldn't be able to see each other so easily. 'It's very soon after your last promotion, though. Why doesn't he want you to stay and do the job you're doing now?'

'He seems to think I've proven myself capable and, like I said, he trusts me. He can see I'm committed.'

'Yes,' said Lucy, trying hard to sound pleased for him. 'I suppose we can still see each other at weekends. Lately we've only been seeing each other at weekends anyway, you've been working such long hours.'

'The thing is…' said Rufus again. He let go of her hand; he didn't seem to want to look her in the eye. '… I'm not sure about us any more.'

Lucy felt a cold chill rush through her. She felt weak and nauseous. Rufus didn't love her. He didn't want her any more. He would be going away and he wouldn't be part of her life. She might never see him again. How could she live with this knowledge? How could her life go on?

Without realising it, they had both stopped walking. Tears began to stream down Lucy's face. She couldn't speak. Her breath started to come in great sobs. She looked up at Rufus and was surprised to see that he was crying too. She turned away from him. There was a wooden bench not far from where they were standing, facing the water, away from the path. Slowly she walked towards it and dropped down onto it. She was aware that Rufus had sat down beside her. For a while they both sat and wept quietly.

'Why?' Lucy asked, eventually, although she wasn't sure she really wanted to know.

'It's just... It's just that you're such an introvert. You have so little confidence,' he replied.

'Oh.' She couldn't really think of a suitable reply. 'Anything else?' Why did she ask that question?

'Well,' he paused, 'sometimes... you don't know things.'

So, that was it. She wasn't confident, the one thing Rufus should have helped her with but had made so much worse. And now... he actually thought she was stupid. Well, perhaps she was. What was it, she wondered, that she didn't know, that she ought to know?

'What don't I know?'

Rufus thought for a moment. 'Well,' he pointed to a tree on the other side of the river, 'for example, what's that?'

'A weeping willow,' said Lucy, surprised at the question.

'Oh, well, I thought you wouldn't know that.'

Lucy clawed back a little of her self-worth.

'Let's go,' she said. She got up and Rufus followed meekly behind. They drove back in silence, Lucy still crying quietly. When they got back to Rufus's house, she said, 'I'll just get my milk out of your fridge.'

'Oh, yes,' said Rufus. 'Perhaps... shall I make a cup of tea? Perhaps you shouldn't go until you feel a bit better.'

Lucy desperately wanted to delay the moment of saying goodbye. 'OK.' She sat on the sofa they had chosen together and looked around the room. She had hoped she would live here with him one day, after their wedding at All Saints. Of course, it had all been in her head. She felt angry with herself for having let her imagination run away with her.

Rufus brought in the tea and sat down beside her. She was surprised to see that he was tearful again.

'Why are you crying?' she asked. 'This is your decision.'

'I know, but it's still sad.' They sipped their tea in silence. Lucy decided that the best way she could get her emotions under control was not to speak.

'I think it's time for me to go home,' said Lucy, sadly. 'I'll just pop up to the loo first.' She went upstairs to the bathroom. As she came down, she remembered she had never asked Rufus where the little door halfway down the staircase led. Rufus was just coming out of his bedroom, blowing his nose on a clean, white handkerchief.

'Rufus, where does that door on the stairs lead to?'

'What? Oh, that door. Oddly enough, it's the airing cupboard,' he said sounding immensely relieved to be talking about something as unemotionally charged as a cupboard with a hot water tank in it. 'Look, not very exciting, I'm afraid.' He opened the door to demonstrate, accidentally dislodging a pile of what turned out to be vests. 'Whoops, sorry,' he said, bending down hurriedly to stuff them back onto the shelf.

'No, wait,' said Lucy, and she suddenly smiled. 'What are these?' She pulled one out triumphantly. 'String vests!' Rufus made a grab for the vest and tried to push it back into the airing cupboard. 'No, stop, stop,' she cried. 'Look!' She pulled out another vest. 'This one is... ugh... yellow!'

'Well, Mother buys me them every Christmas, as a stocking filler. She says they keep you warm because they trap a layer of air between your skin and your shirt. And I have to put them somewhere...'

'You mean, I've been going out with a thirty-year-old man who not only wears string vests, but whose mother does his clothes shopping?'

'I never said I wore them,' said Rufus defensively.

'Then go and get a bin bag.'

Rufus paused for a moment. 'But Mother... oh, I suppose she'll never find out.' He bolted down the stairs, returning moments later with a black bin liner. Lucy took a little comfort from the fact that, just at that moment, Rufus was happy to do anything, even defy Mother, just to make her feel a little bit better.

The following morning Sophie was disappointed to see that neither Lucy nor Rufus had made it to church. A vague notion had been in her mind that she might talk to Lucy about how she and Dominic had been feeling and about them possibly leaving the church, although she hadn't mentioned this to Dominic. She knew that Dominic would probably say that she shouldn't discuss such things with a member of the congregation, but Lucy was her friend as well as a member of the church.

She caught up with Lucy's parents during coffee after the service. 'No Lucy or Rufus this morning,' she pointed out. 'Are they OK?'

'We haven't heard anything to the contrary,' said Shirley. 'I'll give Lucy a ring.'

Sophie thought she might do the same thing, but maybe later on. She knew that Dominic had arranged for Catherine and Robert to come round for a chat that afternoon.

Catherine and Robert arrived at two o'clock. Sophie made some drinks and then sat on the floor with Henry, while they talked generally for a time. However, they all knew there was an issue that they had gathered to discuss and eventually it was Robert who brought the conversation round to the topic at hand.

'Now come on you two, what is it that's on your minds?' he asked.

Dominic began. He told them that the Henderson family had decided to leave the church and how sad and disappointed they felt. He explained how inadequate it made them feel that their one regular family felt they needed to rush off to another church to have their needs met.

'In short,' Dominic said, 'it feels almost impossible to build the church up in Oxley without any young people. The other families who come are off doing other things most Sundays and only come to church when they haven't got something better to do, and a lot of the older people complain about anything we do to try to attract younger people. We feel as if we are failing. Perhaps we aren't really the right people to be doing this job. Maybe we're just not cut out for it and somebody else would be better at it.'

'How do you feel about this, Sophie?' asked Catherine.

'I feel sad, angry, frustrated and, I hate to admit it, rubbish at my job,' answered Sophie. 'Not that it's really my job, but we both felt we were called to this ministry together.'

'But that's it,' said Robert. 'You're here because of what you just said, Sophie. You were called to this ministry together. I have no doubt that Dominic is meant to be leading All Saints with you, Sophie, alongside him. You can't give up just because John and Belinda haven't stuck it out. People are going to come and go. The problems we have at All Saints aren't unique, you know. Take it from me, there will be setbacks along the way. But the right thing to do is to keep going, despite it all. The days of preaching and seeing hordes of people coming to faith are long gone. These days we are digging them out, painstakingly, one at a time.

'Jesus never forced people to follow Him when He walked the earth as a man,' Robert went on, 'so He won't do that now. God isn't asking you to make people follow Him, because you can't. But He is asking you to keep telling people about Him. There may be people at All Saints who see churchgoing as just another activity to be fitted in when they have nothing better to do. There may even be some committed Christians who have a bit of a consumer attitude towards church. People tend to think, "Which church is the best church to serve my needs?" It takes a lot of Christian maturity to ask, "Which is the church where God wants me to serve Him?"

'There are committed Christians at All Saints who want to work with you in bringing the Christian message to Oxley. Don't make any decisions now. Go on holiday. Take an extra week, if you like. We'll cover you. Take some time to think and pray. If you still feel you want to give up when you get back, we won't stand in your way. Just don't make any definite decisions until you get back.'

Robert and Catherine had just left when the doorbell rang again. Sophie went to answer it, to see Lucy standing outside looking forlorn. She ushered her into the living room as Dominic tactfully announced he would take Henry for a walk.

'What's happened?'

Lucy sank down onto the sofa and started to cry, but seemed unable to speak. Sophie sat down next to her and put her arm around her. After a little while of sitting in silence, Lucy finally got her words out.

'Rufus doesn't want to see me any more.'

'Oh… oh, Lucy, I'm so sorry,' said Sophie, feeling as if she could cry herself.

Over about half an hour, in short sentences punctuated by more crying, Lucy explained that Rufus was going to be promoted again, was moving to Maidenhead and would be leaving both her and Oxley behind. Sophie knew she couldn't say anything to make this better for Lucy, though she desperately wanted to. All she could do was listen and sympathise.

'Are you going to be OK for work tomorrow?'

'I think so,' said Lucy. 'If I can sleep tonight, I'll be OK once I get going. I've got to get on with it, haven't I? I don't have any choice.'

'I suppose so. Have you told your mum and dad?'

'Yes, just now,' said Lucy. 'I came straight here from their house. They were so disappointed and that made it even harder, but they were lovely. They suggested we go on holiday together in a couple of weeks and I think I will.'

'That's a good idea.'

Given the circumstances, Sophie didn't feel able to tell Lucy about her own concerns or about John and Belinda leaving the church.

Afterwards, as she told Dominic Lucy's news, she realised that Rufus would be another person leaving their congregation.

What with the Hendersons leaving, Hayley not coming to church, Lucy so sad and Audrey and Geoffrey constantly on the warpath, Sophie felt as if things couldn't get much worse at All Saints. Although she hated to admit it, she also felt ever so slightly cross with God.

Hayley, on the other hand, was feeling positive again. There had been no further knocks on the door from unwanted visitors, and it was nearly the end of term. Her bump was getting heavier and moving around was becoming more of an effort. The recent hot weather made everything much harder work and the summer holidays couldn't come quickly enough for Hayley.

Finally, it was the last week of July and the last day of school. Hayley was delighted to be presented with a beautiful rose tree in a pot and an enormous hand-made card, signed by all the children.

When the children had all gone home, Hayley tidied her desk for the last time and said goodbye to her work colleagues. They all wished her well and she promised to let them know when the baby arrived. One of the teachers dropped her off outside her block of flats with the card and rose tree. She felt tired but happy as she waited for the lift to go up to the third floor. She had much to look forward to.

The following morning Hayley wandered into the kitchen in her dressing gown while Paul was having breakfast.

'It looks as if it's going to be another hot day,' he said.

'Mmm. What would you like for dinner?'

'Don't do anything that takes too much effort. You need to take it easy. It's so hot, a salad would be fine. Whatever you fancy.'

Hayley waved Paul off to work from the balcony, then went back to the kitchen to make coffee and toast. Moments later she returned to the balcony. Setting her breakfast down on the table, she pulled up one of the wooden chairs, but noticed that it had a wobbly leg. Perhaps the chairs did need replacing after all, she thought. She pushed the chair with the wobbly leg into a corner. Then she placed the rose tree on it. It looked as if it was meant to be there, like a feature. She found a chair that was more sound and sat down to eat her toast in the morning sun.

Hayley thought about the future. Her parents were planning to retire this summer and she was anticipating seeing more of them when she was at home with the baby and Paul was at work. They were doing a great job of caring for her grandparents in their home, but Hayley imagined they would appreciate having an excuse to leave the house from time to time, once they were retired. Chloe, her younger sister, would be at work, but was also likely to be a frequent visitor once the baby had been born. Chloe had arranged a holiday to Florida in September with a friend, but she should be back just before the baby was due. Hayley knew that Paul's parents were looking forward to meeting their first grandchild too. She certainly wouldn't be short of company. She felt very fortunate indeed.

Paul had been insisting on doing all the housework since Hayley had been pregnant, so there was very little to do in the flat. After breakfast Hayley washed up and tidied the kitchen. She had her shower and got dressed. Then she wondered what to do. She went into the nursery, but there was nothing that needed doing in there. She found a small pile of ironing, but that didn't take too long. She decided she might as well go shopping before it got too hot and then put her feet up when she got back. Maybe she could sit on the balcony with a book.

She walked past the empty school and passed the play park, already busy with children enjoying the first day of the school holidays. She looked at the mums, chatting while the children played. That would be her one day, she thought. She carried on towards the shops. A black car was approaching. Hayley became aware of it pulling up at the kerb beside her.

'Hayley!'

She turned at the sound of her name. She recognised the driver. She stood speechless, rooted to the spot.

'Hayley, I just want to talk. I don't want to cause you any trouble, but please, just talk to me for a few minutes.'

Hayley turned and tried to start back towards the play park. He couldn't touch her there, not with all the parents and children around. She heard the car door slam and the sound of footsteps running behind her.

'Hayley, really, I just want to talk, just for a few minutes. You owe me that at least.'

She felt a hand on her shoulder.

She stopped and turned, breathless, her heart beating furiously. 'What do you want?'

'I don't want anything. Just to talk. Please. I've been trying to talk to you away from Paul for ages. I tried to see you at church, thinking he wouldn't be there. I came to your flat when Paul was away, but you weren't in. I haven't come to cause trouble between you and Paul, really.'

'OK, just for a minute,' she said. She was aware that she was perspiring uncomfortably. 'Here, though. I'm not going anywhere with you.' She walked to a bench and sat down. He followed her.

'Are you OK?'

'I was,' she replied, 'until I saw you.'

'I just want to ask you…' He was staring at Hayley's bump. 'Please, Hayley, just tell me the truth, is this baby mine?'

'I…' There was no point in lying. 'I don't know.'

'Hayley, I work with your husband. Paul told us all at work what happened. You couldn't have a baby, you went to church and prayed and suddenly you're pregnant and the baby is due in September, nine months after Christmas. He doesn't know what happened at the Christmas party and I have no intention of telling him, but we both know this baby isn't a miracle. It's mine.'

'It might be,' said Hayley, 'but it might not. The doctor said it wasn't impossible for us to have a baby, just unlikely. It's possible that we just got lucky that month.'

'Hayley, this baby is mine.'

'What do you want?' she repeated. Her hands were trembling in her lap.

'I haven't come to make things difficult for you and Paul. All I ask is that you let me see the baby once, when it's born. Then I'll leave you alone, I promise. I'm moving away anyway. I've got a new job.'

'All right,' said Hayley. 'All right, you can see the baby once, but then you leave us alone. Why aren't you at work?'

'Officially, I'm at the dentist. Paul said you were finishing work yesterday, so I said I had an emergency dental appointment. I was intending to call on you this morning and then go in late, but I happened to see you out walking before I got as far as your flat, and I'm glad I did. Please don't worry, I don't want to rock the boat in any way. I'll see the baby once and then I'll leave you alone to get on with your lives.'

He walked away, leaving Hayley alone on the bench.

She sat for a while, waiting for her heart rate to return to normal. She had had a shock, but she had to carry on as normal. There was no reason to think that anything terrible was going to happen. He would see the baby once and then leave them alone. In many ways it was better to have it out in the open, to know what his intentions were rather than worry about him turning up unexpectedly. She would do her shopping and go home and try to relax. Anxiety couldn't be good for the baby.

Sixteen

Sophie had been keeping in close touch with Lucy in the days following Rufus's devastating announcement. Sophie was pleased to hear that her friend had booked a two-week holiday with her parents in Cornwall for the beginning of August. Sophie, Dominic and Henry would be leaving for France just before they returned. They had taken advantage of Catherine and Robert's kind offer to mind the church for three weeks and were not due to return until the first week of September.

Rufus would be leaving Oxley while Lucy was in Cornwall. Sophie was glad Lucy would be spared the agony of watching him go. Rufus had come to church the week after he had broken up with Lucy and had sat next to her that morning. Sophie was thankful that there was no animosity, but there was a definite air of sadness about both of them.

The following Sunday, Rufus had, once again, been missing from church. It was meant to have been his last Sunday with them. Sophie and Dominic wanted to say goodbye to him so, after lunch, they took Henry for a walk and called on him.

Rufus opened the front door, but didn't invite them in.

'We just wanted to say goodbye and that we'll miss you,' said Sophie.

'I'll miss you too,' said Rufus. 'You'll look after Lucy, won't you?'

'Of course,' replied Sophie. 'She's a good friend.'

'I hope you enjoy your new job,' said Dominic.

'I'm sure I will,' said Rufus, smiling brightly.

'And Rufus,' added Dominic, 'find a good church!'

In mid-August Sophie, Dominic and Henry set off for the long-awaited trip to France. They had decided to travel by train, using Eurostar to get to Paris. Once there, they took the Metro before travelling on to Tours. Having been brought up in France, Dominic was familiar with Paris and the Metro. His fluent French meant that communication was one less thing to worry about.

The journey took most of the day. At the end of it they realised that they had done something with Henry that even six months ago they would never have dreamed possible.

Ivor, Dominic's father, was waiting for them at the train station in Tours.

'We bought a car seat for Henry,' said Ivor. 'We've been looking forward to seeing you for such a long time. Harriet has been preparing for weeks. She has the house ready, the fridge and freezer stocked and lots of outings planned. Of course, we want you to have some time to yourselves too. And we would like to spend some time getting to know Henry.'

Ivor and Harriet's home, on the outskirts of Tours, was a spacious four-bedroomed detached house with ample parking in the front, and a large back garden. It was the house where Dominic had grown up and Sophie had visited on several occasions. This, however, was Henry's first visit. Nicholas, Dominic's younger brother, would be home from college in Paris for the first week of their stay, but would then be travelling by train to the coast, to help at a children's holiday camp.

Harriet met them at the front door. 'Hello, my darlings.' She rushed to embrace them all. 'Henry has grown so much.'

'He has,' said Dominic, hugging his mother.

'I've done everything you suggested,' said Harriet. 'I've put safety gates across the doorways and made little cushions for the tops of the doors to avoid slamming.' She pointed to the top of the nearest door, where she had arranged something that looked like a home-made beanbag. 'I borrowed a highchair for Henry and I've put covers over all the plug sockets.'

She showed them upstairs. 'This is Henry's room,' she said. There was a single bed made up with a blue duvet sitting in the middle of a small, white-painted room. Sophie eyed the walls, hoping they would still be white when they left. Harriet opened the next door. 'In the bathroom, I put a step by the toilet for Henry and a non-slip mat in the bath.'

Ivor came up the stairs with their cases and put them in their rooms.

'Now,' said Harriet, 'Nicholas will be home any minute and dinner will be ready in half an hour. I'll leave you to unpack. Let me know if you need anything.'

Sophie felt herself relaxing. She was on holiday, in a lovely place with very kind people. She could feel her tension gradually slipping away.

As they went back downstairs, Nicholas came through the front door – he looked a bit like a younger, slimmer version of Dominic; not that Dominic was overweight, but Nicholas was rather beanpole-ish, thought Sophie.

They all sat down to dinner, Henry in the highchair to keep him contained. There was much to talk about. Nicholas filled them in on his first year studying mathematics in Paris. Ivor and Harriet spoke of their friends and their children, people whom Dominic had known growing up.

'Sorry, Sophie,' said Harriet after a while. 'It must be rather boring for you, not knowing who these people are. Tell us about your family. Are your parents well?'

Sophie told them about Glenda and Patrick and then about Steve, Jane and Freya. 'They all came for Henry's birthday,' said Sophie. 'I wish you could have come too. It's a shame we live so far away.'

'Yes,' said Ivor. 'It is a shame, but we've been thinking recently,' he glanced at Harriet and smiled, 'about taking early retirement! Not right now, but in a year or two. We don't want to leave Tours. This is where we belong and we love the people here and our church, but Nicholas is becoming more independent and we would like to be a bit more free to travel to England. We don't want to miss Henry growing up!'

'That would be great,' said Dominic.

'And what about church?' asked Harriet. 'How are things?'

Sophie knew that Dominic kept his parents informed about the general ups and downs at church, but talking about their emotions was less easy over the phone. She waited for him to respond to his mother's question.

'To tell you the truth,' he began, 'we've been wondering lately whether church leadership is really our thing.'

'What makes you think that?' Ivor looked concerned.

Dominic seemed to be searching for the right words. 'Just... the opposition from within the church, I suppose. We've annoyed some of the older people by trying to attract some younger people and, at the same time, we've failed to attract the younger people. Sometimes it all seems a bit pointless. Either I'm the wrong person for the job... or maybe my job is just to see the church through a managed decline until it fizzles out.'

'I've been reading a book lately,' said Ivor after a pause. 'It's about Elijah. Read it yourselves, while you're here. It might help you see things more clearly.' He went out of the room and came back a moment later holding a book.

Sophie couldn't think how the story of a prophet from the Old Testament was going to help them with their decision, but Dominic took the book and they agreed to read it.

Henry was falling asleep. They gave him a bath and tucked him into the little bed in his room.

The next few weeks were a very happy time for Sophie and Dominic. Ivor and Harriet delighted in hosting their family. Ivor went to the expense of hiring a seven-seater car for a few days.

'There are six of us this week,' he explained, 'so there's plenty of room for all of us plus a space for Henry's pushchair.'

Apart from days out, there were some lovely local walks and lazy afternoons spent in the garden.

'I've always loved the chateaux of the Loire Valley,' Sophie told Dominic one evening.

'I'm glad you're enjoying your holiday. It's good to see you looking so relaxed.'

'Have you noticed, your parents often take Henry off to look at things with them and give us a bit of time alone?'

'They enjoy entertaining him and he's becoming more and more comfortable with them each day.'

At the end of the first week they said goodbye to Nicholas and Ivor returned the hire car. 'We can make do with our car now we are only five,' he said. 'I've checked that you are insured to drive it as well, Dominic, so you can take a few trips on your own too.'

One day they decided to take Henry to a water park.

It was so hot. 'Let's get in!' said Dominic. They went to the side of the shallow pool and jumped in, but Sophie had forgotten to take her sunglasses off.

Dominic laughed, took the glasses and put them on Sophie's towel.

A bit later on, as they were getting out of the pool, Dominic suddenly said, 'Stay where you are and I'll get your towel.'

'Why?'

'Your swimming costume... um... it's got a bit thin in one place,' he said. 'A place you don't usually show to the public.'

Sophie's had to spend the rest of the day being escorted in and out of the pool by Dominic with a towel. At one point she forgot to take off her sunglasses again.

'Glasses, Mummy, glasses,' said Henry, anxiously.

One evening towards the end of their third week, when she had put Henry to bed, Sophie found Harriet in the kitchen, washing up. 'Thank you for looking after Henry so much,' she said. 'He seems to get on very well with you and it has been so good for us to have some time on our own. I really needed to have a break.'

'It's been a pleasure,' said Harriet. 'I know he plays you up a lot and I know that's not your fault – or his, for that matter. What did the social workers say to you about that sort of thing, when you were being prepared to adopt?'

Sophie thought. Sometimes it seemed to take all her energy just to cope with Henry's behaviour day to day, without trying to work out why it was happening. 'They did say,' she began, 'that adopted children these days can demonstrate very challenging behaviour because they have often had a difficult start in life. It all comes down to anxiety, really. A difficult start leads to insecurity, which leads to anxiety. Anxiety breeds anger and bad behaviour. They find it hard to trust adults, so they put themselves in charge and resist authority. I suppose I represent that authority to Henry more than anyone else. Maybe that's why he challenges me the most.

'I put him on the naughty step once,' she went on, 'but I'm really not sure whether that was the right thing to do. If his difficult behaviour is a result of anxiety, then I was pushing him away for being insecure, which is the opposite of what he needs. But, then, how am I supposed to teach him right from wrong? The trouble is that no one really tells you what to do. Perhaps I should get some advice. Anyway, I ended up sitting on the naughty step with him.'

'Well, maybe sitting on the step with him was a way of telling him that his behaviour wasn't right, but that you weren't pushing him away. I'm no expert. Perhaps, as you say, you should get some advice. Anyway, you're giving him security now,' said Harriet. 'And he feels comfortable enough with you to show his anger. Do you see that he's improving?'

Sophie thought again. 'Yes,' she said, honestly. 'I do. Even a few months ago we wouldn't have attempted a trip like this. The day we went to the water park he showed concern when I forgot to take my sunglasses off in the pool. It's such a little thing, but he's never shown he cared before.'

'There you are. He's going in the right direction. It might be slow, hard work, but it will all be worth it in the end.'

'Yes. I have to believe that, otherwise I won't be able to keep going.'

'Changing the subject, how are you feeling about going back to church?'

'We've been reading the book Ivor gave us. We read it together before we go to sleep, but we haven't really discussed it. We must, though, and soon.'

Their last day before travelling home was to be a Sunday. Dominic had been going to church with his parents in Tours. Sophie, not being a French-speaker, had been staying at home on Sunday mornings and enjoying the garden with Henry. Harriet and Ivor had bought a small blow-up paddling pool for Henry to play in. Sophie sat on a garden bench, under a tree, and watched him pouring water from one bucket into another.

'Dear God,' she said, 'please help us to know what to do next. And please help us to both think the same thing. Amen.'

She broached the subject with Dominic after they had put Henry to bed that night. The cases were almost packed, ready for an early start the next morning.

'Have you had any thoughts about the future?' she asked.

'I have,' said Dominic. 'That book on Elijah has inspired me.'

'How do you mean?'

'Well, Elijah worked hard for God and the book of James reminds us that what God did through Elijah, He can do through anybody. But Elijah felt useless sometimes too, just like we do.' Dominic smiled. 'At one point, he also wanted to jack it all in when he felt everything was against him and nobody was interested in God. He felt he was the only faithful one left. He felt abandoned. And what did God do with him when he felt like that?'

'God cared for him gently, met with him and calmly reassured him that He was still in control. Then He told Elijah it was time to go back and continue doing the work God had called him to. So, what do you think?'

'I think,' said Dominic, 'we have to go back and get on with it, like Elijah did.'

Sophie felt relieved. 'I think so too. It isn't easy, but maybe… maybe we've been through a bad patch, like Elijah. I don't think things can get any worse, so maybe things are going to get better now, for us. Onwards and upwards?'

The following morning Ivor and Harriet took Sophie, Dominic and Henry to the station and, after many thanks and tearful goodbyes, they began the long journey back to Oxley.

'Onwards and upwards,' said Dominic.

'Onwards and upwards,' repeated Sophie.

'Onwards and upwards,' echoed Henry.

Seventeen

Robert was waiting at Stafford station when the tired and travel-weary family arrived that Monday evening.

'Welcome home! Catherine has prepared a meal for us all at our house, if you would like to join us. I'll drop you straight home with your luggage after we've eaten.'

'Thank you, that would be lovely,' said Dominic appreciatively.

Soon they were sitting round the table in Robert and Catherine's kitchen, enjoying shepherd's pie. Catherine put a couple of cushions under Henry and sandwiched him between Dominic and Robert so that he couldn't escape from the table, but he was hungry and seemed happy to sit and eat with everyone else.

'Thank you so much,' said Dominic, addressing Robert and Catherine. 'Not just for picking us up and feeding us, but for looking after the church while we were away. How have things been?'

'Fine, fine,' replied Robert. 'That new couple with the baby – Melissa and Daniel – they've been coming along. He's still got a lot of questions, though. It might be an idea to think about running some sort of seekers' course at some point, Dominic. Maybe iron out some of those tricky questions. You know the ones – how do you know the Bible's reliable? Why did Jesus have to die? Why does God allow suffering? All the classics.'

'Yes, it would be great to run a course like that. Everyone else OK?'

'Shirley and Clive came back from their holiday with Lucy. Poor Lucy still seems very melancholy. Anyway, what about you? Did you have a lovely holiday?'

'Yes, we did, thank you.'

'I think, from the conversation we have had so far, I know the answer to the next question,' said Catherine. 'But have you thought any more about the future?'

'Yes,' said Dominic, looking at Sophie for agreement. 'We aren't going to give up; not yet, anyway. We know we need to carry on with the work at All Saints for the time being.'

'Excellent,' said Robert, smiling. 'You just needed to step away from things for a bit, get a bit of perspective. Now, I don't wish to be rude, but let's get you home.'

The next morning dawned bright and clear, with the promise of a hot day. Dominic got up early and went down to the study to start working his way through the answerphone messages and emails that had come in while they had been away.

Sophie, with Henry 'helping', began unpacking the cases and loading the washing machine. 'It's such a nice day,' she said, when Dominic came into the kitchen for a glass of water, 'I think I'll get the laundry washed and dried while the sun's out. Maybe Henry and I could go shopping after lunch and spend a bit of time in the play park on the way.'

'Good plan,' said Dominic. 'Do you know, I've got more than 300 emails in my inbox? So far, I've had two wedding requests, one funeral request, although I know Robert dealt with that, and a request for a burial of ashes from a funeral I did last year. School are asking about dates for assemblies this term and, believe it or not, in 80 degrees of heat, Mrs Fowler-Watt is asking about the Christmas services.'

'Come on, Henry,' said Sophie. 'Let's go outside and hang some washing on the line.'

After lunch, Sophie and Henry walked towards the middle of the village. The new school term had just begun and the play park was quiet. Henry had a go on the swings and the slide and then Sophie coaxed him back into the pushchair, in order to shop for a few provisions to tide them over until she could get to the supermarket in town the next day. They were just passing the pharmacy when the door opened and Paul came out.

'Paul! Not at work today? How's Hayley? Can't be long now.'

'Hi, Sophie. Actually, Hayley had the baby last week! A girl! She was three weeks early, but all OK. We're calling her Alice. I'm on paternity leave at the moment.'

'Congratulations! Maybe I could call round sometime?'

'Yes, definitely. You're very welcome to drop in any time.' He rushed off, clutching what looked like a packet of disposable nappies.

As Sophie was walking home, the shopping loaded under the pushchair, she thought about Hayley and her new baby. She felt slightly hurt that she hadn't received a message from Hayley herself, to tell her that the baby had arrived. Then, maybe she was being unreasonable. Hayley must be very busy, after all. She decided that she would buy a gift for the baby when she went into town tomorrow, then she could ring and ask when it would be convenient to call round.

The other thing Sophie wanted to do, now she was back home, was to catch up with Lucy. However, she knew that Lucy would be at work, so she decided to call her that evening and arrange a time to meet up.

Sophie visited Lucy on Friday evening after tea, leaving Dominic to put Henry to bed. They chatted for a while about their holidays.

'Harriet helped me remember that there are reasons why Henry is as Henry is,' Sophie told her friend. 'He can't help it. I can also see that he is improving, slowly. He might never be quite like his peer group, but he's going in the right direction, at his own pace. As long as I can see progress, I know I can keep going and it will all be worth it.

'Robert and Catherine were very good to cover us for three weeks. They said Melissa and Daniel are still coming to church with the baby. And I expect you already know that Hayley has had her baby too?'

'Really?' said Lucy, sounding surprised. 'No, I didn't. I didn't think it was due yet. When did she have it? Is everything all right?'

'While we were away. I bumped into Paul coming out of the pharmacy on Tuesday, otherwise I wouldn't have known either. She had a girl and they've called her Alice. She was three weeks early but everything is fine, apparently. I'm going to visit tomorrow. Dominic's going to mind Henry for an hour. Why don't you come with me?'

'Wow, great news. I'm kind of surprised she didn't let us know, though. Let's be honest, she didn't really talk about anything else before the baby was born, did she? I thought she would be shouting it from the rooftops.'

'I suppose she's been a bit preoccupied. Anyway, how are you doing, Lucy?'

'Not great. But I'm managing to keep going, you know; I've got a job to do and all that. I get up in the morning and go to work and get on with it. But, if I'm honest, I feel absolutely awful and I can't imagine ever feeling better. I love Rufus and I don't know how to make that stop.'

'I'm so sorry. Have you heard from him?'

'No,' Lucy replied, resignedly. 'Rufus is very much a businessman. He tried me out; it didn't work. I'm sure he's put me behind him. He's probably already got his eye on someone else.'

'I'm sure that's not true. He wouldn't be able to forget you so quickly. Anyway, who says he's going to find someone else?'

'I think Rufus is the sort of person who gets what he wants in life.'

'Well, perhaps that's not a very good attitude.'

'Maybe not, but it's part of his upbringing. His parents expect him to do very well in his career, to marry the right person, who won't be like me, and probably present them with the perfect grandchildren. I would never have been good enough.'

'But is that really what you would have wanted? To be part of all that?'

'Not really. I know his family wouldn't have approved of me. They didn't even want to meet me when I was his girlfriend. But I think I would have put up with it all, put up with their disapproval, because I loved him so much. It's just that I would have wanted Rufus to have been on my side. I mean, I could have put up with his family's disapproval if he had backed me up, but he didn't really.'

'He didn't do much for your confidence.'

'No,' said Lucy, after a pause, 'he didn't. He was so desperate to make me into the person he thought I should be, the person his family would have approved of, the person who would have helped him move in the direction they expected him to move in, he almost ended up trying to bully me into being more confident. And it had the opposite effect. I couldn't be good enough for Rufus. He knows all this stuff about art and antiques and things that I'm not very good at. Even when we went to the zoo he seemed to know everything there was to know about every animal there. I think he thought I was a bit stupid.'

'What about all the things you know about – bones and muscles and nerves? I bet Rufus doesn't know the things you know, does he?'

'We didn't really talk about the things I know about. Anyway, we were walking along near the river, the day he told me he didn't want to see me any more. He pointed to a tree and asked me what it was. I said it was a weeping willow and he said, "Oh, well, I didn't think you would know that."'

Sophie frowned. 'Lucy,' she said, 'in the first place, thinking you wouldn't know something you did know makes *him* look stupid. But, in the second place, it's a tree; it doesn't matter – it's just a tree.'

Lucy thought for a moment. 'I see what you mean. It really doesn't matter, does it?'

'Really, really not! Who cares if it's a weeping willow or an oak? What really matters isn't what you know, it's the type of person you are, the choices you make in life, where your priorities are, your attitude towards God and other people. That's what matters!'

'You're right,' Lucy considered. 'Maybe I started to lose sight of that for a little while.'

'Keep God in his rightful place in your life and everything else will be governed by that. If God's in charge, you won't go wrong.'

'I do try to do that, but I guess it's a constant challenge for all of us. I worry for Rufus, though. Sometimes it felt as if God wasn't always in charge in his life. Sometimes it felt like it was his mother in charge and sometimes it was his career, but I wonder if even that was really a symptom of his parents' priorities.'

'He wasn't the right man for you really, was he?'

'Perhaps not. I thought he was and I loved him… still love him. I prayed for the right man and I thought Rufus was the answer to my prayers, but maybe he wasn't. The bit I don't understand is why God let me meet him in the first place, or why God let him ask me out, if he wasn't the right one.'

'I think a lot of it has to do with free will, but we can't see things from God's perspective. It may be that meeting you was something Rufus needed to do.'

Lucy shrugged. 'I hope he finds a good church in Maidenhead. I hope he doesn't let go of God, but what can I do about that?'

'It's between him and God. All you can do is pray for him.'

'I will,' said Lucy. 'I do.'

The following morning Sophie and Lucy arrived outside Hayley and Paul's flat. A harassed-looking Paul opened the door.

'Welcome,' he said. 'Do come in. Hayley and Alice are in the living room. I've just got to go out shopping again. I'm back to work next week and Hayley has given me another list of things she needs.'

'I can go shopping for you later, if you like,' Lucy offered. 'I don't have much else to do on a Saturday these days.'

'It's OK, Hayley has me running in and out all day,' he laughed. 'Alice absorbs her every waking moment, so I need to have everything organised around the house ready for when I'm not here.'

Hayley was sitting on the sofa with her feet up, holding the sleeping baby, her arms supported with cushions. She looked up proudly as Sophie and Lucy entered the room.

'Hello! Thank you for coming to visit us. This is Alice,' she said, smiling with delight. Sophie and Lucy sat down either side of Hayley, each placing her wrapped gift on the table.

'She's beautiful,' whispered Sophie, looking at the tiny baby sleeping contentedly in Hayley's arms. She was very pale and fragile-looking, with a downy layer of copper-coloured hair on her head.

'She is lovely,' agreed Lucy. 'How are you feeling, Hayley?'

'I'm tired,' replied Hayley, 'but really happy that Alice is here safely. She came a bit early and they kept quite a close eye on her for the first twenty-four hours, but she was fine and we came home the next day. Mum and Dad and Paul's parents have been brilliant. Chloe is in Florida. She was supposed to be back before Alice was born, but Alice was actually born just before she went, so she has seen her.'

They talked for a while about Hayley and Paul's first couple of weeks as parents. It sounded as though Hayley had kept Paul on his toes, washing, ironing, cleaning and running to the shops and back several times a day. Sophie was pleased that Hayley didn't give them a blow-by-blow account of the birth. She didn't want any excuse to open the secret box in her head, with all her sad baby feelings locked inside, just at that moment.

After a little while, Lucy asked, 'May I hold her?'

'Oh…' Hayley hesitated for a moment, then nodded. 'Yes, of course.'

She placed Alice carefully in Lucy's arms. Sophie couldn't help noticing that Lucy looked very contented holding the baby. She hoped that she would find someone with whom she might have one of her own one day. Hayley, however, seemed to be hovering on the edge of her seat, ready to take Alice back. Sophie felt that she hadn't really wanted to let the baby out of her own arms. Lucy appeared to be thinking along the same lines. She gave Alice back. 'Thank you,' she said.

Sophie didn't like to ask if she could hold Alice herself. Then she thought about Dominic, looking after Henry. She knew he had a lot to do, to be ready for Sunday morning. Time to leave.

At that moment, they heard the front door open and Paul reappeared in the doorway.

'We're just going,' Sophie told him.

'Oh, OK,' said Paul. 'Do come again. You could bring Dominic next time.'

'Yes, I'm sure he would love to meet Alice.' Sophie added, hopefully, 'I think there are a lot of people at church who would like to meet her. Why don't you bring her along in the morning?'

'Oh,' gasped Hayley, looking slightly alarmed. 'Well, I'm sure we will at some point. Maybe we're not quite ready yet. But you could bring Dominic round tomorrow afternoon, after church, if you like. And Henry, of course. It would be nice to see Dominic while Paul is here, before he goes back to work next week.'

'OK, thanks,' said Sophie, a little taken aback by Hayley's response. 'I can't think that he's got anything specific in his diary for tomorrow afternoon. I'm sure he would love to come.'

The following morning, in Maidenhead, Rufus left his hotel room with a wrapped parcel under his arm. He wasn't off to church. In truth, he hadn't got around to finding a church in Maidenhead as work had preoccupied him. Rufus had something else on his mind. There was something he needed to

212

do. He got into his sleek, black car and started the engine, the parcel on the passenger seat beside him. In two and a half hours he would be in Oxley. He would just have to be careful not to be seen.

Eighteen

After Sunday lunch at the vicarage, Dominic, Sophie and Henry set out towards Hayley and Paul's flat. They had planned to spend half an hour in the play park on the way, in order to let Henry run off a bit of energy before going to see the baby.

Paul, meanwhile, was being sent out on another errand. 'Pop out and buy a cake,' said Hayley. 'It's nice to have something to offer visitors when they come.'

'Right you are,' said Paul, putting his shoes on for the third time that day and closing the door behind him. He went down the stairs and out of the door, crossed the garden and the car park and walked towards the road. He didn't notice the black car parked in one of the spaces marked for visitors.

The driver was watching him from behind a newspaper. When he was certain Paul had walked away, he got out of the car and walked quickly into the block of flats and up the stairs. He knocked on the door.

Hayley looked at her watch. She hadn't expected Dominic and Sophie for another half an hour or so. She lifted the sleeping Alice on to her shoulder and went to open the door, so focused on not waking the baby that she didn't check the spyhole.

'Hello,' she began, then she stopped. Her blood ran cold. 'What are you doing here?'

'You said I could see her. We agreed.'

Hayley felt weak as the shock of seeing him again washed over her. She tried to recover her composure.

'Yes, I know,' she whispered, 'but Paul is here. You promised… you said you didn't want to rock the boat.'

'Paul isn't here. I've just seen him walk away. Let me come in, I won't stay long. Hayley, you promised.'

She had no choice. She stepped aside to let him into the flat and closed the door behind him. 'Go through,' she said, 'but you can only stay for a few minutes. Paul's only popped out and we're expecting visitors.'

'Let me see her. I want to hold her. What's her name?'

'Sit down, then,' said Hayley, crossly. 'She's called Alice.' She shuddered as she laid Alice in his arms. It repulsed her to do so.

'Alice,' he repeated, gazing down at her. For a few minutes they sat in silence. 'A cup of tea wouldn't go amiss.'

'You said you wouldn't be staying.'

'Don't worry. It's not as if Paul doesn't know me – we've worked together, don't forget. If he comes back, he won't think it strange that I'm here. Anyway, I brought Alice a gift.' He put one hand into his jacket pocket and pulled out a small, wrapped parcel. It was the size and shape of a box that might contain a piece of jewellery. He held it out towards Hayley.

Hayley hesitated before taking the box from his hand. 'Thank you,' she murmured, but she didn't feel very thankful. She didn't want to accept anything from this man. She didn't want to feel under any obligation to him; she wanted him out of her life. She unwrapped it and opened the box. Inside lay a gold bracelet, the size that would fit an adult woman. It was inlaid with jewels – diamonds, rubies and sapphires. A prickling sensation started at the back of Hayley's neck and spread along her arms, then down the backs of her legs. 'I can't accept this.'

'Why? Don't you like it?'

Hayley took a deep breath. 'It's beautiful, but it looks very expensive.'

'My mother gave it to me. It's a family heirloom and I want Alice to have it, because she's my daughter.'

Hayley gritted her teeth. How dare he speak those hateful words? She tried to breathe normally and then spoke slowly. 'And how do you think I'm going to explain it to Paul?'

'Paul doesn't have to know. I wanted to give her something special from me. There's precious little else I can give her and it's for when she's older. Just hide it somewhere for now. How about that cup of tea?'

Hayley felt she had little choice. Reluctantly, she went into the bedroom she shared with Paul and pushed the box into her bedside drawer. She would have to decide what to do with it later. She went into the kitchen, meaning to switch the kettle on, but she heard movement from the living room. She returned swiftly, but there was nobody there. For a few seconds she felt panic rising, then she heard another noise, this time from the balcony.

'What are you doing? Why are you out there?'

'OK, OK, I'll sit down.' He walked back through the open patio door and sat down on the sofa again, Alice still in his arms. 'Kettle boiled?'

Against her will, Hayley returned to the kitchen. She hadn't actually switched the kettle on previously, so she did so. Then she made a decision. Returning to the bedroom, she retrieved the bracelet from her drawer and took it back to the kitchen. There was no time like the present and she didn't want to be caught out. Opening the bin, she pushed the box down underneath the rubbish. An heirloom it may be, but it would never be seen again. As she willed the kettle to boil, she absentmindedly opened the kitchen drawer and took out a knife. She began twisting it round and round in her fingers.

She was startled by another noise from the living room and became aware of what she was doing. She opened the drawer again and put the knife back. Alice had woken and was beginning to cry. Returning to the living room, Hayley took Alice into her own arms. Thankfully he didn't object and Hayley calmed slightly.

'I was thinking,' he said, 'maybe I could just visit from time to time. I could come over when Paul's at work. He wouldn't know. Alice needn't know I'm her real father – I can just be a friend who visits sometimes. Like a friend of the family.'

Hayley became aware of a throbbing in her temple. This wasn't going to plan at all. 'No,' she insisted. 'I agreed to let you see her once. There's too much that could go wrong. It's too much of a risk.' She wanted nothing more than to get him as far away from her baby as possible. 'It would never work. When Alice gets older, she could say something to Paul. How could you possibly make such a ridiculous suggestion? It's insane.' Alice was quietening down. She didn't want him to take her back out of her arms. 'Now, I need to put Alice down for her sleep.'

'Hayley, we need to talk.'

Hayley's panic was now beyond measure. The throbbing in her temple increased and became a tight band around her head. She wanted to cry, but she knew that controlling her emotions was of paramount importance. She needed to deal with this quickly. She didn't want her husband to find this odious man in her home when he came back. She needed to move her baby away from him fast. 'I have to put Alice in her cot. Go out onto the balcony,' she told him, thinking quickly. 'See if Paul is coming.'

'Hayley, she's my family,' he said, helplessly.

Hayley carried Alice into the nursery, opening the door with her elbow and leaning down to put her into the cot. She stroked her downy head and tried to think, but fear overcame her and jumbled the thoughts in her head. The threat to her happiness was becoming intolerable. He had forced her to agree to let him see Alice once. Well, he had seen her now and enough was enough. The thing that was threatening to ruin her happy family, her marriage and her child's secure future was getting out of control. Alice drifted off to sleep and Hayley straightened up. She would shut the nursery door, go back to the living room and tell him to leave.

A noise came from behind her. She turned, then let out a high-pitched squeal. He had been standing behind her – close behind her. He must have followed her silently into the nursery.

At the sound of Hayley's squeal, Alice startled and began to cry loudly. Hayley scooped her up from the cot and held her protectively to her chest.

'You've made her cry. Let me settle her – I can do it,' he said.

'No, she needs her mother.'

'She's my child too. I'm her father, I can look after her.'

'No, go away. It's time for you to leave.'

'Don't take my only child away from me. It's not fair. Can't you understand? I've got nothing left! My mother's dead, I've lost my job and now you're denying me my only child.'

'No! No, David, no.' He was still standing uncomfortably close to her.

'She's my daughter, be reasonable. I should be allowed to see her, to buy her gifts, to take her out when she's a bit older. It can all be done without Paul finding out. I'm starting a new job in Shrewsbury next week – not that it's a job I want, but I haven't got much choice. I don't even work with Paul any more.'

'No! No, that's not the way it's going to be! I agreed to what you asked. You said you wanted to see her once. You've seen her, now get out!'

Hayley watched David's anger burn. The muscles tightened in his reddening face and he clenched his jaw. For a moment they both stood still, Alice's cries filling the room. Then, with a swift movement, David grabbed the baby from her arms and ran from the room, across the hall, into the living room and out onto the balcony, Hayley fast behind him. He stopped at the edge of the balcony and turned to face her, Alice screaming in his arms.

'How dare you speak to me like that!' he shouted. 'You used me. You knew, didn't you, at the Christmas party, that you couldn't have children with Paul? He got drunk and you came into my room at the hotel and you used me to get pregnant, to solve a problem, to get what you wanted. Well, you got what you wanted, but she's mine too. Now, I've been reasonable, but if you won't agree to my terms, I'll make this public. I'll take you to court and I'll force you to get a paternity test for Alice. I want access to my child!'

Hayley stood in front of the patio doors, facing him, the table between them and the sun in her eyes. She became aware that she was perspiring uncomfortably. A sudden breeze caused the leaves on the rose tree Hayley had placed on the chair to rustle. David glanced towards it. He had a frenzied look about him and beads of sweat were forming on his forehead.

Hayley was no longer aware of the piercing pain in her head. She no longer cared that Paul might come home to find David in the flat. At that moment, all she cared about was taking Alice away from David. She took a step sideways in order to move around the table. David took a step in the opposite direction, towards the chair and the rose tree. She took another step and so did he. Like boxers in a ring, they circled each other.

'David...' she tried to speak calmly. She could feel sweat trickling down her back.

'How would you feel, Hayley, if you were me?' He took another step sideways. 'How would you feel if someone took Alice away from you?' With one swift movement, he kicked the rose tree off the chair. The pot crashed to the ground, smashing into pieces as a wave of earth spilled out across the balcony. 'How about this, Hayley? If I can't have her, then neither can you!' He stepped onto the chair. It creaked under him.

'No!'

'I've lost everything dear to me and I've got nothing left to live for. Now you are going to lose what is dear to you. You're a deceitful, selfish woman! You care only for yourself and you deserve nothing better. This is your punishment, Hayley!' He suddenly turned and held Alice over the edge of the balcony.

Hayley screamed. 'Please, no, please, David, don't do it! Please, please, don't hurt our little girl. I'll give you whatever you want!' The chair leg made a grating sound. 'Please, David, you don't really want to hurt her. She's your daughter, your baby, you love her.' She held her arms out towards him, imploringly, her breathing coming in short, quick breaths. 'Please give Alice back to me and let me keep her safe. Please don't hurt her, she's just a baby, she hasn't done anything wrong.'

'Why should I? I've got nothing left to lose. I'm going down and I'm taking her with me.'

'You can have whatever you want! You can see her. I'll tell Paul the truth – just please, please, don't hurt her. Please give her back to me. David, if you care about her, you'll give her back to me.'

As he looked at Hayley, the chair made a creaking sound. He looked at Alice, then back to Hayley. Slowly he placed Alice into Hayley's outstretched arms. Hayley pulled Alice towards her and stepped back towards the patio doors. 'Now get down from the chair, David. Come inside and we can talk.'

The chair gave another creak. David didn't move. Then, with a crash, the leg splintered and the chair collapsed backwards, tipping David back over the edge of the balcony. He shrieked, but managed to catch hold of the bottom of the balcony. He looked up, their eyes met, but Hayley didn't move. Seconds passed.

'Hayley! Help me!' he begged. Still she didn't move. 'Hayley, please!'

Holding Alice, Hayley walked slowly to the edge of the balcony. She made her decision. Reaching her foot under the edge of the railing, she pressed her shoe down hard onto David's fingers. There was another shriek and a sickening thud.

Suddenly she heard footsteps behind her. Hayley turned, still clutching Alice, to see Paul.

Nineteen

As Sophie, Dominic and Henry prepared to leave the play park they heard sirens approaching from behind. In the space of a few minutes an ambulance and two police cars went past.

'That can't be good news,' remarked Sophie, grimly.

They walked on towards Paul and Hayley's block of flats. As they rounded the corner, the sight that met their eyes at first alarmed then terrified them. The ambulance and police cars had taken over the car park. They were met by a young policeman who had seen them coming and had started running towards them.

'Please could I ask you to step back and keep the area clear?'

'But, that's our friends' flat,' said Sophie, pointing up to the third floor. 'There are people on the balcony. What's going on?'

'I'm afraid there's been an accident. If you could just wait where you are, I'll get someone to come and speak to you.'

After a little while, Paul appeared and was escorted by a policeman into the back of a police car. The policeman who had approached them previously then reappeared, and Dominic called to him.

'We know that man. Is he OK?'

'I'm terribly sorry,' said the policeman, 'but this is going to be very bad news.'

Briefly, but kindly, the policeman explained to them that there appeared to have been some sort of accident involving a man falling from the balcony and losing his life. 'Paul

McDurney is going to come to the station to answer some questions. The man who died appears to have been one of his work colleagues, a man by the name of David Stubbs.'

'What about Hayley and Alice, their baby? Are they OK?' stammered Sophie.

'Mrs McDurney is being treated by the paramedics for shock. Then we'll need to talk to her too, as she is a witness. The baby is fine. I really am very sorry to have to give you this news, but there is nothing you can do here at the moment. It would be best if you went home.' He looked down at Henry. 'This isn't the right place for a child just now.'

'Please could you tell them that we're here for them if they need us?' The gesture seemed rather futile in the circumstances, thought Sophie, but she didn't know what else they could say.

'I will,' said the policeman. 'May I just ask your names?'

Dominic spoke. 'Dominic and Sophie. I'm the local vicar. Hayley McDurney is a member of our church.'

'Right you are. I'm sorry to have to move you along but, as you can see, we're trying to seal off the area.'

Numb with shock, Dominic and Sophie began to move away. The whole thing had a sense of unreality about it. They both felt there was something they should be doing to help.

The walk back to the vicarage passed in a blur. Finally, Dominic opened the front door and they went inside. There was a rather stuffed-looking brown paper package on the doormat. Dominic wondered how it had fitted through the letterbox. He picked it up before Henry could get to it and threw it into the study, shutting the door. 'I'll make us a cup of tea,' he said.

Sophie removed Henry's shoes and took him into the living room. She opened the toy box and switched on the television, finding the children's channel, praying that Henry would entertain himself while they pulled themselves together. She could feel her mobile buzzing in her pocket. Taking it out, she looked at the screen. There was a message from Hayley: 'I know you came. Please get people to pray. Paul's been arrested.' Sophie felt a wave of nausea surge over her.

Dominic came in with two cups of tea. 'It just got a bit worse,' Sophie told him, as she showed him the screen. 'If he's been arrested... Do you think... You don't think he pushed...?' She couldn't finish the sentence.

'I think we need to let people know,' Dominic said, 'and then I need to open up the church in case people need to come and talk and pray. Hayley has told us he's been arrested and she's asked us to get people to pray, that's all we know, but that's what we have to do.'

'Yes... yes, you're right,' said Sophie. 'Why don't you ring Robert and Catherine first? You probably ought to ring Geoffrey and Audrey too, being as he's churchwarden. When you've done that, I'll call Lucy. The word will soon get out. We can open up the church room, make cups of tea and just give people a space to come and pray and support each other. But, Dominic...'

'Yes?'

'Please could you pray with me first?'

Dominic did as she asked, made some phone calls and then went over to church. Soon people began to appear. Audrey, Geoffrey, Robert, Catherine, Lucy, Shirley and Clive were among the first to arrive. Mike and Sarah came in soon after them. After a while, Lucy came back from the church and offered to mind Henry so that Sophie could go too.

By nine o'clock the church had finally emptied. Dominic locked up and walked back to the vicarage.

'I've never felt so tired in all my life,' he said, as he sat down on the sofa. Then the house phone rang and he got up again to answer it.

'That was the policeman we were talking to earlier,' he said, when he came back. 'He said that Paul is still with them. Hayley is going to be staying at her sister's flat for the time being.'

'Oh, yes, I know where that is – it's in Lucy's block. Chloe's away on holiday at the moment, but Hayley has a spare key.'

'Well, Hayley's mum and dad are with her. Her mum is going to stay with her overnight, but she has asked if you would go and see her tomorrow afternoon.'

'Oh… Dominic… What on earth am I going to say?'

The following morning Sophie and Dominic were awakened by the phone ringing. Dominic sprang out of bed and rushed down the stairs to answer it. Sophie sat up and looked at the clock on her bedside table, memories of the previous day flooding into her consciousness. To her surprise it was eight o'clock. Sophie got out of bed and went to Henry's room. A few minutes later she was lifting him into the highchair in the kitchen when Dominic came out of the study. Stepping over the safety gate easily, he sat down at the kitchen table.

'That was Robert, just ringing to see if there was any news. He said he was sorry to ring early, but he knew I'd be up! I didn't like to say he'd woken us, but I can't believe we slept so late. I didn't think we'd sleep at all after yesterday.'

'Neither did I, but I think we must have both been emotionally exhausted. What about Henry? He hasn't slept until eight o'clock since… well, ever. Anyway, what did you say?'

'I said Hayley's mum had been with her overnight and that you were seeing her this afternoon. Then I said that I presumed Paul was still at the police station, but we don't actually know.'

'Shall I send her a message? Hopefully she'll just answer when she can. I can ask her what time I should come over this afternoon.'

'Good idea.'

Sophie fished her phone out of her dressing gown pocket and sent Hayley a message. Hayley replied very quickly.

'She says Paul is still at the police station and she will let us know if that changes. She asked me to go at two o'clock.'

Robert's call was the first of many that morning, and Dominic and Sophie spent all morning juggling answering the phone with looking after Henry and trying to get dressed. Sophie was feeling very anxious about what she would say to Hayley. What if Paul had...? She couldn't bear to consider the possibility. At least the busyness of the morning might stop her having to think too much about it but, as time wore on, she realised that her stress levels were getting higher. By lunchtime, she was barely able to swallow. She forced down a couple of biscuits and a cup of tea and then put her shoes on. 'Maybe the walk will help,' she said, hopefully, as she left the house.

The walk didn't help. By the time Sophie reached the middle of the village, she had started to feel dizzy. Spotting a wooden bench on the green near the play park, she dropped down onto it, leaned forwards and lowered her head into her hands. The last thing she wanted to do right now was pass out. Moments later, she became aware of someone sitting next to her and putting a hand on her shoulder.

'Sophie?' Audrey's voice.

Somebody else sat down on her other side. 'Where's Henry?'

Great, thought Sophie. Audrey and Geoffrey! What excellent timing! They were probably wondering why she wasn't looking after Henry and whether she had left him with Dominic when he should be working. Then she remembered that Monday was supposed to be their day off, so Audrey and Geoffrey couldn't really say anything. 'Henry's with Dominic. Hayley asked me to go to see her. But...'

'Are you feeling all right?' asked Audrey, kindly.

'I just came over a bit dizzy and I needed to sit down.'

'Would you like me to go and get the car and drive you home?' offered Geoffrey.

Sophie was slightly taken aback. 'Thank you, but I'm supposed to be seeing Hayley at two o'clock. She's staying at her sister's.'

'Ah,' said Audrey. 'Well, in that case, it's probably just anxiety. Right, put your hands on your tummy and breathe in slowly and deeply through your nose... that's it, very good. Now, relax your shoulders and blow the air out slowly through

225

your mouth. Excellent. Now, keep doing that for a few minutes and you'll start to feel better.'

Audrey was right. Gradually the dizziness passed and Sophie sat up. 'Thank you.' She looked at her watch. 'I'd better go.'

'Geoffrey and I will walk with you, but we won't come in. I'm sure she doesn't want to see… well, anyone other than you at the moment.'

'I don't know what I'm going to say,' Sophie blurted out.

'You'll be fine. I'm sure you'll think of something,' said Audrey.

Slowly they walked towards Chloe's block of flats. Audrey and Geoffrey kept Sophie talking as they walked. She could tell they were trying to keep her from hyperventilating again and she was grateful.

'Are Dominic and Henry well?' asked Geoffrey, as they rounded the corner and walked towards the entrance to the flats.

'Yes, although the phone's been ringing all morning. Henry doesn't like it when the phone rings, but I had to leave Dominic with Henry and the phone, so I could come here.'

'We know Henry can be difficult, but you are doing very well with him,' said Audrey.

Geoffrey nodded in agreement. 'Now, off you go. Don't hesitate; just go in.'

'Thanks, you really helped,' said Sophie, honestly. She turned and did as Audrey had instructed, walked straight up the stairs and knocked on the door.

Twenty

As Hayley opened the door, Sophie was taken aback by her appearance. Normally immaculately turned out, Hayley's face was pale and blotchy and she had dark circles around her eyes. Her hair was pulled back roughly into a ponytail. Hayley took one look at Sophie and burst into tears.

Going in, Sophie closed the door behind her and put her arms around her friend. She still didn't know what to say to her, but she found it didn't matter. After a few moments she took Hayley by the hand, led her into the small living room and sat down with her on Chloe's sofa. Tears were streaming down both their faces and Sophie pulled a box of tissues on the coffee table towards them, taking some for herself and offering them to Hayley.

'Thanks. Everyone's being so kind.'

'Is your mum here?'

'No, she went home half an hour ago. She stayed with me all night, but she didn't sleep, so she's gone home, and Dad's coming over later to stay with me tonight. They don't seem to want to leave me on my own, so they're working out some sort of rota. Chloe is supposed to be coming home tomorrow night, but Paul should be back by then, shouldn't he?' Sophie didn't answer. 'I mean, they can't keep him indefinitely.'

'Hayley, everyone's so sorry that this has happened to you. Everyone's praying and the phone hasn't stopped ringing because people are worried about you. Is Alice OK?'

'Yes, she's asleep in the travel cot, in the bedroom.' Hayley started crying again. 'Everyone's being kind and I don't deserve it.'

'Why don't you deserve it? You didn't do anything wrong. Do you know what happened?' The question hung in the air.'

'Sophie, I *did* do something wrong.' Hayley stopped crying and took a deep, shuddering breath. 'I did something really wrong and I don't know if Paul will ever forgive me. Everyone will think I'm a terrible person and everyone is going to know.'

'I'm sure you can't have done anything that bad.'

'I have, Sophie. I've done something terrible and I must tell you.'

Bit by bit, Hayley told Sophie her story, starting from the night of the Christmas party. It seemed to take an age for Hayley to put each part of the story into words. 'I kept telling myself that everything would be all right as long as Paul didn't find out what I'd done. David was just as ashamed as I was... at least, he said he was. He said he wanted to keep it a secret. I know I've been completely stupid and utterly selfish. I even managed to convince myself that this was God's way of giving me a baby. But then David turned up yesterday afternoon. He'd obviously been waiting for Paul to leave the flat. He started threatening me that he would tell Paul everything if I didn't let him see Alice. He was talking about wanting to take her out and buy her presents. Then, when I said no, he got mad and took her and stood on a chair on the balcony, as if he was going to throw her down.'

'Oh, how awful. You must have been terrified.'

'It was terrible, but I managed to stay calm. I said we could work something out. Then he gave her to me, but the chair collapsed and he fell over the balcony. It was just an accident.'

'But then why have the police arrested Paul?'

'He came back across the car park to see David standing on the chair at the edge of the balcony, holding Alice over the edge. He ran up the stairs as fast as he could, but by the time he got here, David had given Alice back to me and then fallen. Paul looked down and could see he was dead…' Again, they paused for a fresh wave of tears.

'Paul told me not to look. Then he called the police and they came really quickly. I told them about the accident, but then Mrs Solomons next door came round. She's so nosy. She can't see our balcony from hers, but she can hear everything. She's always eavesdropping. She had heard David shouting at me and saying I'd used him to get pregnant and then she had seen Paul running across the car park to come up the stairs. She said she'd heard David shout, "Hayley, help me," because that's what he shouted when the chair started wobbling. She told the police that, but then the police decided that Paul must have pushed him, in a fit of rage or jealousy, because he was calling out to me for help… But Paul didn't do anything. It was just an accident – the chair collapsed and he fell. And now our flat is a crime scene, so I've come here. Chloe won't mind. Mum and Dad thought it best I didn't go to stay with them, because they're trying to keep this from Grandma and Grandad until Paul comes home.'

For a little while, they both sat in silence, weeping. Eventually, Sophie broke the silence. 'Hayley, I'm not going to deny that what you did with David was wrong. God can forgive anything, but I have no idea how Paul is going to react when you see him. What I do know is that Paul didn't deserve any of this. We must pray for the police to let him go, for them to know the truth.'

'Yes, I do need people to pray. Sophie, please can you tell Dominic about David and Alice? I know he thinks Alice was an answer to prayer, but he's going to have to find out what really happened at some point. And tell Lucy, because she's my friend, but please don't tell anyone else yet. I know I won't be able to hide it for much longer, but just Dominic and Lucy at the moment.'

'OK, I will. But first I'm going to pray with you now, for the police to know the truth, to realise that Paul is innocent and let him come home.'

Just as Sophie said 'Amen', Alice began to cry. Hayley jumped up. 'I need to feed Alice.'

'Would you like me to stay with you until your dad comes, or would you prefer a bit of space?'

'No, you go home… though, actually, could you do something for me?'

'Of course.'

'Please could you pop to the pharmacy and get me some formula milk? I don't feel as if I can face going out and seeing people yet. Anything suitable for newborns.'

'No problem.' Sophie gave Hayley another hug. Alice was still crying. 'You go and see to Alice and I'll see myself out. Send me a message if anything happens, but I don't think the police can hold Paul for very much longer without making a decision one way or the other. There's no reason for them to charge him, apart from what Mrs Solomons said, so we'll just keep praying for them to know the truth.'

'Thanks, Sophie, for everything.'

As Sophie walked down the stairs she acknowledged to herself that she was rather glad that Hayley didn't need her to stay. Her head was throbbing painfully and she suddenly felt so tired that all she wanted to do was get into bed. Then she felt guilty. Poor Hayley must be feeling a hundred times worse. She headed for the pharmacy and bought a packet of baby milk formula, making sure that it was suitable for newborns. As she paid at the counter, it occurred to her that she had been sure that Hayley was breastfeeding Alice. Maybe things changed after a shock, she thought. What did she know about such things, having never had a baby?

Sophie left the pharmacy just as the bus stopped outside. She turned to retrace her steps, back to Chloe's flat, when a familiar figure stepped off the bus.

'Lucy!' she called.

'Hi, Sophie. How're you?'

'Tired. Bad headache, actually.'

'I'm not surprised after yesterday. I found it really hard to concentrate at work today. My last patient cancelled, so I left the clinic early. I normally get the later bus. Any news from Hayley?'

'Let's sit down on the bench for a minute,' said Sophie, leading the way. As briefly as she could, she told Lucy Hayley's story. 'Hayley asked me to tell only you and Dominic for the moment. We need to pray for the truth to come out. Paul is innocent.'

'The police will have to make a decision to either charge him or release him very soon.'

'That's what I thought,' said Sophie, wearily, as she stood up. 'I'm just going to drop this baby milk off for Hayley, so I'll walk back your way.'

'Sophie, you look exhausted. Chloe lives in my block, so I'm virtually passing the door on my way home. I'll take the baby milk. I don't need to go in if she doesn't want me to. I can just tell her I'm still her friend, and that I'm praying for her. You go home.'

'Actually, that would be great, thanks. I'll send her a message to say you're coming and I'll let you know if I hear anything else.'

'Ditto.'

Lucy climbed the stairs to find Hayley waiting in the doorway. 'Come in,' she said, tearfully. Lucy followed her into the living room. 'Sit down, I need to talk to you.'

Lucy sat. 'Hayley, I'm so sorry,' she began. 'Sophie told me everything, about David and the Christmas party and him threatening you and your neighbour hearing everything. Whatever happens, I'll be here for you.'

'Sophie didn't tell you everything...'

'Yes, I saw her coming out of the pharmacy.'

'Sophie didn't tell you everything, because I didn't tell her everything.'

'She didn't... what? What do you mean?'

'Lucy, ten minutes ago I had a phone call from the police station. Paul's been charged with David's murder.'

'What? But he's innocent. No, they can't do that... We'll have to...'

'Lucy, stop talking... Please, stop talking.'

'But...'

'No, stop talking. Lucy, I need to tell the truth. I must tell the truth,' Hayley sobbed. 'It was me. I did it.'

Lucy shrank back from her. It was an involuntary movement, but she knew Hayley had seen it. 'You... pushed him?' Lucy whispered. 'No, surely not, he fell... The chair collapsed...'

'No, I mean, yes, it did, but...'

Lucy's heart was beating very fast. 'It's OK, take your time, breathe.'

Hayley steadied herself a little. 'The chair collapsed and he fell backwards, but he managed to grab hold of the bottom of the balcony. That's when he shouted for help and Mrs Solomons, our neighbour, heard. But I didn't help. I was so frightened and this terrible rage came over me. I looked at him and I felt pure hatred, Lucy. All I could think of was getting rid of him, so I... so I stepped on his fingers, hard, and he let go.' Hayley began crying again. 'I'm a terrible person. The forensic people found David's fingerprints on the floor of the balcony. There were marks with earth on the top of David's fingers. They confronted Paul with that information and he confessed, but it wasn't him – it was me.'

Lucy paused to let the full horror of Hayley's words sink in. 'What are you going to do? What do you want me to do?'

'I can't lie any more, Lucy. I hoped the police would decide it was an accident and no one would have known what really happened. I mean, it wasn't as if it would bring David back. But now I have to tell the truth. I have to call the police and tell them what really happened, before my dad comes. Mum and Dad will know the truth when the police come and take me away, but I don't want my dad to hear me say it. Alice is asleep and I've said goodbye to her, for now.'

'You might be able to take her with you.'

'No. Sophie prayed that the police would know the truth, and that's when I knew that I might not be able to keep up with the lies for much longer. That's why I asked Sophie to buy the baby milk. I'm not taking Alice with me; it isn't right. Paul will be able to come home and look after her.'

'What do you want me to do?'

Hayley's voice suddenly became calm. 'Wait with me while I make the phone call. Then please go and tell Sophie and Dominic the truth, the real truth.'

Sophie was lying on her bed with an ice pack on her head, when Dominic came into the room with a tray.

'I've put Henry to bed and I've brought you something to eat. Do you think you could tell me what happened?'

'Thank you. I do feel a bit better now the paracetamol has kicked in.' She sat up and picked up the plate of reheated food that Dominic had brought her. As she ate, she told Dominic about Hayley and David and the accident. 'I felt so relieved when Hayley said it was an accident and that Paul hadn't done anything wrong. Actually, I was so worried on the way there, I felt a bit ill. I had to sit down on the bench by the park to stop myself from fainting. Then Audrey and Geoffrey turned up. They've both had personality transplants overnight, by the way. They were really kind and walked the rest of the way with me!'

The doorbell rang and Dominic went downstairs to answer it. A moment later, Sophie heard Lucy's voice. She got up and went downstairs herself.

'Lucy, any news?'

'I've got something to tell you. You had better both sit down.'

Twenty-one

The following morning, after very little sleep, Sophie sat at the kitchen table with Henry and his paints. But her heart wasn't in playing with him. She did her best to join in, but her attention kept wandering to the clock on the wall as she waited for Dominic to return from visiting Paul. Paul had taken Alice to stay at his parents' house in the village when he had returned from the police station the previous evening. Dominic had called on him there.

At length, she heard the front door open and Dominic walked into the kitchen, stepping straight over the safety gate as usual, and sank down onto a kitchen chair.

'How was he?' Sophie asked, anxiously. She got up and poured Dominic a cup of coffee as she waited for him to speak.

'In a terrible state, as I'm sure you can imagine. He's going to be allowed to move back home tomorrow and his parents are going to stay with him for a little while, which will help. He knew Hayley had been desperate to have a baby, but he's struggling with the thought of...' Dominic drank his coffee.

'I can't say I blame him... Will he be allowed to keep Alice, if she actually isn't his?'

'No one has suggested otherwise. Most importantly, Hayley's family haven't... Paul's name is on the birth certificate and David had no living relatives. But how Paul will move on from this point, I really don't know.'

'You can't even offer to pray with someone in those circumstances, can you?' Sophie lowered her eyes.

'That's the odd thing, though,' said Dominic. 'Just as I got up to leave, he *did* ask me to pray.'

She looked up, surprised. 'What on earth did you say?'

'First, I prayed in my head that God would give me the words to say. Then I just prayed for peace, protection and a way forward. I'm not sure what else I said. I asked him to stay in touch, but it will be up to me to stay in touch with him. Please pray for him, Sophie. Pray for all of them and for me to know how to help.'

Over the coming weeks Dominic, sometimes accompanied by Sophie, visited Paul as much as he could. They couldn't do anything to change the past, but they could offer friendship and love. There were often tears, and much time was spent just listening to Paul as he felt the need to recount the events leading up to and including that terrible Sunday. Lucy also called on Paul to offer practical help, whenever she could. They all knew that he had not yet been to visit Hayley. So far, Hayley had only allowed her parents to visit her.

David's funeral took place in the middle of October. As David had no religious conviction, it was a short humanist ceremony at the crematorium, attended by a few friends and David's work colleagues. Paul did not attend. Neither did Rufus.

Lucy had a plan. The Saturday morning following the funeral, she walked to Paul and Hayley's flat and knocked on the door. Paul opened the door with Alice over his shoulder. Lucy thought he looked tired, but not unhappy to see her.

'Hi, Lucy, come in.'

'Thanks.' They went into the living room and sat down. 'How are you?'

'OK, well... you know... coping.' He lifted Alice off his shoulder and cradled her in his arms.

'Sorry, it was a silly question really. Maybe I should just get to the point – there's something I want to ask you.'

'Go ahead.'

'Do you mind if I visit Hayley? If she is happy for me to, that is. Sophie said she has only allowed her parents to visit her so far, but I would like to try to talk to her. I want to try to help her if I can.'

Paul sighed. 'You're probably wondering why I haven't been to see Hayley myself. At the moment I just feel so angry with her, so alienated from her. And I'm not sure she could face me, either. It's actually up to Hayley who she will and won't see, but yes, of course I don't mind you seeing her. You are a good friend and you were with her when she rang the police to confess.'

'I was.' Lucy paused, then took a deep breath. 'Paul, while we're on that subject, can I ask you something else?'

'Sure.'

'When did you realise Hayley was responsible for David falling from the balcony?'

'Not until the police charged me. They told me that the forensic team had found David's fingerprints on the edge of the balcony and crush marks and earth on his fingers. That was when I put two and two together. There was some spilled earth on the balcony which had both our footprints in it. The police blamed me, but I knew it had to be Hayley.'

'But you let them think it was you. Why did you do that?'

'Because... because I love her.'

Lucy paused to let him think about what he had just said.

After a moment, Paul continued, 'I know I need to see her too, and I will, just not yet.' He bit his lip. 'Lucy, there's something I need to ask you.'

The following Tuesday Lucy arrived at the vicarage early for study group, as had become her tradition. She followed Sophie into the kitchen, took a small box out of her pocket and opened it.

'What have you got there? Wow, is that real? It's not another present from a patient, is it?'

'No, it belongs to Alice. It was David's mother's, apparently. They found it in the bin – Hayley told the police she'd thrown it away. Anyway, Paul doesn't want it in the flat, so he asked me to look after it. Audrey and Geoffrey have a safe in their basement, so I'm going to ask if I can put it in there.'

'It's very pretty. It must be worth a small fortune.'

'Sophie, I went to visit Hayley.'

'Oh! I didn't think she was seeing anyone except her parents at the moment.' Sophie felt a mixture of surprise and hurt that Hayley had allowed Lucy to visit, but not her.

Lucy read Sophie's expression. 'She wasn't, but she allowed me to visit on Sunday afternoon. I think it's just that I was the person who happened to be there when she rang the police to make her confession. She doesn't have to explain herself to me, you see, because... well, she already has.'

'I can see what you're saying. Anyway, how was she?'

'Very tearful, obviously. Struggling with guilt and shame, as you can imagine. She's missing Paul and Alice terribly. I think, at the moment, she hates herself. She said she wanted to be sent to prison because she wanted to be punished, but now she's realising that being punished isn't making her feel any better because it can't change what she did. Then she said she didn't deserve to feel better. She needs to find her way back to God, but it's going to take a very long time for her to realise that she can be forgiven. Sophie, do you remember when David turned up at church with his mother's ashes in a box?'

'Yes, of course.'

'And then Rufus mentioned that David had been taking the box to work and that he had had an outburst when someone dropped something on it?'

'Yes. I was worried that he wasn't coping too well.'

'So was I. And Rufus told me that David had been underperforming at work and coming in late, smelling of alcohol. Rufus said he was having to take disciplinary measures and that he might have to let him go. What I'm trying to say is, I think there were other reasons why David became so unstable, other than Hayley and Alice, I mean.'

'Maybe David became fixated with the idea of filling the gap his mother had left in his life with Alice.'

'I agree. Anyway, I thought Hayley needed to understand that, so she could start to come to terms with how she reacted. That's why I went to see her. I've encouraged her to speak to the prison chaplain and I'm going to keep visiting. I'm working on getting Paul to visit too. I'm sure she will see other people, eventually, but I thought maybe I could encourage people to write to her first, help her realise she still has friends.'

'That's a good idea – I didn't think of that. I'll write a letter tomorrow and I'll get Dominic to write too.'

'Great. Sophie, if I'm honest, I nearly rang Rufus to try to find out more about David, but I realised that I would have had mixed motives in doing that. Ringing Rufus wouldn't have been good for me.'

'I think you're very wise. Anyway, speaking of Rufus, what about you? How are you, Lucy?'

'Oh, you know, not great in myself, but I do feel God has a purpose for me at the moment – to support Hayley and her family in whatever way I can.'

'I feel bad that I'm not doing more.'

'You can't do everything, Sophie. You've got Henry and he has to be your priority. I've got time that I can dedicate to helping Hayley and Paul. I know I'm in for the long haul.'

'And I greatly admire you for it, but I'm sorry you still feel so awful in yourself. I'm sure you'll start to feel better, in time.'

'Are you?' said Lucy, doubtfully. 'I'm not so sure myself. I've acknowledged that Rufus wasn't right for me. He wasn't a bad man and he never set out to hurt me; he just had his priorities wrong, that's all. It's just that…'

'Just that…?'

'Just that I still love him, with all my heart. I don't think the pain of losing him will ever go away.'

Twenty-two

Lucy continued to visit Hayley regularly. With reassurances from Lucy, Hayley also received a visit from Sophie and Dominic. Eventually, with all their encouragement, Paul also visited, with Alice. Sophie, Dominic and Lucy knew that it was going to take a long time for them to repair their relationship, but at least they had made a start.

Paul was given paid leave from work until after Christmas. His parents had gone back to their own house, leaving Paul to look after Alice by himself, but they were regular visitors, as were Hayley's parents and Chloe. So he had a very supportive network of family and friends around him.

Sophie had felt that life at All Saints, indeed life in Oxley, might be changed forever after that fateful Sunday. In some ways she was right: certainly the lives of Paul's and Hayley's families and friends would never be the same, but gradually the church and the village began to return to normal.

One Sunday morning in November, Sophie and Lucy were sitting on the floor, packing the children's toys away in the crèche at the end of the service. They had been looking after Henry and Jessica, who was now crawling, between them.

'Do you know what?' said Lucy. 'Church seems a more loving place than it used to be.' She looked over her shoulder and whispered, 'Even Audrey and Geoffrey seem less – well, you know – fierce!'

'I know,' whispered Sophie. 'A number of people seem to have changed. It's as if the tragedy has made people realise that the *church* is the *people*. It has reminded people to love each other more than themselves and their traditions. Catherine thinks it was Audrey and Geoffrey who had riled other people in the first place. She thinks they've been affected by watching others share Paul and Hayley's troubles and now their hostility has been replaced by compassion. I know you've been helping Paul too, by the way. He mentioned that you babysit once a week so that he can get out of the house on his own. I think that's so important for him.'

'It's great to feel I can do something useful for him,' said Lucy. 'I love looking after Alice anyway – she's gorgeous. Sometimes Paul just goes round to his mum and dad for the evening, but last week he went out with his friends from work. When he goes back to work in January, Hayley's parents and Paul's parents are going to look after Alice between them.'

'It's amazing that they can do that, in the circumstances. It might have turned out very differently,' said Sophie.

At that moment the door opened and the sound of Mrs Fowler-Watt striking up the opening chords of the last hymn filled their ears. Melissa came in to collect Jessica.

'How was she?' asked Melissa.

'Fine,' said Lucy. 'She settled really well.'

'Thanks, Lucy.' Melissa looked relieved. 'Actually... there was something I wanted to ask you.'

'Go ahead,' said Sophie, as she wrestled Henry into the pushchair. Audrey handed her a biscuit for him through the hatch from the kitchen.

'Here you are, Henry, darling,' said Audrey, smiling at him. 'Good boy.'

'I was just thinking, I'm really enjoying the women's Bible study group on Thursdays and I'm learning loads,' Melissa started to explain, 'but Daniel still has lots of questions and I'm not very good at answering them. I was wondering – is there, maybe, a men's group? Sort of… like the ladies' group, where you can ask any question without feeling stupid?'

'Oh,' said Sophie. 'No, we don't have a men's study group. I suppose most of the men who want to, come to one of the evening Bible study groups.

'I'm not sure Daniel's really ready for that yet,' said Melissa. 'He's still got questions. He says things like… hmm… let me think… he gets that Jesus died for our sins, but he doesn't understand why that should change the way we live, or why we need to come to church. He thinks that if Jesus has already died for the sins of the whole world, it shouldn't really matter what we do and everyone should be able to go to heaven, if you see what I mean?'

Mary Brown's children, Emma and Euan, making one of their rare appearances at church that morning, wandered in from the impromptu Sunday school group that swung into action whenever children turned up on a Sunday morning. They started taking toys back out of the boxes that Sophie and Lucy had neatly packed away.

'Yes, Jesus did die for all our sins,' Sophie started to say, 'but there's a "but" – and it's a big "but".'

'Big butt, big butt,' giggled the Brown children.

It was unfortunate that, at that moment, Doris walked through the door in search of coffee, her massive bottom swaying from side to side.

Sophie tried not to get distracted. Lucy tactfully pointed the Brown children in the direction of the biscuits, taking the toys out of their hands and packing them away. 'The thing is,' continued Sophie, 'yes, Jesus did die for all our sins.' She tried to avoid the word 'but'. 'We can't undo our own sins.' She tried to think how to put it. 'Erm… I suppose it's more that trying to live God's way is done out of love and gratitude for what God has already done. Does that help?'

'I think so.' Sophie thought Melissa didn't look completely convinced.

She tried again. 'I guess the bottom line…'

'Bottom, bottom,' shouted the Brown children, gleefully.

Sophie ploughed on, '... is that, if you choose to follow Jesus on earth, you will spend eternity with Him. If you choose not to follow Him on earth, why would you want to spend eternity with Him?'

'You explain it better than me,' said Melissa.

'Whatever you do,' encouraged Sophie, thinking about Hayley and Paul, 'don't nag Daniel into coming to church. Just be a loving example, and if he asks questions, answer as best you can.'

'But sometimes I don't have the answers.'

'But you are a loving example and you can always ask the questions yourself and go back to him with the answers. I do have one idea, though,' said Sophie, thinking back to the conversation they had had in Robert and Catherine's kitchen the day they had come back from France. So many things had been pushed to the back of their minds with the catastrophic events that had taken place since then. 'We had talked about running a seekers' course, where we could go through questions like this. Maybe that's the right thing for Daniel. Do you think he would be interested?'

'I do,' said Melissa. 'I think I'd be interested too.'

'I can babysit,' volunteered Lucy, immediately.

'Ask Daniel what he thinks and I'll talk to Dominic,' said Sophie.

Over lunch, Sophie mentioned the idea to Dominic. 'I'd love to do that,' he said. 'I think it would have to be in January, but we could announce it to the congregation generally and see if we get more takers. It's a great idea and it's good to have something to feel positive about.'

'It is,' agreed Sophie. 'You never know, you could get someone who wanders into one of the Christmas services who might be looking for something like that too. Lucy has already offered to babysit so that Melissa and Daniel can come together.'

'She's a good girl,' said Dominic. 'She told me something else earlier too. She's quite nervous about it, so don't mention it to anyone, but ever since she came back from her holiday in Cornwall, she's gone back to playing the piano. She goes to her parents' house in the evenings and plays the piano she used to play when she lived at home. She's thinking about playing at church some of the Sunday mornings after Christmas!'

'Well, that's another thing to feel positive about.'

'True. I'll just pop into the study and check some dates for January and we'll see which days are best for Melissa and Daniel. I bought a wall planner for next year. It's time I put it up and started thinking beyond Christmas anyway.'

Dominic went into the study, but a few minutes later Sophie heard a shout. 'Sophie, come here and look at this.' She went to join him. 'I was hunting around on the shelves for the wall planner. I knew it was rolled up somewhere. The study has got rather messy lately, with so many things going on. I moved a few files and books and found what I was looking for, but then I noticed this brown paper package. I pulled it down and realised it was that rather stuffed-looking envelope that was on the mat when we came home that Sunday afternoon, when everything happened. I had thrown it into the study, meaning to open it later, but I forgot about it in all the chaos. I've just opened it, and... look...'

He held it out. It was stuffed with £50 notes. There was a small, folded piece of paper in the envelope with the bank notes. Dominic opened it and read it, then passed it to his wife. It simply said, 'For the church drive.' There was no signature and nothing else inside the envelope. Dominic did a quick calculation. 'Just enough money to cover the quote,' he said. 'Someone with inside knowledge of All Saints must have given us this, but wanted to remain anonymous. It's been sitting here for such a long time, whoever gave it to us must wonder why we've never said anything about it.'

'If it's someone from church, I'm sure they must have realised we've all had our minds on other things,' said Sophie.

'True. Maybe it was Audrey and Geoffrey, after all. I think I'd better ring Geoffrey right away.'

'It's another little bit of good news.'

'It is.'

Sophie shut the study door and let Dominic make the phone call. A moment later he came back out of the study. 'He was really pleased. He thinks he can even get the drive fixed in time for Christmas. And, if it was them that gave us the money, he's a really good actor. He sounded genuinely very surprised.'

'Well, whoever it was, they obviously didn't want us to know, so let's stop guessing and just be grateful!'

By the beginning of December, preparations for Christmas at All Saints were well underway. The mood was more sombre than previous Christmases, but Christmas was still Christmas. Geoffrey was as good as his word and arranged for the new church drive to be laid in time for the many people who would be walking up and down it in the weeks leading up to Christmas Day.

Two weeks before Christmas, Dominic, Sophie and Henry were sitting at the kitchen table at teatime when Sophie said, 'I'm very sorry to tell you, when you have so much to be thinking about, but the oven door has broken.'

'Oh,' said Dominic. 'That is a nuisance.' He thought for a moment. 'Don't worry. I'll have a look at it this evening when Henry's in bed. You're going to be busy this evening, aren't you?'

'Yes,' said Sophie, looking at Henry. She had been planning to spend the evening wrapping presents while Henry was asleep. 'I wanted to steam the Christmas pudding this evening too, but I can do that another day.'

'No problem. The hob will still work. I can keep an eye on the pudding while I'm looking at the oven door.'

A little while later, Henry had been bathed and was tucked up in bed. Sophie had waited for him to drop off to sleep and had begun work with the wrapping paper and sticky tape. This year Henry had a little more understanding of Christmas than he had done the previous year and he was getting excited.

In the kitchen, Dominic had taken out his toolbox. The Christmas pudding was bubbling in an old saucepan, kept especially for the purpose, on the hob. Dominic opened the kitchen window to let out the steam. Despite the cold weather outside, the kitchen was hot and the stream of cool air across his face was welcome. He knelt down on the floor and opened the oven door, peering closely to try to work out the problem. He could see a loose screw in the hinge. He tried to tighten it with a screwdriver, but the screwdriver was too big. He reached round for a smaller one, but it was difficult to get it into the gap and the door kept dropping down. He knew he had another smaller screwdriver, but now the door had become even more loose and was in danger of falling off the oven completely. He tried to reach the smaller screwdriver, without letting go of the oven door, but he couldn't quite manage it. With a clang, the oven door dropped onto the floor.

In frustration, Dominic put his hand up onto the top of the cooker to pull himself into a standing position. Unfortunately, as he stood up, he caught the handle of the old saucepan, dislodging it slightly and spilling boiling water onto his hand. He rushed to the sink, uttering several loud swear words on the way, and thrust his smarting hand under the cold tap.

Sophie, hearing the shouting, rushed into the kitchen. 'What's the matter? Are you hurt?'

'Stupid saucepan! I burned my hand.'

Sophie looked at his scalded hand. 'I think it will be OK. You just need to keep it under the cold tap until it stops stinging.'

'Sorry about my language, but it really hurt.'

'Don't mind me, but the window is open!'

'Oh no! What if someone heard me? What will they think of me? I'm supposed to be the vicar.'

'You are the vicar, there's no "supposed to be" about it!'

The doorbell rang. Dominic looked horrified.

'Stay there,' said Sophie. 'Keep your hand under that cold tap. I'll get the door.'

A moment later, she returned to the kitchen with someone behind her. 'Dominic, Paul is here,' she said. 'Do come through, Paul. Dominic just had a bit of a mishap with the oven door.'

'Sorry, Paul. I was trying to mend it and I stupidly spilled boiling water on my hand. Do sit down, but do you mind if I stay standing at the sink?'

'Are you OK?' asked Paul, looking concerned.

'He'll be fine,' said Sophie.

'I'm just on the way back from Mum and Dad's,' Paul told them. 'Lucy's babysitting and I don't want to keep her waiting, but I had something I wanted to ask you and I thought I'd call in, as I was passing.'

'Fire away,' said Dominic.

'Well, I was wondering about having Alice christened, or baptised, whatever you call it. It's just... It's what Hayley wants.'

'Oh, yes,' said Dominic. 'I'm glad Hayley wants Alice baptised and I'm sure we can arrange it, but it has to be what you want too. You will be the one bringing her for baptism and you will be making some quite big promises about bringing her up in the Christian faith and the life of the church. Why don't I call round one morning and we could chat about it, then you can decide if it's what you want?'

'OK, thanks, that would be great,' replied Paul. 'I'd better get going, but I'll see you soon, then.'

Sophie saw him out, then came back into the kitchen. 'How's the hand?'

'The hand is fine,' said Dominic, taking it out of the cold water and looking at it. 'The oven door isn't, but it will be. I just need a different screwdriver. But I really, really hope he didn't hear me. How embarrassing!'

The following Tuesday was to be the study group's last meeting before Christmas and it had been decided that they would put down their Bibles for the evening and have a meal together instead. Everyone was to bring something for the table. Lucy arrived early, as she often did, with a tray of home-made mince pies. She found Sophie in the kitchen, stirring a steaming pan of mulled wine.

'Hi, Lucy,' said Sophie, through the steam. 'How are you?'

'Let's not talk about me,' Lucy replied. 'I have something rather interesting to tell you.'

'Mulled wine?'

'Yes, please.'

'Go on.'

'Well, you know Paul called on you the other night and asked about having Alice baptised?'

'Yes,' said Sophie, handing Lucy a glass of mulled wine. 'Be careful, it's hot.'

'Thanks. Well, I was babysitting Alice that night, so he told me Dominic was going to visit to explain what it was all about. Anyway, he called round with Alice when I got home from work yesterday, with a present to say thanks for all the babysitting. He was really sweet and said that I'd helped him a lot. Then he told me that Dominic had been round and helped him understand about bringing up Alice in the Christian faith and that he wanted to understand it better. He said – now let me get this right – he said that he didn't understand why Jesus would die to take the blame for the sins of the world, when it was Him we had sinned against in the first place. So I said – actually, Sophie, I'm quite proud about this bit – I said, "Remember when I asked you why you had taken the blame for what Hayley had done and you just said that it was because you loved Hayley? Don't you think it's a bit like that?" Anyway, he just stood there for a moment and then he said, "Ohh…" And it was a bit like watching bits of a jigsaw puzzle fall into place! Then I mentioned the seekers' course you're planning for January and he said he knew he'd never been interested in the past, but he thought he'd like to come.'

'That is interesting!' said Sophie. 'Who would ever have thought that Paul would consider something like that, especially after everything he's been through?'

'I know,' said Lucy. 'So I asked him what had made him change his mind and he said that people at church had been so kind... and...'

'And?'

'And that when he came to see you, apparently, just as he was walking up the drive he heard Dominic swearing his head off... and realised that Christians are normal people too!'

'Oh, how embarrassing! How terribly, but wonderfully, embarrassing,' giggled Sophie.

'I know,' said Lucy. 'Anyway, I'm going to babysit Alice so he can come. I know I said I would babysit Jessica, but I've already asked Mum to do that for Melissa and Daniel. Mum and Dad have got to know them at church and Melissa and Daniel are fine about it, so you've got a group of three already!'

'That's brilliant. You're a star. But Lucy...'

'Yes?'

'I do still want to talk about you.'

'I still miss Rufus terribly,' admitted Lucy, 'but something is different. I prayed a different prayer a few nights ago. Instead of praying, "Please, God, help me," which really meant, "Please, God, bring Rufus back," I prayed, "Please, God, help me stop loving Rufus."'

'And?'

'And there's still a big Rufus-shaped hole in my heart, but now I've stopped thinking it won't get better. I've known for a while, in my head, that Rufus wasn't good for me. You helped me realise that.'

'Did I?'

'Yes, that day when I told you about the conversation I'd had with Rufus, when he didn't think I would know that tree by the river was a weeping willow. You said, "Lucy, it's just a tree, it doesn't matter." That was when I realised – I mean, really realised – that his values weren't my values and he wasn't the one for me, and, actually, it's better to have no man than the wrong man. I've just got to wait for the feeling to move from my head to my heart.'

'It will. Just give it time.'

'I'm still praying that I might meet the right man one day, but if I don't, then God will show me what He wants me to do. That's what really matters.'

'I think, for the moment, He already has. He's given you plenty to be getting on with for the time being!'

'Yes. Speaking of which, I've got something else to tell you.'

'Oh?'

'I've decided to learn to drive! Mum and Dad are going to get me lessons for Christmas.'

'How did you make that decision?'

'I keep having to ask Dad to drive me when I go to visit Hayley. He doesn't mind, but it made me realise that it would be good for me to be a bit more independently mobile.'

'Excellent plan!'

As Sophie finished speaking, the doorbell rang and she went to open the door to the rest of the group.

Twenty-three

It was Christmas Eve afternoon, just one more sleep until Christmas. Sophie, Dominic and Henry walked back to the vicarage at the end of the afternoon service. Henry had taken part in the nativity this year, proudly playing his part as a shepherd.

'How wonderful that we had Paul and Alice with us this afternoon,' said Dominic.

'Lucy brought them. Nice not to be walking back through muddy puddles this year, isn't it?'

'It certainly is, thanks to Geoffrey's efficiency and our unknown benefactor. Speaking of Geoffrey, shall I tell you something else?'

'Go on.'

'You know how Audrey and Geoffrey haven't been so… Lately, they've been so much… nicer?'

'I do know, yes.'

'Well, I saw Robert just now. Apparently, Geoffrey had a chat with him the other day and he said, "I still can't understand some of Dominic's wild ideas, but I can see he wants the best for the church. I suppose I ought to let him try to do things his way."'

'I can hardly believe it,' said Sophie, in amazement. 'Well, I never. A lot has happened this year.'

Dominic looked thoughtful. 'We've certainly seen some changes. Some people left us and some new people joined us.

We lost the Hendersons, but we gained Melissa, Daniel and Jessica. Rufus came and then left again. Lucy got hurt, but has come out stronger in herself and in her faith. You, Sophie, have dealt with some difficult issues yourself and come out stronger too. One member of our congregation did something terrible and a lot of people suffered for it. But, as a result, the whole congregation seems to have learned to love each other more. And now we have three people signed up for a seekers' course, which must be good.'

'What about you, Dominic, how do you feel about everything that's happened?'

'I think it's been a very difficult year. In fact, there was that time when we thought things couldn't get any worse, and then we came back from holiday thinking about Elijah. And…'

'It got a lot worse.'

'It did,' said Dominic. 'But through it all I think I've learned to stop worrying and just trust God. That's what Elijah had to learn when he got completely depressed. Elijah did some spectacular things for God but, at the end of the day, he was just human. We don't have to be Elijah for God to work through us.

'I don't know what will happen next,' he continued. 'But I've decided I need to stop worrying about the church of the future and let God do that. We're here to look after the church of the present. It's God's church, so whether it grows or declines is up to Him. Our job is to serve God here and now, to preach and teach, to encourage church members and welcome new people in, and to do it to the best of our ability. And we have some very supportive people here with us. I'm very thankful for them all. As long as we're doing our best and praying, of course, whatever happens next is up to God. I'm just going to do my job and trust God to do the rest.'

'I couldn't agree more,' said Sophie.